The LAST RENEGADE

Jan Lindsey

pages I was hooked. I couldn't put the book down and finished it within 24 hours. ***All the Dogs of Europe Barked*** connects on many different levels. I can truthfully say that this book is worth the buy, and you'll never regret it."

*****

"It's hard to properly explain the writing talent that created this book. It's akin to the author Wilbur Smith, who can, in just a few short pages, paint a 3 dimensional, fully colored picture that puts you right into the story. I became Kristopher in all that filth in the barracks: I smelled the fragrance of Hannah's hair as they made love: I felt the blood running down the head of the old Jewish shopkeeper that Kristopher had hit with a brick. I thank Jan Lindsey for an experience I will never forget."

*****

"Since the author is a friend of mine, I wasn't sure what to expect, but I can honestly say I was drawn into the book from the minute I started reading it. The story is intriguing and suspenseful: the history interwoven throughout is a great educational bonus, and I'd recommend this to anyone, young or old. This period of German history was horrible, and the author has captured the peoples' hopes and fears as if she had experienced it herself. It's a marvelous book, and I'm proud of her, but I must admit that this isn't what you expect when a friend comes up to you and says, 'I just wrote a book!' It's much much more than just a book!"

The LAST RENEGADE

In 1994, the Yakama Indian Nation in central Washington State changed the spelling of its tribal name from Yakima to Yakama in order to return to its original spelling. With no disrespect meant to the Yakamas, I have chosen to spell their name YAKIMA, which is how it was spelled in the 1950s, the setting for this story. I also refer to the Yakamas as "Indians," as most Whites did then.

JAN HOUGHTON LINDSEY

TWOHARBORS
WWW.TWOHARBORSPRESS.COM

Two Harbors Press
322 First Avenue N, 5th floor
Minneapolis, MN 55401
612.455.2293
www.TwoHarborsPress.com

This book is fiction. Names, characters, places, and incidents are entirely products of the author's imagination. Because the story is set in a town on the Yakima Indian Reservation, some names of actual places and locations are used, but what happens to the characters there is entirely fictitious.

The cover picture is based on a 1910 bronze sculpture made by Cyrus E. Dallin. Paintings of the sculpture have appeared over the years with various backgrounds and colors. This rendition was copyrighted in 1921 by the John Drescher Co.

ISBN-13: 978-1-63413-643-3
LCCN: 2015910401

Distributed by Itasca Books

Cover Design by Ross Patrick
Typeset by Lois Stanfield

Printed in the United States of America

BOOKS
Authored, co-authored,
or edited by Jan Lindsey

Satan is Alive and Well on Planet Earth

The Liberation of Planet Earth

There's a New World Coming

The Promise

The Guilt Trip

Fed Up With Fat

All the Dogs of Europe Barked

The Last Renegade

Dedicated to my sister, Ellen Houghton Tengesdal,
and
my cousin, Jack Labbee, founder of
Labbeemint on the Yakama Indian Reservation

AUTHOR'S NOTE

This book is fiction, and Derek Abrams is a fictional character, but the early mistreatment of the Yakama Indians by the U.S. Government is *not* fiction: it is fact.

For at least a thousand years before any White-man stepped foot into the Pacific Northwest, it had been home to 125 different native tribes and cultures, but when white settlers began moving westward in the 1800s looking for furs, horses, silver, gold, and land, the rights of these native inhabitants were consistently violated.

By 1848, the United States Government claimed ownership over most present-day parts of Washington, Oregon, and Idaho, and with it the authority to govern the lives and movement of anyone who lived there. In 1855, the fourteen Indian tribes of Central Washington—led by Chief Kamiakin of the Yakamas—were forced by the U.S. Government to sign a treaty giving more than eleven million acres of their ancient tribal lands to the Government, in exchange for the promise that they could continue to fish and hunt there for the next two years, but would then be moved to an area with equal resources in another part of the territory.

Two weeks after this treaty was signed, gold was discovered on the Yakama Indian Reservation, and Isaac Stevens, the governor of the Northwest Territories, broke the treaty with the Indians by allowing immediate White settlement on the Reservation.

Outraged, Chief Kamiakin called on the other Indian signers of the treaty to join him in opposing this unlawful act, and for three years they battled the U.S. Army to get back their stolen lands, but were ultimately defeated. Kamiakin was gravely wounded, but managed to escape. The thirteen other rebel Chiefs were caught and executed. The surviving Yakamas were confined to a small area on their own Reservation, and their children were taken from them and put into boarding schools to be indoctrinated into White culture.

With federal agents now running the Reservation, the Yakamas were forced to give up their hunting and fishing, and ordered to learn to farm. But this way of life was foreign to them, and few were successful at it. Before long, ill health, alcoholism, lawlessness, infant deaths, and the breakup of families became commonplace on the Reservation. As the years went by, the Yakamas were left with only dim memories of their carefree past.

In this story, Derek Abrams, a brilliant Indian schoolteacher, is forced to become a renegade in order to keep those memories alive for himself and the Yakamas.

CHAPTER 1

1956

Derek Abrams's algebra class was on its lunch break, and he had just sat down at his desk to correct some tests when he noticed a piece of paper sticking out from under his desk blotter. He pulled it out, and as he read the words—***the only good Indian is a dead Indian***—he flinched. Those were the same ugly words someone had taped to his school locker twelve years earlier when his father had just been killed by a drunk white teenager who ran into him on the Fort Road. He had finally come to terms with that terrible loss, but now those same words threatened to open that old wound.

It had not been easy for Derek growing up on the Yakima Indian Reservation, but as poor as his family had been, Jason Abrams always managed to keep food on their table by breaking and selling the wild horses that he and Derek brought down from the Horse Heaven Hills each spring. Then, in the late autumns the two of them would ride their *cayuses* deep into the foothills of sacred Mount Adams, often camping out in the open for days at a time. On those trips they lived—as the Ancient

1

Ones had—on prairie hens and jackrabbits, roots, berries, and trout and salmon caught in the many streams that pocketed the Cascade foothills.

It was also on these trips that Jason had opened his heart to his son about his Indian heritage. Lying on blankets under the stars, he had filled Derek's head with all the legends of the Great Spirit, and stories of the mighty deeds of their ancestors, and reminded him that he was a direct descendant of Chief Kamiakin—the last great chief of the Yakimas—and it would be his responsibility one day to lead the Yakimas back to their days of greatness.

Derek had eagerly promised to do all he could to lead the Yakimas, but as he sat there now, looking down at the ugly note in his hand, he wondered if there were enough Yakimas left who really cared about the old ways to make it worth the effort. Most of the ones he knew didn't.

There was a tap on his classroom door, and he swiveled his chair to see who it was. One of his Indian students, Angie Tall-bear, poked her head in. "I don't mean to bother you, Mr. Abrams, but I know who put that stupid note on your desk, and he's a jerk. Don't pay any attention to it. All your students love you."

He motioned her in as he tore the note into pieces and dropped it into the wastebasket. "I don't even want to know who wrote it, but thanks for the encouraging words."

Angie's gaze was pure adoration. "You're the best teacher in this whole school. Everybody says so."

Derek let out a little laugh. "Being an Indian, you might be slightly prejudiced."

"No! My dad said you got job offers from all over the country, but you came back to the Reservation because you love our people. He brags about you all the time."

"He must be a Washington State Cougar fan."

"Oh, he is! He used to drive over to Pullman for all your games, but he's also one of our Elders, and he's very proud of you. Don't let some stupid white kid make you feel bad with his dumb criticism."

He gave a dismissive flip of his hand. "I won't, and I don't want you too either. Life is too short to worry about what people think of you, but I've gotta finish correcting these tests now, and you need to get back to lunch. Don't worry about the note. I'm not going to."

"Okay," she said, reluctantly backing out the door.

Derek took an apple from his backpack and sat down at his desk. Angie's devotion was sweet, but he was going to take his own advice and not let the note get to him. He'd dealt with things like that all his life, but he knew who he was. His great-great-grandfather on his mother's side had been the legendary Yakima Chief, Kamiakin, and his great-great grandfather on his father's side had been the famous Indian agent, Joshua Abrams, who had married one of Kamiakin's daughters in hopes of bringing enlightenment to the savages. But Derek's father had often reminded him that white frontiersmen like that had brought more than just their enlightened ways. They had robbed the Indians of their land and corrupted their sacred traditions, and it was hard to forgive them for that, no matter how noble their aims had seemed to them.

But Derek had learned from what his father had taught him. If he wanted to excel in the White-man's world, he needed to adapt to their cultural ways without losing his own identity. And to ensure that his spiritual roots went deep, his father had taken him to the religious services at the Indian longhouse each week. His earliest memories were of his father drumming and chanting their special family chant in the sacred Washat service there, and his heart would burst with pride as his father led them in their praise and worship of the Great Spirit.

But it had all come to a terrible end twelve years ago. That was when his father had been run down and killed on the Fort Road by Morgan Cullen, a drunken white teenager. Morgan was only fifteen at the time, but well known as a wild, unruly kid, so no one really believed it when his father accused Jason Abrams of being drunk and causing the accident. No one believed the elder Cullen, but no one dared defy him either. Too many people on the Reservation depended on Andrew Cullen for employment in the hop fields at The Oaks, and he held too much power for anyone to cross him.

Derek looked up from the papers he was correcting, remembering how all the dreams he'd nurtured from childhood had died with his father that day, and in order for him and his mother, Lucy, to survive, she'd had to go to work as a housekeeper for the Lamonts—a rich white family who lived a mile down the Fort Road from them.

After his mother had been working there a few months, Helen Lamont invited them to visit her church in Harrah where she taught a Sunday school class, and they began attending. He liked their summer camps and church picnics, but their teachings about God were so different from what his father had taught him about the Great Spirit, that he stopped going to this new church when he was sixteen. Some of his church friends told him he just thought he was better than everyone else. But his father had always told him he *was* better than most kids his age, so he set out to prove it by lettering in basketball, baseball, and football during his last two years at White Swan High School, and never made a grade below an A.

It had been a grueling two years, but it changed the course of his life. He received a full athletic scholarship to Washington State College, where he was selected as an All-American on their championship football team in his junior year. He also met some Indian activists whose religious beliefs were similar to his, and he let his hair grow long like they had. His braids got a few snickers on campus, but basically no one seemed to care as long as he continued leading the Washington State Cougars to victory.

But he *had* run into a problem with the braids when he'd applied for the job here at his old high school in White Swan. When the School Board told him he'd have to cut them if he wanted the job, he told them he'd get a job somewhere else. But after a hurried conference, they'd decided they could live with the braids. Where else were they going to find an All-American football star with top academic honors who was willing to teach in a backwater town like White Swan?

Now that he was back on the Reservation and settled into his job at White Swan High School, he'd started attending the longhouse again, but although he enjoyed being around people who believed like he did, he was beginning to have serious doubts about his promise to his father that he would become their spiritual leader. Maybe sometime in the future his old fervor would come back, but, right now, all he wanted to do was make algebra as much fun as he could for his students, and keep winning championships with his football team.

So he was perplexed as he sat there now, thinking about the stupid note he'd just gotten. He knew there were Whites who honestly believed that most Indians were drunks, but everyone who'd known Jason Abrams knew he had never touched a drop of liquor in his life, and Derek decided it was time to make sure Andrew Cullen knew that. Whether he would finally admit that it was his drunken son who had caused the accident, Derek would just have to wait and see, but he wasn't going to be satisfied until he and Andrew Cullen had a long talk about it, and Cullen admitted the truth to him.

CHAPTER 2

Gus Styvessan leaned his battered chair back against the front of his gas station and pulled his baseball cap down over his eyes. A persistent horsefly kept dive-bombing at him, and he grabbed the cap off his head and took a swipe at it, then fanned himself a couple of times before plopping it back on his head. This heat was really getting to him. It had been over one hundred degrees on the Reservation for more than three weeks, and things were slow at the station. Not many people wanted to be out unless they had to.

Gus gave a little snort as he thought about this crazy old town. Plopped right in the middle of the Yakima Indian Reservation, Harrah's four blocks of commercial buildings, his service station, a tavern, and four churches served an outlying population of a couple thousand Whites and Indians. It wasn't much of a town, but it had been home to him for fifty-two years, and there was no place on earth he'd rather live. He glanced across the sizzling asphalt to Tiny's Cafe and was just about to go over and get an iced tea when he suddenly saw a battered old truck come barreling through the intersection without stopping at the light.

Gus jerked his chair forward. "Oh, blast it all!" he muttered. "There goes Johnny again. I bet he's drunker'n a skunk."

The old truck raced past Gus's station, weaving from side to side as it headed south on the Harrah Road in the direction of the Fort Road, three miles away. Gus jumped up and ran to his pickup, but by the time he got to the Fort Road, the old Indian was nowhere in sight.

As he passed The Oaks on his way back to the station, he glanced up at the high wall of evergreen oaks that completely hid the famous three-story mansion built nearly fifty years ago by Cyrus Barron, and as always when he passed here, his thoughts went to Barron's daughter, Laura. How he wished it were possible to just drop in and say a friendly hello to her. Just a glimpse to see how she was doing. But even as he wished it, he knew it could never be. That painful chapter in his life had been closed for him twenty-six years ago.

A familiar melancholy settled on him as he thought of Laura Barron. She'd chosen her own hell when she'd married Andrew Cullen instead of him, and there'd been nothing he could do about it then, and certainly nothing he could do about it now. Still, after all these years, he couldn't help but worry about what it must be like for her, married to someone like Andrew Cullen. He wouldn't wish that on his worst enemy.

But, he had other worries, now, and Johnny Birdsong was one of them. Gus had known him since they were kids, and he was a harmless old Indian, but he couldn't stay off the booze. Where he was getting it, Gus didn't know. Charlie wouldn't take the chance on losing his tavern's liquor license by selling to an Indian. But Johnny was getting someone to buy it for him, and Gus was gonna have to find out who and put a stop to it, or Johnny was gonna end up dead. This was the part of being the local deputy sheriff that he hated.

Just then, his eyes were drawn to some skid marks in the gravel on the side of the road. A little apprehensive, he pulled his pickup off onto the shoulder and looked down into the canal that ran alongside the road. He groaned as he saw the back of Johnny's truck sticking out of the muddy water, the cab nearly obscured by the tall cattails that grew along the bank.

"Oh, no! He's done it this time!" Gus moaned as he jumped out of his pickup. He called the old Indian's name as he slid down the muddy bank, but there was no answer.

The cab of the truck was submerged, and as Gus waded, chest-high, into the brackish water, he could see Johnny's head lying against the steering wheel, just above the water. He jerked frantically on the door, but it was jammed. Reaching through the open window, he grabbed one of Johnny's braids and pulled his face out of the water. His eyes were rolled back under half-closed lids, and blood ran out of his nose and open mouth.

"Oh, Johnny, what've you done to yourself?"

He let go of the Indian's braid to pull at the door again, but as he did so, Johnny's head fell forward and hit the steering wheel. To Gus's complete shock, Johnny suddenly began sputtering and thrashing at the water. "Where am I?" he mumbled thickly.

Gus let out a sigh of relief and almost laughed. "You're in the canal, you old drunk. Are you hurt anywhere?"

Johnny looked around in a stupor and suddenly saw the water that was up to his chin. "Where'd this water come from?"

"I told you. You're in the canal, and you're lucky you didn't kill yourself." He jerked at the door again. "I can't get this thing open, so you'll have to come out through the window. Gimme your arms, and I'll pull you out."

Johnny looked up at Gus through bleary eyes. "Is that you, Gus?"

"Who do you think it is? Your fairy godmother? Of course it's me, you idiot! Now c'mon. Gimme your arms."

"What am I doin' in the ditch?"

"Johnny! I'll tell you all about it when I get you outta here. Now gimme your arms, or I swear, I'm just gonna leave you here to drown."

Gus finally managed to pull him through the window and up onto the bank. He looked him over and saw that his nose was bleeding, but otherwise, he didn't seem to be hurt too badly. He was too drunk to even stand, so Gus dragged him into the back of his pickup and took him to Doc Stevens's office in Harrah.

Doc Stevens was a kindly man in his early seventies. His thick hair had turned completely white and stuck out in unruly clumps above his bushy brows. He had grown up in Harrah and was as much an institution in the town as were the Brethren Church, Charlie's Tavern, and Tiny's Cafe. He'd seen many of the towns-people into the world, and a good many of them out of it.

Doc was in the process of giving one of the old-maid Carpenter sisters her regular checkup when Gus came barreling up in front of his clinic. He looked out his window and saw Gus struggling to get Johnny out of the back of the pickup and rushed out to help him, leaving a horrified Miss Carpenter sitting on the examining table with a sheet draped over her bare torso.

Doc and Gus carried Johnny into the examining room and wrestled him up onto the table while Miss Carpenter huddled in a corner, frantically clutching the sheet over her bare bosom. Gus doffed his cap to her. "Afternoon, Miss Clara," he said, and heard a muffled shriek as she pulled the sheet up over her head.

"'Scuse us, Miss Carpenter," Doc said, "but we've got an emergency here. I'll be right back with you in a few minutes. Just make yourself comfortable on that chair over there, and don't pay us any mind."

Doc looked Johnny over and pronounced him whole. "He just needs to sleep it off," he told Gus. "He's one lucky Indian."

"He's gonna be one *dead* Indian if he doesn't get off that booze," Gus retorted.

Johnny was still unsteady on his legs, so Doc helped Gus get him out to his pickup and stuff him into the passenger seat. "Don't be too hard on him," Doc said. "He hasn't got anything but liquor to keep him company since his wife kicked him out, and you know his kids won't have anything to do with him either. Where's he getting all this liquor anyway?"

Gus gave a disgusted snort. "There's always somebody ready to part these Indians from their money. Sometimes I think it was a big mistake for the government to dam up their rivers and give them all that money instead. They just don't know how to handle it."

"I'm not so sure that's their fault," Doc said. "What would you do if you got a free handout every year when you'd never had a pot to pee in? You'd probably go a little berserk yourself."

Gus chuckled. "I wouldn't mind having the chance to find out, just the same."

Doc laid a hand on his shoulder. "You're the wrong color, Gus."

"I know," he laughed. "Thanks for looking at Johnny, and give my apologies to Miss Clara. I think she might be a little undone."

Doc Stevens chuckled. "You don't know how many years it's taken me just to get her to take her top off when I examine her. I'm probably the only man alive who's ever seen her buck naked, and I can assure you, it's nothing to get excited about."

Gus tried to keep a straight face. "Shame on you, passing on gossip like that."

Doc laughed sheepishly. "Yeah, you're right, but I just thought that, being an old widower, you might have some ideas about her, and I wanted to spare you if I could."

"That's all I'd need is to have her start chasing me. Folks have been trying to fix me up with one or the other of those two sisters ever since Emily passed away, but I've got enough grief without that. Thanks anyway."

Gus was still chuckling as he drove over to his gas station and hauled Johnny out of the pickup. Harrah didn't have a jail, so Gus usually handcuffed drunk Indians to the telephone pole in front of the station until they sobered up. He didn't wanna do that to an old friend, so he dragged him into his cottage behind the service station. Putting a blanket on the sofa, Gus laid him down to sleep it off. Even though he was a drunk, and an Indian, in the final analysis he was just a lonely old man that nobody had much time for. Gus knew that feeling.

CHAPTER 3

The next morning, Gus was having a tough time trying to pull Johnny's truck up the muddy canal bank with the tractor he'd borrowed. Johnny stood peering down at the back of his truck, too hungover to be much help. Gus yelled at him disgustedly. "If you're not gonna help, then get outta the way. Of course, you could get down in there and straighten out the wheels. This is your truck, you know."

Johnny gave him a pathetic look. "You know I can't swim."

"You shoulda thought of that before you drove the blasted thing in there. I'm surprised you haven't killed yourself before now, the way you pour that booze down."

Johnny gave him a sheepish look. "Aw, c'mon, Gus. Yesterday was just a bad day. You have days like that, don't you?"

Gus pursed his lips and shook his head. "You really beat all. You know that? How many times—just this week—have I had to get after you about your drinking? You gotta face it, pal, you give all the Indians a bad name when you're tanked, and you guys have little enough to be proud of as it is. You're a grown man, and it's time you acted like it."

Tears began running down Johnny's rough brown cheeks, and

he turned his face from Gus, wiping at his eyes with the back of his hand.

"Aw, shoot!" Gus muttered. He turned the tractor off and climbed down, putting his arm around the quivering man's shoulders. "I know your wife kicked you out, but doggonnit, John, I've been your friend for forty-five years, and I hate to see you like this. You weren't so beat down when we were kids. You were a real fiery young buck. What turned you so sour on life?"

Johnny wiped his nose with the back of his hand. "I dunno. It don't seem like nothin' I ever done worked out. I couldn't keep a job up at the mill, and my wife is always naggin' me about not havin' any money, and my kids all took off the Reservation as soon as they could." He shook his head. "I don't belong nowhere, Gus, and the only thing that stops the pain is a little drink now and then." He looked up sheepishly. "Is that really so bad?"

Gus gave a disgusted shake of his head. "It may stop the pain for a few hours, but it's gonna kill you one of these days." He jerked his thumb down toward the truck. "If I hadn't come along when I did yesterday, you'd be dead right now. Is that what you want? You wanna kill yourself?"

Johnny hung his head dejectedly. "Maybe everybody'd be better off if I did. I'm sure nobody'd miss me."

Gus dropped his arm from Johnny's shoulders and walked back to the tractor shaking his head. He started to climb up to the seat, then turned back to Johnny. "Maybe I'm nobody to you, John, but I'd miss you."

Johnny started to cry in earnest now, great heaving sobs that shook his whole body. Gus went back over to him and pulled his head to his shoulder. "C'mon now, buddy. It'll be okay. C'mon."

An old Ford pickup pulled up as they stood there. It was Derek Abrams, the young Indian teacher and coach out at White Swan High School. He climbed out of his truck and came toward them. "What's going on?" he asked. "What's wrong with Johnny?"

Gus pointed down to the truck. "He had a little accident with his truck yesterday."

Derek went over and looked down at the truck. "Anything I can do to help?"

"I know you're working at The Oaks this summer, but if you could spare a few minutes, we'd both appreciate it," Gus said.

"Sure. What do you want me to do?"

"I hate to ask it, but could you get down in there and straighten out the wheels while I try to pull it up? Johnny's scared of water."

"No problem," Derek said. He stripped off his shirt and shoes and handed his wallet and watch to Johnny, then slid down the side of the ditch and squeezed through the window into the driver's seat. As Gus gunned the tractor, Derek straightened out the wheels, and after a couple of tries the back of the truck slowly inched up the bank onto the road, water pouring out of the cab and from under the hood.

Gus unhooked the chain, then walked back to where Derek still sat in the cab. "I hate to take any more of your time, but could you stay in there till I pull this thing into my station? I know it's gonna make you late to work, but I'll call Cullen if you like."

"Don't worry about it. I don't answer to him for my actions."

Gus started to say something, but thought better of it. If the kid was willing to stick his neck out with Andrew Cullen, that wasn't any skin off *his* nose. Gus hooked the chain to the front of the truck, and with Johnny on the tractor behind him, and Derek still in the cab of Johnny's truck, he started off toward Harrah a mile away. When they got to his station, Gus unhooked the tractor as Derek climbed out of the cab. Johnny handed him his shirt, and he put it on, then took his watch, wallet, and shoes.

"I wish I could take you back to your car," Gus said, "but I left my pickup over at Jim Swick's and told him I'd get his tractor back as quick as I could. Johnny can stick around the station, but you'll have to walk back to The Oaks. What're you doing working there this summer anyway?" Gus asked. "I thought there was bad blood between you and the Cullens."

"I'm just taking care of some unfinished business," Derek replied.

Gus bit back the admonition he wanted to offer about not getting on the wrong side of Andrew Cullen. No one ever won that game.

CHAPTER 4

It was only eleven o'clock in the morning, but the broiling sun was raising little wisps of heat off the surface of the searing asphalt on the Harrah Road. Cassie Hampton peeled her sticky back from the leather upholstery of her aunt's Cadillac. "I can't believe this heat," she said.

Helen Lamont looked over at her and nodded. "It's the hottest summer we've had in years. I'm sure grateful to Laura for the invitation to use their pool."

"I didn't know you were such good friends with the Cullens."

"We're not, but once in a while Uncle Hank does some business with Mr. Cullen, so we get an occasional invitation to dinner or to use their pool."

Cassie gave a little laugh. "It seems so weird to actually be visiting this place after all these years of driving by here and wondering what's behind that mysterious wall of oaks."

"Well, you're in for a real treat," Helen said. "There are very few places like it in the whole country. Cyrus Barron wanted the best, and he got it."

"It seems like a strange place to build a mansion like this—right in the middle of an Indian Reservation."

Not at all," Helen said as she slowed down near the high wall ɪf native stone and thick evergreen oaks. "He knew he'd always have plenty of cheap labor."

"Do you think their daughter's going to be here today?" Cassie asked.

"I hope so. Laura wants her to get to know some of you local kids while she's home from boarding school this summer."

Cassie frowned. "I'm not sure I want to meet some stuck-up little debutante."

"Lily's not stuck-up. She's just a lonely little rich girl who doesn't know anyone here in the Valley, so if she does join us, I want you to be nice to her. I'd like to get another invitation to use their pool this summer."

"Oh, you know I will, but I look awful today. My swimming suit's three years old."

"It looks just fine," Helen said as she turned in at the gate and honked her horn. In a few minutes the heavy oak gate was slowly opened, and an old Indian man stood aside as the car passed onto the winding brick lane that led to the three-story, country French chateau just barely visible through the trees.

Cassie leaned forward eagerly as she saw the gardens and grounds of The Oaks for the first time. Off to the left, behind arbors of gnarled wisteria vines, she could just make out the marble columns that surrounded the swimming pool, and up ahead loomed the limestone-clad mansion. Cassie's mouth dropped open as they pulled up on the cobblestone motor court in front of the marble steps that led to the front entrance. "Oh my gosh!" Cassie exclaimed. "This is unreal!"

Helen grinned over at her. "I told you it was pretty special."

"Special isn't a big enough word for it. It's unbelievable! Are the Barrons still alive?"

Helen shook her head. "Only Laura. She was born here, but her mother died when she was very young, and Mr. Barron raised her alone. Then, about a year after she married Andrew Cullen, Mr. Barron was killed in a freak accident with a horse, and Laura inherited the house and the ranch, and she and Andrew and their three kids have lived here ever since. At least twenty-five years."

Helen and Cassie had just gotten out of their car when an elegant woman in her mid forties came out onto the front portico. Her blond hair was done up in a casual Victorian twist, and blue eyes dominated her beautiful face. She smiled as she came down the wide marble steps.

"Hello," Helen said, reaching out for Laura's hand. "It's so good to see you again. I'd like you to meet my niece, Cassie. She's going to be teaching out at White Swan this year and living with us."

Laura shook Helen's hand, then Cassie's. "I'm sure your aunt is thrilled to have you," she said. "We couldn't get along without our girls."

"Is your daughter here?" Cassie asked. "I'm really looking forward to meeting her."

Laura gave an apologetic shrug. "I was hoping she would be, but she got an invitation to visit an old friend in Yakima, so I let her go. I'll make sure she's here the next time you come. With this heat the way it is, you're both welcome to use the pool all summer. Just give me a call to make sure no one else is using it."

"We don't want to make a nuisance of ourselves," Helen said. "We'll just take a quick dip and get out of your way."

"You won't be in anyone's way. It sits here with no one in it most of the time."

"Don't your kids use it?" Cassie asked.

"Not very often. They're usually working or away at school, and Mr. Cullen doesn't like Lily running around in a swimming suit with all the young men who work on the ranch."

Cassie gave a little laugh. "I'm sure the sight of me in a swimming suit isn't going to tempt anyone."

"You don't need to worry about that. None of the ranch hands are allowed anywhere near the pool, so you two just enjoy yourselves, and I'll have Sam bring you some iced tea." She turned and went back up the steps as Helen and Cassie started along the path toward the pool.

They passed under a marble arch and came out into the pool area. White marble columns with connecting slabs surrounded the pool, and gnarled old wisteria vines had wound their way up the pillars and along the slabs, ending in a profusion of color on the roof of the pool house. Lounge chairs with blue and white stripes had been placed around the deck, and the pool itself was long and wide—the water crystal clear under the blazing sun.

Cassie's hand flew to her mouth. "Oh, my gosh! Look at this! It's like something you'd see in the movies!" She turned to her aunt with a giggle. "I can't believe I'm actually here." She quickly stripped off her shorts and shirt, and dived into the water, emerging in the center of the pool. She called out to Helen, "Come on in, Auntie. It's great!"

"I'll be there as soon as I change," Helen said, heading for the pool house.

Cassie climbed out and stepped up onto the diving board at the pool's end. She took several tentative bounces, then dived in with hardly a splash and surfaced to the sound of applause. Laughing, she turned her head, expecting to see her aunt, but was startled to see a young man in faded jeans and a sweaty tee shirt standing at the edge of the pool with a grin on his face.

"Very nice," he said.

Cassie treaded in place and wiped the water from her face with one hand. "Who are you?" she asked.

"I was about to ask you the same thing."

She swam to the steps and climbed out, tugging at the bottom of her suit as she looked around for her towel.

The boy grinned as he held it up. "Is this what you're looking for?"

She reached for it, but he playfully put it behind his back.

"May I have it please?" she asked.

"Not until you tell me who you are and what you're doing in my pool."

"*Your* pool?" Cassie said.

"Well, my mother's pool."

Cassie's mouth dropped open. "Mrs. Cullen is your mother?"

"She was the last time I asked."

"Oh my gosh! The way you're dressed, I thought you were one of the ranch hands. I'm really sorry."

He grinned as he handed her the towel. "Don't be. I consider that a compliment."

Just then, Helen came out of the dressing room, and the young man greeted her. "Hi, Mrs. Lamont. I don't know if you remember me or not, but I'm Max Cullen. Is this your daughter?"

"No, it's my niece, Cassie Hampton. She's going to be teaching out at White Swan this fall and living with us. Have you come out to join us?"

"I wish I could, but I'm running the kiln this summer, so I've gotta get going." He grinned at Cassie. "I hope you'll both come back though. It's nice to see someone using the pool."

"I'm sure we will," Helen said. "Your mother's invited us to use it all summer."

Max gave Cassie an appreciative grin. "Great! I'll look forward to seeing you both again, then." He gave them a little wave, then took off toward the hop kiln.

Cassie turned to her aunt with a grin. "Gosh! He's sure cute. He's not the one who ran into Derek's father, I hope."

Helen shook her head. "No. That was their older son, Morgan. Max is a nice young man. He's always been very friendly to Uncle Hank and me at their Christmas parties. He goes to college somewhere back East, then comes home in the summers to work on the ranch."

"Does their other son live at home?" Cassie asked.

"Yes, but no one sees much of him. He was badly crippled in the accident, and can't get around without a cane, but he does have a specially-built car that he speeds through Harrah in, and that's made him very unpopular around town."

Cassie lowered her voice. "I hope *he* doesn't show up down here. If he does, we're leaving."

"I don't think he will," Helen said. "He probably can't even swim."

She slipped into the pool and swam across the width, then grabbed the edge and called back to Cassie. "Better get back in, honey. We shouldn't stay too long."

They swam for about a half hour, then sat and drank the iced tea that the Indian servant had brought out to them. The sun had dried Cassie's suit, so she pulled her shorts and shirt on over it while Helen changed in the pool house. They were just leaving the pool area when something made Cassie glance up toward the back of the mansion, and she caught a glimpse of a girl looking down at them from the third-floor balcony. When the girl realized she'd been seen, she jumped back out of sight.

Cassie said nothing to her aunt until they were in the car. "Did you see that girl looking down at us from the balcony up on the top floor?" she asked.

Helen looked over at her. "When?"

"While we were leaving the pool. She jumped back when she realized I'd seen her. Do you suppose that was Lily?"

"I don't think so. Her mother said she wasn't home."

"Didn't you say Lily had long blond hair?"

"Yes."

"Well this girl had long blond hair. I bet she just didn't want to meet me, so she had her mother lie about not being here."

Helen gave her a quick frown. "You're making way to much out of this. Maybe she simply wasn't feeling well and asked her mother to make excuses for her, or maybe she's shy. You mustn't jump to conclusions, honey."

Cassie looked back at The Oaks as they drove away, and grinned. "Well, that was fun anyway, and that Max is sure cute. I hope I see him again."

Helen smiled over at her, but suddenly realized she felt no mirth. She had thought for some time that something was terribly wrong with that whole family, and she didn't want Cassie getting involved in any way with any of them.

CHAPTER 5

Max Cullen grinned as he walked back to the hop kiln and climbed to the upper deck. That Hampton girl was cute. His years of schooling back East, and travels in the summers, had kept him from getting to know any local kids as he'd grown up in the Valley, so he hoped he'd get to see her again. He wiped the sweat from his forehead. He'd forgotten how hot the Valley could get in the summers.

This was the first summer he'd been home in several years, and he was only now realizing how fractured his family was. They rarely shared meals together, and when he did see any of them, they never had time to just sit and talk like families are supposed to do. His big brother, Morgan, didn't get out of bed until noon, and was usually in a foul mood the rest of the day, and his mother and Lily spent most of their time in their rooms. It was obvious that there was no relationship between them and his dad.

His dad had always been emotionally remote with him too, so it was going to be a real challenge working for him full-time. It wasn't that he hadn't tried to build a relationship with him in the past; he just seemed incapable of any real affection for anyone in the family, except Morgan.

But Max felt it was time to make peace with his dad. He knew he was still mad at him for deciding not to go to law school in the fall as he'd wanted him to, but Max felt the time had come to take his future into his own hands, and since one of Andrew Cullen's sons would one day have to run this ranch—and Morgan wasn't interested in anything that made him get out of bed before noon—Max intended for that son to be him.

He looked down as a truck loaded with tall racks of hop vines slowly backed into the open end of the kiln. A well-built young Indian, with long braids, jumped out of the driver's seat and easily pulled himself up onto the back of the truck. Sweat glistened on his bronzed arms as he began hooking the racks onto a metal bar that Max had lowered. When the boom was loaded with vines, the driver motioned to Max to take it up, then jumped down from the truck bed and climbed back into the cab. He glanced up at Max as he pulled out of the shed, and Max gave him a little wave, but he didn't respond.

Max had little in common with any of the guys who worked on the ranch, but Derek Abrams had intrigued him when he'd first applied for the summer job. He'd told Max that he taught math and coached out at White Swan High and needed a job to tide him over till school started in September. Max figured he'd be a good influence on the kids who worked there in the summer, so he hired him. Later, someone told him that Derek had been an All-American football star at Washington State College, and Max had been impressed, but not surprised. Over six feet tall, Derek was one of the most well-built men he'd ever seen. He wasn't someone he'd like to tangle with—on or off the football field—but he might be someone to get to know, now that he was going to be living back home full-time.

Lily Cullen had also spotted the attractive Indian who was driving a truck at The Oaks this summer. He obviously wasn't a full-blood Indian, because he lacked the broad nose and wide cheekbones most Yakimas had, and his skin was nearly as light as hers. She made a mental note to ask Max about him.

It was nice having Max home again. He was so upbeat about everything and always brightened things up when he was here. She was thrilled that he'd decided not to go on to law school, but stay home and work full time on the ranch. She needed him here to keep her safe from Morgan. Earlier today, she'd watched Max flirting with some girl down at their pool, and it reminded her that she couldn't even use their pool anymore. Morgan might show up and try to put his dirty hands on her again.

The first time he'd tried something was the summer she was fourteen, and he'd gotten into the pool with her one day and begun teasing her about how big her breasts were getting. She was in boarding school most of the year, and barely knew her big brother, so she was flattered that he was taking time to notice her. He began splashing water at her and tickling her, and it was fun at first, but then he put his hands on her breasts and that scared her, and she started to cry. He put his arm around her and told her it was just an accident, but begged her not to say anything about it to anyone, so she hadn't.

But after that, she never went down to the pool when he was there, and when she was home on vacations, she spent most of her time in her room with the door locked. Two summers ago, when she was sixteen, she'd just come back from lunch one day, and he was waiting in her room. He pushed the door shut behind her and locked it, then shoved her onto her bed and forced himself on her. When she finally found the courage to tell her mother what he'd done, Laura immediately told Andrew, and he said he'd take care of it. But nothing was ever done about it, and Lily was too scared of her father and Morgan to ask why.

As a result of all this, she rarely left her room when she was home on vacation. At eighteen, she was a prisoner in her own home. But it was all going to stop soon. She had already decided that no matter what it took, Morgan was never going to put his dirty hands on her again.

CHAPTER 6

The day's blistering heat had finally cooled down as Cassie slid off of her aunt's golden palomino and led him by the reins toward the corral gate. She loved these late evening rides along the canal bank that wound its way through Uncle Hank's 600 acres of farmland and pasture. It gave her time to think. And, as usual, her thoughts were about Derek Abrams. All of her college friends thought she was crazy for going back to the Reservation to teach when she could go anywhere in the world with her teaching degree, but she had to see whether there was any possibility of a relationship developing between her and Derek.

Not many white girls on the Reservation got romantically involved with Indians, but other than the slight difference in their skin color, she and Derek had so much in common. Both had lost their fathers when they were young: Derek's in a car accident, and Cassie's to pneumonia when she was four. That's when she'd gone to live with her aunt. With Uncle Hank off fighting the Nazis, Helen had been delighted to have her company, and Cassie had ended up staying with them clear through high school. And now that she'd graduated from college, she was back with them again, excited at the prospect of teaching with Derek at White Swan High School in the fall.

Helen watched through the kitchen window as Cassie led the big palomino into the corral. She reminded her so much of herself at that age; so innocent to the ways of the world. She frowned as she thought about Cassie's reaction to Max Cullen today. He might be a nice enough boy, but you could never tell about someone whose father was a notorious womanizer. A boy like that could easily take advantage of someone as innocent as Cassie.

Helen knew she worried too much about her, but she'd been like a daughter for so many years that she sometimes felt like she was. She'd known when she married Hank Lamont that they would probably never have children. Hank had had mumps when he was young, and the doctors had told him he might never be able to father a child. He'd told Helen about it before he asked her to marry him, but neither of them fully realized how much they'd miss having a child of their own. Helen had tried to make up for it by gathering all the stray children in the neighborhood every Sunday morning and taking them to the Sunday school class she taught at her church in Harrah, but the longing for a child of her own had never left her.

Cassie had filled that void, especially during Hank's frequent absences over the years. The son of French immigrants, he was blunt and unsophisticated, but his six-foot-four height and 240 pounds gave him an intimidating presence. Helen never doubted that he loved her, but his extensive business dealings with wealthy ranchers and politicians all over the state often took him away from home for days at a time. His wealth had provided her with every physical comfort, but so many nights she went to bed alone, longing to snuggle into the curvature of his massive body, his strong arms wrapped around her, his heavy breathing filling her with contentment as it lulled her to sleep.

CHAPTER 7

Andrew Cullen relished the feeling of power he got from patrolling his 300-acre hop ranch in his silver Army-surplus Jeep. He loved to brag that his Jeep had once belonged to General Patton, so his men called him "General" behind his back. He knew they did, and secretly loved it. He pulled alongside the truck Derek Abrams was maneuvering down the rows of vines and laid his hand on the Jeep's horn. "What do you think you're doing?" he yelled up at the young Indian. "You've missed half the vines in that row."

Derek stopped the truck and looked through the back window at the rows behind him. One vine still dangled from the overhead wires where the cutters had failed to cut it cleanly. He looked down at the angry face of the older man, but he kept his response civil. "Maybe you should talk to the guys on the back. It's their job to cut the vines. I just drive."

"Don't give me any of your lip!" Cullen said. "As the driver, you're supposed to see that all the vines are cut cleanly before you move on. If you wanna keep your job, you'll see to it. You Indians all seem to think it's a free ride around here. Well, it's not, so you do the job right, or I'll get someone who will!" Cullen gunned the Jeep and whirled around, heading back to the kiln.

He roared up in front of the kiln in a cloud of dust. A truck had just backed up to the kiln, and the men who were unloading their vines jerked their heads in his direction. Cullen spotted Max on the upper deck and motioned to him. "Get down here!" he bellowed.

Max turned to say something to the man beside him, then came down the steps. "What's up, Dad?"

"What's the name of that big buck who drives the blue Ford?"

"You mean Derek Abrams?"

"Abrams?" Cullen shot back, his brows raised in surprise. "Is he the kid that belonged to the Indian who ran Morgan down?"

"Yeah."

"Why'd you hire him, for God's sake? You know how I feel about that family."

"He's the coach up at White Swan, and all the kids here like him. Why? What's he done?"

"He's leaving half the vines on the wires."

Max frowned. "That doesn't sound like Derek, but I'll talk to him about it."

"Do more than talk. You let him know he's outta here if it happens again." He glanced around. "Where's Morgan?"

Max looked at his watch and gave a rueful snort. "It's only noon. He's probably not up yet."

Cullen shot him a disgruntled look. "His leg is probably acting up again. When you see him, tell him I wanna see him in the kiln office."

Cullen drove off, and Max shook his head. It wasn't Morgan's leg that was bothering him. It was another hangover.

Max had never felt close to his older brother. Morgan had picked on him as they were growing up, and although he didn't actually hate him, when the car accident happened, and his parents told him that Morgan might die, Max was sure it was his fault for wishing him dead. When they finally let him see Morgan lying there in the hospital in such pain, Max begged his brother to forgive him for being so mad at him all the time. In a moment of uncharacteristic camaraderie, Morgan told him not to worry about it. "We've both gotten into each other's hair, and we'll probably keep right on doing it till the day we die."

And that pretty much summed up the relationship they'd had ever since. They had no friends in common, no mutual interests, and no great love for each other, but there was an unspoken agreement between them that each would do his own thing without interference from the other. More than once Max would have liked to talk to Morgan about his drinking and gambling, but as long as it didn't affect him personally, he minded his own business. Morgan was twenty-six years old, and if he chose to throw his life away on such stupid things, it wasn't Max's responsibility. As far as Morgan being the old man's favorite, Max had come to terms with that a long time ago.

It was nearly one o'clock when Morgan came limping up to the kiln, his scowl making it obvious that he was in a bad mood. Max spotted him and yelled down, "Dad wants to see you in his office."

Morgan glanced up, the scowl deepening. "I suppose you told him I wasn't out here yet," he shouted back.

Max shook his head. "Nope, but he's not in the greatest mood."

"Well, that makes two of us then," Morgan grumbled, limping off in the direction of the kiln office.

Morgan pushed open the door of the office, and Dorothy looked up from her desk, then down at her watch. "Good afternoon," she said.

He gave her a sour look. "You're not my timekeeper," he said, pushing open the door of his father's office.

Cullen's eyes never left the papers he was looking at on the desk. "Shut the door and sit down," he growled.

Morgan flicked the door shut with his cane, then took a seat in the green leather chair in front of his father's desk. "Max said you were looking for me. What do you want?"

The older Cullen finally looked up, and his eyes were blazing. He shoved the papers he'd been looking at toward his son. "Take a look at these and you'll see what I want. To start with, I want the truth, not the lies I usually get from you."

Morgan reached over and took the papers. The letterhead read, "Law Offices of Felder and Keith." His eyes widened in alarm as he read down the page. "This is a lie! I never touched that girl. I hardly know her."

Andrew's angry eyes were riveted on his son. "What kind of fool do you take me for? I know you've been seeing her for months. Your brother told me that, and I'm sure you didn't keep your hands to yourself, so how do you know this baby isn't yours? It could just as well be."

Morgan shrugged indifferently. "Well, I'm sure I'm not the only one who's had her. Plenty of other guys have too."

Cullen slammed his fist on the desk, and Morgan flinched

slightly. "Well, 'plenty of other guys' aren't being sued for a hundred thousand dollars. I'm tired of bailing you out of one scrape after another. You're on your own on this one."

Morgan leaned forward, pretending concern. "You don't mean that."

"Oh, yes I do. It's time you learned to take responsibility for your actions."

A smirk turned up the corners of Morgan's mouth, and he slouched back in the chair. "You mean, like you did with Grandpa Barron and his horse?"

His father's eyes narrowed. "If you're gonna use threats like that, you'd better be prepared to back them up with more than just words. There's gonna come a time when you threaten me once too often. Do you understand me?"

Under the onslaught of his father's rage, Morgan backed off a little. "I'm not threatening you, Dad. I'm just reminding you that we all make mistakes. If you'll recall, you're the one who told me that."

"I told you a lot of things I wish now I hadn't, and I've been paying for it for years." His eyes bore into Morgan's. "But I'm serving you warning, young man. I'm not gonna take it forever." He flipped his hand toward the door. "Go on, now. Get outta here, and at least try to give the appearance that you're pulling your weight around this place."

Morgan picked up his cane from the floor and stood up. "What're you gonna do about that?" he asked, pointing his cane at the papers on the desk.

Cullen gathered up the papers. "What do you *think* I'm gonna do? I'll give the girl something to soothe her father's ruffled honor, but not a hundred thousand dollars, you can be sure of that." He glared up at Morgan. "But get one thing straight, Morgan. This is definitely the last time I'm bailing you out. Is that clear?"

Morgan smiled to himself as he limped out of the office. It wouldn't be the last time. He and his father both knew that.

Andrew Cullen sat motionless at his desk for a long time after his son left. He was thinking back to the night in the hospital when he'd told Morgan about his involvement in his grandpa Barron's death. The boy had been close to death himself from the car accident and was riddled with worry about the consequences of having killed the Indian in the other car, and Cullen had sought to ease his son's conscience by telling him that everyone made mistakes. He, himself, had done something he wasn't proud of. Old man Barron had fancied himself a great bronco buster, and although Cullen was married to Barron's only child, the old man still treated him like a hired hand, so Cullen had seen a chance to humble him one day when they were breaking some wild broncos, and he put a burr under the saddle of one especially wild one. When Barron got on, the horse bucked him into the railing, and Cyrus Barron died a day later from a broken neck.

In all the confusion, Cullen removed the burr before anyone found it, and no one ever knew that Andrew Cullen had been the cause of his father-in-law's death. No one, that is, except Morgan, and he had never let his father forget that he knew.

Cullen got out his checkbook and grudgingly wrote out a check for twenty thousand dollars.

CHAPTER 8

Lucy Abrams watched her weary son lying on the living room rug working on some school plans for the coming year. The rug, like everything else in the house, was old, but clean. When she'd married Jason Abrams, she'd known that life would be hard married to an idealist with little formal education, but an over-abundance of Indian pride. She herself had finished high school and wanted to go to college, but her parents didn't have the money to send her, so when Jason asked her to marry him, she decided it was the best she could do. Derek was born in that first year, a beautiful, light-skinned boy with dark hair, and eyes that seemed way too observant, even as a baby.

Jason loved to tell Lucy how beautiful she was, but she had never thought of herself as such. Many Yakima women were short and squat with high cheekbones and broad noses, but Lucy's height and sculptured features were gifts from a white ancestor who'd married one of Kamiakin's daughters a hundred years before. Jason had never tired of telling her how proud he was that she had taken such good care of herself, and he'd once knocked down a White-man who had called her a *squaw*, a supreme insult to his beautiful Lucy.

Jason Abrams had been tall: his hair chestnut brown, his eyes hazel, and his nose straight and narrow—gifts from his own white ancestor, Joshua Abrams, an Indian Agent who had also married one of Chief Kamiakin's daughters.

Derek was a blend of both with Lucy's black hair and dark eyes and Jason's fair skin and Caucasian features. Few people ever knew exactly what he was thinking, but without a word passing between them, Lucy always knew, and she knew now that something was bothering him.

She motioned for him to get up so she could measure for the buttons on the shirt she was making him. He slipped it on, and she began marking where the buttons needed to go. "I swear, your chest and arms are getting bigger every day," she said. "Are you lifting weights again?"

"I'm lifting 200-pound racks of hops," he replied dryly.

She looked up at him. "How are things going at The Oaks?"

"About the way I expected."

"And?" she asked, aware that there was more.

"Max and his old man chewed me out today over something I wasn't responsible for."

"I'd expect that of Andrew, but I thought you said Max liked you."

"He can take me or leave me, but he isn't going to stick his neck out for me with his old man, that's for sure."

Lucy's expression darkened. "Have you had any run-ins with Morgan?"

Derek let out a derisive grunt. "I've barely seen him. He

doesn't show up till noon, and then he's so hungover he keeps out of sight the rest of the day."

Lucy had been worried ever since Derek told her he was going to work at The Oaks this summer. In all the years since Jason had been killed, she'd done her best to avoid any contact with Andrew Cullen. He'd stopped by her place numerous times in the months following the accident on the pretext of seeing how she and Derek were doing, but his real intentions had been to get into her bed. The thought now—as then—nauseated her. She'd never told Derek about it, fearing what he might do, so when he'd decided to get a summer job at The Oaks, she'd tried to talk him out of it, but he'd made up his mind. One way or the other, he was going to get Andrew Cullen to admit that Morgan had caused the accident that killed his father.

A shadow crossed her face now. "I wish you'd leave this thing alone, honey. Revenge was not your father's way. He believed in forgiveness, just like they teach in the longhouse *and* in our church. He'd want you to forgive the Cullens."

"I *can't* forgive them. They put a stain on Dad's name by saying he was a drunk, and it's my responsibility to remove it. Can't you see that?"

"All I can see is that you're going to get hurt if you take on Andrew Cullen."

"I'm not going to 'take him on'. I just want him to tell me to my face that Morgan was the one who was drunk—not Dad."

"Why is that so important to you? You know the truth."

"Yes, but most people don't, and I want to be able to tell them

40

that Andrew Cullen looked me in the eye and admitted that his son caused the accident. Don't you think Dad deserves that?"

She put her hand on his arm. "Let it go, honey. Let God deal with him for what he did."

"Your God has had twelve long years and hasn't done anything about it yet."

She folded the shirt she was working on and laid it in her sewing basket, staring down at it for a long moment. "Sometimes you frighten me," she said. "You really do."

"Why?" he demanded.

She looked up at him. "Because you're going to throw away everything you've worked so hard for just to get revenge on someone who isn't worth it."

He reached out and gripped her shoulders. "I don't know how to make you see this, but by labeling Dad a drunk, they not only put a stain on our family, but on every Indian on this Reservation, and I have to remove that."

"Why is this so important right now, when everything is going so well for you?"

"Because too many Whites think *all* Indians are drunks, and I want them to know that my father was the most righteous man who ever lived on this Reservation. Don't you think he deserves that?"

She cupped his face in her hands. "Of course he does, but be careful with those Cullens. I don't want to lose you too."

"You won't," he said, then grinned as he flexed his right arm. "I'm not an All-American for nothing."

CHAPTER 9

Several days after Helen and Cassie had been guests in the Cullen pool, the temperature soared to 105 degrees and Cassie begged her aunt to call Mrs. Cullen and see if they could come for a swim. Helen called, but Laura said they were going to be out of town for a couple of days and it would be better if they came on Friday. Helen said that was fine, but as luck would have it, she woke on Friday with with a runny nose, and reluctantly told Cassie they'd have to put off going to the Cullens until she felt better.

"Oh, darn!" Cassie said. "I was really looking forward to going today. It's so hot, and I want to try out my new swimsuit. Do you think it would be alright if I went alone? I'd just jump in for a few minutes and get cooled off. I wouldn't bother any of them."

"Let me call Laura and see what she says."

Helen called and explained that she wasn't feeling well enough to come for a swim, and Laura said it was fine for Cassie to come by herself.

It was about three in the afternoon when Cassie pulled up to the gate of The Oaks and honked the horn as her aunt had done. After ten minutes had passed and no one came, she honked again, and Sam finally opened the gate. He nodded at her as she started down the lane toward the parking court in front of the house. She got out and waited for a few minutes to see if Mrs. Cullen would come out as she'd done before, but when no one came, she walked around the house toward the pool.

Passing under the arbor, she saw that someone was floating in the pool at the far end. She paused for a moment, worried that it might be Morgan, but since she was already there, she called out cheerily, "Hi."

When she got no response, she continued along the deck and saw that it was a man, and he was floating face down. She waited for him to come up for air, then suddenly realized that something was wrong. Without thinking, she dropped her towel and purse and jumped into the pool and swam over to him, grabbing him by his trunks. He was heavy, but she managed to pull him over to the steps on the shallow end and saw that he was bleeding from his head. She began yelling for help, but when no one responded, she climbed out of the pool and ran around to the front of the house and pounded on the front door.

Sam was scowling as he opened it. "What's all this noise about?"

"Someone's in the pool, and I think he's been hurt. Come quick!"

His eyes widened. "Who is it?"

"I don't know, but hurry!"

Sam turned and yelled up the stairs. "Mrs. Cullen! Someone's been hurt in the pool!"

He pushed past Cassie and ran down the path toward the

pool, Cassie right behind him. "It's Morgan!" Sam gasped, jumping down onto the steps where Cassie had dragged him.

"Is he okay?" she cried.

Sam felt for a pulse, then looked up and shook his head.

Cassie noticed that one of the lounge chairs was lying on its side near the edge of the pool, and she pointed to it. "There's blood on the chair."

Sam looked up and saw the blood. "He must've hit his head on something and stumbled into the pool," he said.

Just then, Laura and Lily came running up. When Laura saw Morgan, she let out a cry and jumped down onto the steps beside him, cradling his head in her arms. "Oh, Morgan!" she cried. "Morgan! Morgan!" She looked over at Sam. "Is he dead?"

The Indian nodded.

"No!" she cried. "No!"

Lily knelt on the edge of the pool and put her arms around her mother. "Don't cry, Mother. Please. Don't cry." She turned to Sam. "Go get Dad and Max. Quick!"

Sam got out of the pool and took off running toward the kiln. Cassie watched helplessly as Laura sat half submerged on the steps, rocking back and forth with Morgan in her arms.

"Shouldn't we call an ambulance?" Cassie said.

Lily whipped around. "Who are you?"

"Cassie Hampton. Mrs. Lamont's niece. I was here a few days ago with my aunt, and your mother invited me back today."

"Did you see what happened?"

Cassie quickly shook her head. "No. He was in the pool when I got here."

"Well, he was probably drunk and fell in," Lily said.

Cassie gave her a stunned look. There was no remorse in her voice at all, and yet this was her brother lying there dead. Cassie began to have an uneasy feeling.

"I'll call the police," Lily said, heading for the pool house.

Cassie stood there shivering, not knowing what to do. She looked down at Mrs. Cullen who was still on the steps, sobbing as she caressed Morgan's face.

Lily was back in a minute. "I called Deputy Styvessan at the station, and he said he'd call the Toppenish sheriff, then get right over here." She knelt down beside her mother and tried to disengage her from Morgan. "C'mon, Mother," she begged. "The sheriff's coming, and he'll take care of Morgan. You can't do anything for him. He's obviously dead."

"Don't say that!" she sobbed. "He might not be!"

"He *is*, Mother. You can see he's not breathing."

Just then, Andrew Cullen and Max came bursting through the arbor with Sam at their heels. Cullen's face was ashen. When he saw Morgan, he let out an agonizing moan. "Not Morgan! Oh God! Not Morgan!"

He shoved Laura and Lily aside and pulled Morgan up onto the deck. He put his ear to his son's chest and listened, then turned him over on his stomach and began trying to pump the water out of him. He stayed at it for about ten minutes, but only a few spurts of water came out of his mouth. He turned him onto his back and put his ear to his chest once more. After a few minutes, he looked up forlornly. "There's no heartbeat." He stood up, his eyes wild with pain. "How did this happen? Who found him?"

"I . . . I did," Cassie muttered.

Cullen turned on her, his rage beginning to mount. "Who are you?"

Cassie could barely control her voice. "I'm Hank Lamont's niece. Your wife invited me to swim today."

Cullen looked down at Laura. "Is that true?"

Laura was still sitting on the pool steps, her eyes glazed with grief, but she gave a little nod.

Max came to Cassie's defense. "She and Mrs. Lamont were both here a few days ago, Dad. I talked to them myself."

Cullen turned back to Cassie. "Did you see who did this?"

Cassie quickly shook her head. "No. All I saw when I came in was someone floating in the far end of the pool, and when I got closer and saw he wasn't coming up for air, I jumped in and pulled him over to the steps."

"Was he still alive?" Cullen demanded.

"I don't know. I didn't stop to find out. I just ran for help."

"You didn't stop to find out?" Cullen roared. "What kind of idiot are you? You might've been able to save him if you'd given him artificial respiration."

Cassie's shivering increased under his onslaught, and Max put his arm around her shoulders. "For God's sake, Dad! She didn't know what to do."

"Any fool would know enough to check to see if someone's breathing if they're found unconscious in a pool. If she'd used her head, she might've saved him."

A rush of indignation suddenly shot through Cassie. "I did the best I could. I pulled him over to the steps and ran for help."

Max knelt down beside Morgan and saw the jagged tear in his scalp. "Look at this, Dad! There's a gash on his head!"

Cullen knelt down beside Max and pulled Morgan's hair back. "He must've hit the edge of the pool when he went in."

Max looked over at the overturned lounge chair and saw the blood on it. "Then why is there blood on the chair? He was definitely bleeding before he went into the pool."

Cullen got up and turned the chair right side up and looked at the spatters of blood on it. "You're right. He must've fallen over here."

"He was drinking at lunch today. Maybe he was trying to get into the pool to cool off and slipped and hit his head."

"He couldn't have gotten a gash like this from just falling down. He was hit with something." Cullen looked around, his panic mounting. "Was someone out here with him? Sam, did you see anyone out here today?"

Sam shook his head. "I was in the house all day. I only went out to let the young lady in the gate. I didn't even know Mr. Morgan was at the pool."

Cullen whipped back to Cassie. "And you're sure you told me everything you saw?"

"Why would I hide anything? I don't even know you people."

"Leave her alone, Dad," Max said. "She wouldn't have any reason to lie."

"That remains to be seen. Did someone call the police?"

"I called Deputy Styvessan at the gas station," Lily said. "He's gonna call the Toppenish sheriff and an ambulance."

Cullen seemed to notice his daughter for the first time.

"Where were you when this happened? You're always spying on everyone from up there on your balcony."

Max piped up again. "For God's sake, Dad. Lay off! We don't know if somebody did *anything* to him. It could easily have been an accident."

The sound of a car horn could be heard at the gate, and Cullen turned to Sam. "That's probably Styvessan now. Go let him in."

Sam dashed out and returned in a moment with Gus right behind him.

"What's happened here?" Gus asked, kneeling down by the body. "Morgan drowned?" He felt for a pulse on the boy's neck, then slowly shook his head. "There's no pulse." He saw the blood on Morgan's forehead, and parted his hair. "Looks like he hit his head when he went in the pool."

"I thought so too," Cullen said, "but look at this."

Gus looked up. "What?"

Cullen showed him the lounge chair. "There's blood over here. If he'd hit his head going into the pool, there wouldn't be blood on the chair."

Gus examined the chair and the deck around it. "It looks like he was hit with something."

"I think so too," Cullen said, "but what? There's nothing here with blood on it."

"Who found him?" Gus asked.

"I did," Cassie said.

Gus turned to her. "You're Hank Lamont's niece, aren't you? How'd you happen to be here?"

Cassie explained about the swim invitation and how she'd found Morgan in the pool and pulled him over to the steps.

Gus looked at the others. "Did any of you see anyone around here today who didn't belong?"

They all shook their heads.

Gus wiped the blood from his hands with his handkerchief. "Well, it looks like something might've gone on out here, and I'm gonna need some help sorting it all out. Is there a phone I can use?"

"In the pool house," Cullen said. "I'll show you."

"I called an ambulance in Toppenish when your daughter called me," Gus told Cullen as they walked to the pool house. "It shouldn't take too long for it to get here. Why don't you take everybody into the house while I call Sheriff Lucas in Toppenish? I'm sure he'll wanna question all of you. I'll stay out here with Morgan."

Cullen nodded and went back out to the pool. He glanced down at his son's body, and his voice was raw. "Gus wants everybody in the house till the sheriff gets here."

Cassie had been watching all this in disbelief, but the enormity of what had happened was just beginning to sink in. She turned to Max. "I've gotta call my aunt. She'll want to know about this."

"You can call her from the house," Max said. He was about to ask his father to gather up his mother and bring her in, but Cullen had stormed off toward the house without another word.

Max went over to his mother who was once again cradling Morgan's head in her lap. He motioned to Sam. "Give me a hand with Mom, will you?"

Laura shook her head vehemently. "I won't leave him."

Max knelt down beside her and tried to disengage her arms from Morgan's body. "C'mon, Mom. You can't do anything more for him. The ambulance'll be here soon. They'll take care of him."

Laura looked up at Max, her face a stricken mask. "I can't leave him, Max. He needs me."

"Please, Mom. Gus said he'd stay out here with him."

Max got his hands under her arms, but she refused to let go of Morgan.

"I'll take her," Sam said. He lifted the sobbing woman into his arms and followed the rest of them into the house.

CHAPTER 10

Word that there had been an accident at the pool spread quickly around the ranch, and the workers began making their way to the pool area. Derek Abrams stood at the back of the group and watched the scene with keen interest.

Gus Styvessan began questioning the men, but no one had seen anything out of the ordinary, or anyone who didn't have a reason for being on the ranch. He was still questioning them when Tom Lucas, the county sheriff from Toppenish, and Carl Perkins, his deputy, arrived. Lucas was a country boy who'd made his way up through the ranks to the post of County Sheriff. He greeted Gus, then took a look at the body while Gus briefed him on what they knew so far.

"I want Carl to get pictures of all this," Lucas said, pointing to the body and the bloody lounge chair. "And get names and pictures of all these guys. I wanna make sure they all belong here."

Carl began snapping the shots that Lucas wanted, then got out a pad and pencil and asked the men to write down their names.

Lucas turned to Gus. "I think we've got everything we need out here as soon as Carl gets all these names. He can stay with the body till the ambulance gets here. I'd like to talk to those in the house."

Gus looked at his watch, then turned to the men. "After you've put your names down, why don't you boys go on home? It's almost six."

"Is Cullen gonna want us back tomorrow?" Billy Aimes asked.

"I'm sure he will, but call the office in the morning, and they'll let you know."

The men began drifting off until they'd all left. The sheriff looked at the pad of names Carl had gotten, and showed it to Gus. "Do you think any of these guys coulda done this?"

Gus glanced down the list and shook his head. "I don't think so. I know all of 'em, and they've worked for Cullen off and on for years. It's no secret that Morgan wasn't very popular with a lot of people, but it'd be pretty hard for someone to get in here and kill him in broad daylight without being seen. Maybe it was an accident."

Lucas knelt down by the body and parted the matted hair on Morgan's head. "I s'pose it could be, but this looks more like he was whacked with somethin'."

"I didn't see anything around here that could put a hole like that in his head," Gus said. "Besides, it would take someone pretty darned strong to do it, no matter what he used."

"From what I just saw, there's some big guys workin' here," Lucas remarked.

"Yeah, but they're all local guys. When you get the pictures developed, I'll show them to Cullen or Max and see if there was anybody here that shouldn't have been."

The sheriff stood up and tucked the notepad into his shirt pocket. "You know everybody in Harrah, Gus. Can you think of anyone who wanted him dead?"

Gus pursed his lips thoughtfully, then shook his head. "Not off hand. He was always getting into trouble in Yakima, but that was mostly for drunk driving and disorderly conduct. He did do some gambling, and maybe he got in over his head. I know he wrecked his dad's car a couple times, and I'm sure you remember the time he ran into that Indian there on the Fort Road and killed him. That's the accident that messed up his leg."

"Yeah, I remember that. I was only a patrolman then, but as I recall, there was some question around the station about who was really to blame for that."

"There was more than just a question," Gus said, looking around to make sure no one was listening. "Morgan was drunk and under age, and everyone knew he was responsible, but Cullen claimed the Indian was the one who was drunk, and Cullen's buddy, Judge Harmon, let Morgan off."

Lucas gave a little snort. "That Harmon's some piece of work. How he ever got to be a judge, I'll never know."

"Well, Morgan didn't get off scot-free," Gus said, pointing down to the body. "You can see how messed up his leg is."

Lucas threw Gus a questioning look. "Did he need a wheelchair to get around? I don't see one out here."

Gus thought for a moment. "I don't think so. All I've ever seen him use is a real fancy cane with a heavy gold handle on it."

"Can he walk without it?"

"I don't think so. Why?"

"Well, a thing like that could put a pretty good dent in someone's head if a strong enough guy was swingin' it."

Gus nodded thoughtfully. "Yeah, I guess it could."

"Did you see the cane anywhere out here?"

Gus shook his head. "I wasn't looking for it. One of the family must've picked it up."

"I think we'd better get into the house and start askin' some questions," Lucas said. He turned to Deputy Perkins. "I don't know how long this is gonna take, Carl, but I'd like you to stay out here with the body and get a few more pictures before the ambulance gets here, then go on back to Toppenish with them. I'll catch up with you at the station. Okay?"

"I'll have the pictures ready when you get there."

"Great. We shouldn't be more than another hour or so here."

"Take your time. I've got my work cut out puttin' all these names in the order in which they were standing so I can match 'em with the pictures when I get 'em developed."

The mood in the Cullen living room was grim as they waited for the sheriff and Gus to come in. Sam had helped Laura up to her room to change into dry clothes, and Andrew Cullen was in his study with the door closed. The three younger ones sat in the living room waiting for the two sheriffs to come in.

No one seemed inclined to talk until Max finally said to Lily, "I know you and Morgan never got along, Sis, but he wasn't all bad. You know that. He just felt like he had to prove that he was as good as everybody else with that leg of his."

He waited for Lily's response, but her expression remained

impassive, so he went on. "He tried to act like being crippled didn't bother him, but I know it did."

Cassie's clothes had dried, and she was seated beside Lily on the sofa with her legs tucked up under her, but couldn't control her shivering. "I'm sorry I never got to know him," she said.

"You don't know how lucky you are," Lily quipped.

Max dismissed her comment with a flick of his hand. "Don't pay any attention to her. She and Morgan never did get along." He paused a moment, then added as an afterthought, "I guess the truth is, Morgan didn't get along too well with most people. All he could think about was getting out of this Valley as soon as he could." He gave a half-hearted laugh. "He hated hops worse than anybody I ever knew."

"Unless they were in a bottle," Lily muttered. She got up and walked over to the window, drawing back the corner of the drape.

"Knock if off!" Max fired at her. "I mean it! There's no need to involve Cassie in your personal feud with Morgan."

Lily whipped her head around. "It's the truth, isn't it? He was a drunk, and everybody knew it, although you'd never get Dad to say anything against his precious pet."

Max shrugged. "Well, maybe he did drink more than he should've, but he had a lot to cope with."

"Don't we all?" Lily snapped. She pulled the drape aside and looked out again. "The ambulance is here."

Max jumped up and went to the window. He shook his head as he watched Morgan being loaded into the back of the ambulance. "It's just so hard to think of him being dead," he said. "He was so excited at lunch today about a new car Dad was getting him."

Lily exploded. "Oh, that's just great! What's that for? Employee of the month?"

Max pointed toward the door of his dad's study. "For God's sake, Lily! Dad's gonna hear you."

"What do I care? They're two of a kind."

Max was about to respond when there was a knock on the front door. He glowered at Lily as he went to open it. It was Gus Styvessan and Sheriff Lucas. "C'mon in," Max said. "I'll go get Mom and Dad."

Gus and the sheriff stepped in and stood there awkwardly, apparently too awed by the grandeur of the room to sit down without being asked. Sheriff Lucas had his Stetson in his hands, and Gus nervously fingered his baseball cap as his gaze took in the opulent furnishings. His eyes stopped at a large oil painting of a young Laura Barron that was hanging over the fireplace, and he smiled to himself. How well he remembered her at that age. His first love. Who knows what might've happened if Andrew Cullen hadn't come along and stolen her from him? He'd stopped brooding about that years ago, but now, seeing the fragile girl on the canvas looking down at him, a flood of memories came rushing back.

Gus and Sheriff Lucas turned as Andrew Cullen came out of his study. Twenty-six years had still not made Gus like the man, but this was no time for that. He was obviously shattered by his son's death. Gus stepped toward him and stuck out his hand and Cullen shook it. "I just want you to know that we're all real upset about this," Gus said to Cullen. "I know how much Morgan meant to you." Gus turned to Sheriff Lucas. "You know Sheriff Lucas, don't you?"

Cullen reached out and gave Lucas's hand a perfunctory shake. "We've met."

"I'm sure sorry about this," Lucas said. "As soon as your wife gets down here, there's a few questions I need to ask all of you. Why don't we sit down?"

They had just taken their seats when Laura came down the staircase assisted by Sam. She'd changed into a long white robe, but her face was pale and drawn, and her eyes swollen from weeping. Sam helped her into a chair, then left the room. Gus looked over at Andrew, expecting him to get up and go to Laura's side, but he made no move toward her. It was all he could do to keep from going to her himself, but this was no time to open old wounds.

Sheriff Lucas walked to the fireplace and turned to face them. "Well, folks, Morgan's death was probably an accident, but with that hole in his head, it raises some questions on how it got there. Gus has told me what all of you told him, but there's a few questions I'd like to ask. Did Morgan need a wheelchair to get around?"

"No," Cullen said. "All he ever used was his cane. Why?"

"Well, Gus and I looked for it, but we didn't see it out there. Did any of you pick it up?"

They all looked at one another and shook their heads.

"I'd appreciate it if you'd look through the house and see if he mighta left it in here," Lucas said.

"He wouldn't have left it in the house," Cullen said. "He can't walk without it." He suddenly leaned forward. "Do you think someone might've used it on him, then took off with it?"

Lucas gave a little shrug. "We don't know, but Gus says the handle on it is a heavy gold ornament with a sharp point that could cause some serious damage. Of course, we don't know if that's what put the gash on his head or not, but since we didn't find it out there—and you say he can't walk without it—somebody may have used it on him, then took off with it or tossed it somewhere here on the ranch." Lucas looked over at Gus. "Maybe I'll get a couple of my guys out here tonight to look for it."

Cullen suddenly jumped up. "I will not have strangers running around my property, poking their noses into private areas. I've got my own men, and we'll look for it ourselves."

It was obvious that Cullen was on the edge of coming unglued, so Gus spoke up quickly. "Why don't we continue this tomorrow, Lucas? This has been a rough experience for these folks, and they look like they need some time for themselves."

Lucas turned back to Cullen. "Why don't we discuss this tomorrow when you've all had a chance to calm down? In the meantime, there are a couple of things I'd like you all to do. First, look through the house and see if Morgan's cane mighta been left in here. If we can rule that out as the cause of his wound, we'll know better how to proceed. And secondly, I'd like to have all of you think about whether Morgan had any enemies who mighta wanted him dead."

Lily let out a caustic laugh. "Are you kidding? Half the Valley hated him."

Andrew whipped his head in her direction. "That's a lie, and you know it. Everyone liked him."

"Well, let's be honest, Dad," Max put in. "Not *everyone* liked him."

"You don't know all his friends," Cullen shot back. "You've

been having a high-old-time in college while he's been working his butt off here on the ranch."

This was quickly degenerating into a family squabble, so Lucas turned to Gus. "I think we've got all we need for now," he said, "but I'd like for both of us to come back in the mornin' and talk to each of these folks individually. Maybe somebody'll remember somethin' that'll help us."

The two men said goodbye to the women, and Cullen walked them to the door. As Lucas shook Andrew's hand, he said, "I really need to put a couple of my deputies on watch here tonight, Mr. Cullen, at least for a few hours, but I'll tell 'em to report to you before they set up. I know this has been a terrible ordeal for you and your family, but I want you to know I'm countin' on your cooperation. We both wanna find out if this was an accident, or someone did this to him, and it'll only help if we work together. Can I count on you?"

"I'll give you guys a chance, but if you can't find out who did this in the next day or two, then I've got some plans of my own."

"Just don't take things into your own hands," Gus said. "We can handle it."

Cullen turned on Gus. "Easy for you to say, since you don't have any kids."

Gus winced. Cullen's remark was a deliberate jab at the fact that he and Emily had never had any children. "I know I don't," Gus said, "but if I did, and one of them had been killed, I'd want the best possible help in finding out who did it. All we're asking is that you don't withhold any information that can help us make that determination. That's not too much to ask, is it?"

"I'll be the judge of that," Cullen snapped.

Lucas could see that Gus was getting heated up, so he put a hand on his arm. "Let's go," he said. As they went out the door, Lucas turned back to Cullen. "I'm real sorry about your loss, Mr. Cullen, because I *do* have a son, and he's just Morgan's age."

Cassie Hampton followed the two men out, and they all walked down the steps to their cars, leaving Cullen standing in the doorway scowling.

CHAPTER 11

Gus was frustrated that he couldn't get to sleep. He tossed and turned restlessly, visions of Laura Cullen's tragic face refusing to leave his head. He'd seen that precious face in his dreams far too often in the past twenty-six years. His dear Emily—who'd shared his life for twenty of those years—was dead now, lost to a stroke five years ago, so he no longer felt guilty when these dreams of Laura intruded into his sleep.

Gus had had his first glimpse of Laura Barron just after he'd returned from the trenches in France in 1919. Harrah had had a rally to welcome home her hometown heroes, and Laura's father, Cyrus Barron, had presented all the young veterans with a special plaque and a key to the "city" of Harrah. Laura had been on the platform with him and given a sedate kiss to each of the seven young men. She was only sixteen years old, but to a love-starved twenty-year-old just back from the front, that kiss left an indelible impression on Gus.

He traded in his soldier's uniform for that of a gas station attendant in his father's little service station in Harrah. There were few automobiles in the Valley in 1919, but those were enough for Anders Styvessan to know that it was the up-and-coming thing of the future. Had it not been for Cyrus Barron's fleet of trucks, tractors, and Model T Fords, Styvessan's bold venture would probably never have gotten off the ground, but seeing the advantage of having gasoline a mile from his ranch, Barron had backed Styvessan's station and kept it afloat until he could get it on its feet. Eventually other ranchers in the Valley began to see the value of having motorized transportation, and soon a steady stream of Model A and Model T Fords, Chevrolets, Packards, Hudsons, Cadillacs, and assorted trucks patronized Styvessan's gas station, the only one within ten miles.

Gus loved working at the station. It sat at the main crossroad of Harrah, and sooner or later everyone in town stopped by either for gasoline or just to shoot the breeze with Gus and his dad. He loved to tell his war stories, and always had an eager audience. A good-looking young man with a mass of dark unruly curls, Gus was a war hero—especially in the eyes of the girls.

Over the next couple of years, Gus watched with growing interest as Laura Barron transitioned from a winsome young girl into a beautiful young woman. She was away at school in the East for most of each year, but in the summers she often came in to the station with her father.

In 1921, when Laura Barron was eighteen, she got her first car, a red Stutz Bearcat. Gus loved to watch her fly through town, her long golden hair whipping around her head in the open air. He took to waving at her, and she began waving back. Soon she was dropping in for gas more frequently than necessary, and often found some imagined defect on her Stutz for Gus to fix.

One day he asked her if she'd ever seen the old Indian fort up in the hills above White Swan, and she said no. After an awkward few moments, he gathered his courage and asked her if she'd like to drive up there some Sunday afternoon and look at it, and to his utter amazement, she said she'd love to. They set a date, and his mother packed a basket of fried chicken, potato salad, and German chocolate cake. At the last minute, his father produced a bottle of wine.

Since prohibition was in effect, Gus was startled. "Where'd you get this?" he laughed.

His father gave him an amused look. "I've been saving it for a special occasion, so keep it out of sight till you get to your picnic. But for God's sake, don't get that little filly drunk. Her dad would never let me hear the end of it."

The outing was a great success. Laura let Gus drive her Stutz, and he couldn't keep the grin off his face as he sat behind the wheel. When they got to the fort they found a picnic spot under some lovely old oaks near a natural spring. As they ate, they talked about their years of growing up in the Valley, and Gus told her some war stories that left her gasping in horror, and others that brought tears to her eyes.

Gus was amazed at how easy it was to talk to her. She wasn't at all like he imagined she'd be, having been raised with so much money and privilege. She was natural and funny, yet charming and demure at the same time. It boggled his mind to think that she might like him, but she obviously did, because before they parted she accepted another date with him for the following Sunday. For the next two months, they saw each other every Sunday, and often during the week when she came into the station for gas.

They'd progressed to holding hands and kissing, and Gus knew he was falling in love.

That's why it nearly destroyed him when Laura came in one day with tears running down her cheeks and told him she couldn't see him anymore. Her father was insisting that she marry someone he'd picked out for her, and there was nothing she could do to change his mind.

Gus went into a deep depression. He couldn't eat, he couldn't sleep. He put gas in people's cars and went back into the station, often without a word. His parents were worried sick, but his mother told Anders that she'd known all along that Cyrus Barron would never let his daughter get involved with someone like Gus. The families simply weren't in the same league.

The day of the wedding, Gus sat sullenly in front of the gas station and watched the parade of fancy cars pass through Harrah on their way to The Oaks. His grief had turned to smoldering rage. *Those high and mighty Barrons! They just used people then disposed of them!* Well, he hoped Laura would be miserable the rest of her life. That she could prefer some flashy cowboy to him was galling. He might not have been able to give her a life like she was used to, but what could this fortune-hunting drifter offer her? Nobody knew where he'd come from, and people said he hadn't even been in the war.

Three months later, when Gus was putting gas into Cyrus Barron's car one afternoon, he glanced into the back seat and was shocked to see Laura sitting there, *very* pregnant. He suddenly realized why she'd married Andrew Cullen. He must have gotten her pregnant sometime before Gus began dating her, and old man

Barron—*ever mindful of his family's reputation*—had forced her into a wedding she didn't want. But why hadn't she told him she was pregnant? He would've married her. Unless she hadn't known she was. *That was it! She was too innocent to have known.*

He stared at her bulging stomach, and she looked down at it, then up at him with the saddest expression he'd ever seen, and it was all he could do to keep from ripping the door open and gathering her into his arms. Her heart-wrenching look nearly tore his guts out, but it told him all he needed to know. She *had* loved him, and perhaps still did, and maybe there was a chance for them after this baby was born. Surely she could get free of Andrew Cullen then.

But when old man Barron died suddenly a couple of months after the baby was born, and Barron's new son-in-law took over The Oaks, Gus knew it was not to be. He had lost her forever to an arrogant fortune hunter who had manipulated his way into Cyrus Barron's home and fortune, and now, with an heir of his own securing that future, Andrew Cullen would never let Laura go.

In his sorrow, Gus had turned to Emily Sawyer, a local girl who'd been infatuated with him for years. After a short courtship, he married her and settled into the routine of married life, but his thoughts were never far from Laura Cullen.

As he lay there in bed now, remembering these things, he could still see Laura sitting on the steps of the pool today, numb with grief at the loss of her firstborn, and he could not get her stricken face out of his mind.

Who had caused his beloved Laura so much pain? He couldn't begin to imagine who it might be, although he'd had to admit that when he first heard that Morgan had been killed, it hadn't really surprised him. He was disliked by many people—and with good reason—but being the deputy sheriff in Harrah, he intended to use the authority he had to find Morgan's killer, if only for Laura's sake.

CHAPTER 12

When Gus and Lucas arrived at The Oaks the next morning, the family was waiting for them in their sunroom. Cullen's mood was foul. "Let's get down to business," he said. "We searched this house from one end to the other, and Morgan's cane is not here. Whoever used it on him still has it, and I want him found *today*. But I'm telling you both right now that if I catch him before you do, I'm going to make him wish he'd never been born."

Lucas frowned. "We don't like the idea of a killer runnin' loose on this Reservation any more than you do, but you'll only slow us down if you take things into your own hands."

"Well, the two guys you left here last night were useless," Cullen said. "They just stood around shooting the breeze. The guy who did this could be 200 miles away by now."

Lucas frowned. "Whoever did this to your son is someone who had a personal grudge against him, so let's have some names of people who mighta had it in for him." He looked from one to the other. "Who wants to be first?"

No one said anything, so Gus leaned over to Lucas and lowered his voice. "I think we'd better talk to each of them individually. Why don't you take Andrew first, and I'll start with

Mrs. Cullen? We've known each other for years, and she might feel more comfortable talking to me."

"Good idea," Lucas said. He turned back to the others. "Gus thinks you'd all be more comfortable if we talked to you individually, and I agree. I'll start with you, Mr. Cullen, and follow up with your son, and Gus can talk to your wife and daughter."

"Is that alright with you, Laura?" Gus asked.

She gave him a grateful nod, and the two of them started upstairs to the sitting-room off her bedroom.

Cullen led Lucas into his study and sat down behind a massive oak desk. He motioned for Lucas to take the leather chair in front of it.

Lucas sat down and cleared his throat. "You don't seem to like me very much, Mr. Cullen. Is there something I've said or done to offend you, or are you just disagreeable as a general rule?"

"I don't like anybody poking his nose into my family's business, and that goes for you, as well as anyone else. As for me not liking you personally, I can tell you right now that I'll like you a whole lot better if you find my son's killer."

"I appreciate your frankness," Lucas said, "so I'll be frank too. If you know anything about your son's activities that might've made someone want to kill him, I suggest you tell me now and don't jerk me around. Keeping secrets won't help us find who did this to Morgan."

Cullen leaned back in his chair and stared at Lucas, trying to decide whether to tell him about the letter from Felder and Keith. He'd been thinking about it all night, and it occurred to him that the girl's father might've been so angry that Cullen hadn't paid him what he was asking, that he'd had Morgan killed. He reluctantly explained the blackmail letter to Lucas, emphasizing that Morgan adamantly denied the girl's charges.

Lucas took down all the information on a notepad, then looked up when Cullen had finished. "Did Morgan ever get himself in trouble with any other girls?" he asked.

Cullen shook his head. "Nothing that I know about. I tell you right now, when this girl's father heard the name Cullen, he just saw dollar signs. I've gotten that before."

"Someone else has blackmailed you?"

"No, but there was a situation a few years ago when a drunk Indian ran into Morgan out on the Fort Road and got himself killed, and the Indian's squaw pestered me for months trying to get money out of me. I finally told her I'd run her and her brat off the Reservation if she didn't get off my back." He suddenly leaned forward in his chair. "Why didn't I think of it sooner? Her kid's working out here on my ranch right now. He must've done this." He started to get up. "Come on," he said. "You've got to arrest him before he takes off for the hills."

Lucas motioned for Cullen to sit back down. "Hang on a minute," he said. "I know Derek Abrams, but what I don't know is why you hired him if you thought he might be a danger to your son."

"I didn't hire him. Max did."

"Well, if Derek's out here today, we'll talk to him, but I'd like to talk to the rest of your family first. Your daughter's attitude toward Morgan seemed pretty hostile yesterday. Didn't they get along with each other?"

Cullen was caught off guard by the question, and it obviously made him uneasy. Yes, Lily had every reason to hate Morgan, but he couldn't imagine her getting up the courage to kill him. Cullen shook his head. "They had their squabbles like all kids do, but they got along fine."

"Did Morgan have any problem with any of the men on the ranch?" Lucas asked.

"He didn't deal with them directly, but Max told him the Abrams kid was working here this summer, so I'm sure Morgan was keeping his eye on him."

"Was he worried that Derek might try to do something to him?" Lucas asked.

"You've always gotta keep your eye on an Indian with a grudge."

Lucas cocked his head slightly. "I seem to recall that there was some controversy at the time of your son's car accident over who was really responsible. Wasn't there?"

"Not as far as I'm concerned. Judge Harmon ruled that the Indian was at fault."

"Oh, yes. I forgot that you know Judge Harmon. Do you and he still go on fishing trips every year?"

Cullen's eyes narrowed. "Are you trying to suggest something?"

Lucas's brows shot up innocently. "No, no, not at all! I was just confirmin' that you and Judge Harmon know each other." He wrote something on his notepad, then looked up at Cullen. "Did Morgan and Derek have any run-ins with each other since he came to work here this summer?"

"Not that I know of, but I'm sure that Indian was just waiting for the right time to have it out with him."

"Why didn't you fire him if you were worried about something like that?"

"I almost did last week, but I let Max talk me out of it. If I had, Morgan would still be alive."

"Well, that remains to be seen, but that's all the questions I've got for you now." He flipped his notepad shut and stood up. "I'm sure I'll have more after I've talked to the others, but if you think of anything you haven't told me, gimme a call. I'm gonna keep my men out here the rest of the day lookin' for that cane."

"It's not in the house," Cullen said. "We searched everywhere, and it's not in here. It had to be out at the pool because Morgan couldn't have gotten out there without it. I tell you, that Abrams kid has it stashed somewhere. He'd never throw something that valuable away. You need to get over to his house and search for it before he tries to pawn it."

"Well, I can't do that without a search warrant, and I'd rather wait to get that until I've talked with him personally. Did he come in today?"

"I don't know. He's probably taken off for the hills. Those Indians know them like the back of their hands, and if he gets up there, you'll never find him."

Lucas smiled indulgently. "Well, we'll cross that bridge when we get to it. Right now I'd like to talk to Max, and then I'll see if Derek's here." He reached across the desk and received a lukewarm handshake from Cullen.

CHAPTER 13

Gus had followed Laura upstairs into her sitting room, and as they sat down on the sofa, Laura reached over and took his hand. "I know this can't be easy for you," she said, "but you don't know how much it means to me that you're here. You're the only real friend I've ever had."

Gus looked into her stricken face and saw that she was on the verge of tears again. "You knew I'd be here if you ever needed me. You've always known that."

"I always hoped you would, but I wasn't sure after what I did to you. Things were completely out of my control back then, Gus. You know that, don't you?"

"I figured they were, but I just didn't feel like I could butt in unless you asked me to, and you never did."

"You'll never know how many times I wanted to stop and pour my heart out to you, but I didn't have a right to expect any sympathy after what I'd done to you." She reached up and brushed at a tear that had slipped onto her cheek. "If I'd only known then what I know now, things would've been so different, but I was young and stupid—and I guess we have to learn by our mistakes."

"I've often wondered why you didn't just leave Andrew."

"I would have, but after Daddy died, Andrew warned me not to even think about leaving him, or he'd take Morgan from me."

Gus shook his head. "How did you get mixed up with someone like him in the first place? I thought we had something special going on between us."

Her eyes brimmed again. "We did, but before I even knew you, Andrew had come to work at The Oaks, and I was young and stupid, and when he forced himself on me one night, I thought I must've made him think I wanted him, and afterwards, I was too ashamed to tell anyone—even you." She reached over and took his hand. "You must know that when I began seeing you, I had no idea I was pregnant, but when I found out I was, Daddy made me marry Andrew so there wouldn't be a scandal that would soil my mother's memory."

"*I* would've married you! I loved you!"

"I know you would've, but Andrew told Daddy how much he wanted me and our baby, and it was just easier for Daddy to believe that than have an unwed mother on his hands. I knew Andrew didn't love me, but I thought I could divorce him after the baby came, and then when Daddy died so suddenly, and Andrew found out that The Oaks had been left to me in a trust that he couldn't get his hands on if we divorced, he told me he'd take Morgan away from me if I ever tried to leave him. So after awhile I just gave up trying to get away, and he gradually took complete control of the ranch . . . and all of us." Tears began spilling down her cheeks in earnest, now. "Oh, how I've paid for that one stupid night when I let him into my bed. You'll never know, Gus."

His grip tightened on her hand. "I knew you were suffering, but I couldn't do anything unless you reached out to me first."

"Well, I'm reaching out now. Please help me get away from him before there's nothing left of me or the kids. Can you do that?"

He leaned over and brushed at her tears. "I'll do what I can, but you need to be sure this isn't just grief over Morgan that's talking."

She shook her head. "It isn't. I've known for years that I had to get out of this marriage, but I really felt Morgan needed me here to counterbalance Andrew's influence on him. Now that he's gone, everything's changed. Andrew will never get over his bitterness at losing Morgan, and he'll just take it out on the other two kids and me."

"How will Max and Lily react if you leave him?"

"They'll be fine. Lily and her dad hate each other anyway, and Max knows what his dad's put me through. Of all the children, he's been the only one whose love I've been sure of."

"I'm sure Lily loves you."

"In her own way she does, but it's hard for her to show her feelings. She's got so much anger bottled up inside her about Morgan."

Gus gave her a questioning look. "Did he do something to her?"

She hesitated a moment, then reluctantly told him about the rape.

"Oh, Laura!" he moaned. "Does Andrew know about it?"

"Yes, but Morgan told him it was a lie, and he believed him."

"Do you think she's angry enough to have killed him?"

"I don't know. I've tried to keep her away from the ranch as much as I could so she wouldn't have to deal with him, but Andrew insisted she be here this summer so he could go over her college plans for next year. Morgan may have tried something again, and it might've been more than she could take."

He reached over and took her hand. "I'll talk to her and see what she's willing to tell me. If she had anything to do with it, after what you've just told me, I'm sure the courts would go very easy on her."

Laura's eyes widened in alarm. "Do you have to bring all this out into the open? There's no telling what Andrew will do if people find out that Morgan molested his own sister, but I know he'll take it out on her. Please don't say anything to anyone. I don't think she could bear having people know."

Gus gave a reluctant sigh. "I'll have to tell Sheriff Lucas, and I'll need to talk to Lily about it too. This is too important not to follow up on, but I don't really think she's strong enough to put a hole like that in Morgan's head. More than likely it was a man, and a strong one at that."

Laura clutched at his hand. "Please don't tell Andrew that you know about this. He'd be furious with me for telling you."

"I won't say anything at this point, but you implied that there were others who might've wanted Morgan dead. Who else besides Lily?"

"This is just speculation," she said, "but I've always worried about the Indian man that Morgan killed in that car accident when he was fifteen. You remember? Morgan got drunk and took our car, and ran into the Indian on the Fort Road. I heard that he had a son about Morgan's age, and I'm sure he must've been very bitter against Morgan all these years, but whether he hated him enough to kill him, I don't know. In fact, I don't even know if he's still on the Reservation, but you asked me who might've hated Morgan enough to want him dead, and this boy popped into my head. I don't even know his name."

"His name is Derek Abrams, and he's working here at The Oaks right now."

Laura's mouth fell open. "What?"

"Yes. He's a teacher and coach out at White Swan, but the last time I saw him he told me he had a summer job here."

"I can't imagine Andrew hiring him. He must not know who he is. Have you talked with this boy about Morgan?"

"Not yet, but I plan to. What about Max? Did he and Morgan get along?"

Laura's face finally brightened a little. "Max gets along with everybody. I think he got my genes, and Morgan got Andrew's. And Lily got a little of both."

Gus smiled. "Well, she sure got your looks. Looking at her is like looking at a carbon copy of you twenty-six years ago. I can still see you flying through town in that old red Stutz. You'll never know what the sight of you did to me." He squeezed her hand lightly. "I never got you out of my system, but I think you know that."

She managed a weak smile. "Selfishly, I always hoped you hadn't, but I can't make any promises to you right now, Gus. I'm too torn up about Morgan. You understand that, don't you?"

"You won't get any pressure from me. I just want you to know that I'm here for you if you need me."

She reached out and touched his cheek. "I'd forgotten how dear you are."

A wry little smile played at his mouth as he leaned over and kissed her on the forehead. "I'll do my best to keep reminding you," he said, then took both her hands in his. "Now, why don't you lie down for awhile and try to get some rest? There's gonna to be some rough road ahead."

When Gus came downstairs, Lily was sitting alone in the sunroom. She told him that Sheriff Lucas had taken Max outside on the patio to talk.

"Good," Gus said. "We'll just talk here then. Okay?"

She nodded. "How's Mom doing?"

"She's pretty broken up, but she's resting."

"Did she have any idea who might've done this to her precious Morgan?"

Gus dipped his head with a little frown. "That isn't a very nice way to talk about your mother. Are you mad at her for some reason?"

"No. I just thought that the point of all these private little chats was to see if one of us might confess to killing the family pet."

Gus's frown deepened. "You really *didn't* like your brother, did you? Do you wanna tell me why?"

Lily let out a disdainful little laugh. "Sounds like my mother already did. I knew she would."

"What would she have to tell me?"

"Don't be cute, Mr. Styvessan. I'm sure she told you about

77

Morgan putting his hands on me every chance he got. Does she think I killed him because of that?"

He shook his head. "No, she doesn't, but she did tell me that he molested you a few years ago, and she's been very upset about it."

"Not enough to have stopped him."

Gus frowned. "Did he do it again?"

"He tried, but I guess he believed me when I told him I'd kill him if he ever touched me again."

"And did you kill him?"

Lily let out a little laugh. "No, Mr. Styvessan. I wanted to, but I didn't."

"Do you have any idea who did?"

"No, but I wish I did, so I could send them a big bouquet of flowers."

Gus frowned again. "I hope your mother never hears you talk like that. It would break her heart."

"Don't get me wrong, Deputy, I love my mother very much, but when it comes to men, she has lousy judgment. She knew Morgan was a drunk, but she continually made excuses for him. And as for my father, she's never understood what a loser he is. I'd never let a man treat me, like he treats her."

"I'm sure your father's not the easiest man in the world to be married to, but I think she thought that staying with him was the best thing for you kids. That makes her pretty special in my book."

Lily's tone softened a little. "She is special, but I hate the way she's let Dad beat her down. He's done his best to do the same thing to me, but I won't let him get to me anymore. I did when I was too young to fight back, but I'm through with all that now."

"What are you planning to do?"

"Well, I'm not going to Vassar, like he wants. That's for sure. I'm getting out of here and getting a job. I won't take another dime from him."

Gus raised his brows. "That's very commendable, but it won't be easy out there without an education or money. Do you think you can do it?"

"I'll figure out a way. I hope Mom doesn't stick around here either. Now that Morgan's gone, she doesn't need to be here to try to keep him in line, and Max can take care of himself. She should get out while she still can."

"Well, I can't speak for her, but maybe it *is* best for you to get out on your own. I'm sure it'll break your mother's heart if you don't go to college, but we've each gotta do what we think is best for ourselves, so I wish you luck." He hesitated a moment, then asked bluntly, "Is there anything else you want to tell me about any of this?"

She paused for a minute, then shook her head. "Not really. I guess I just have one final question for you though: Do you think I killed him?"

Gus gave her a long sober look, then shook his head. "No, but I think if I'd been in your shoes, I would've wanted to. The only thing I'd worry about is that some innocent person might get blamed for it, and in that case, I'd have to own up to what I'd done. Think about that, Lily, and if you want to talk to me again, I'll be happy to listen."

She suddenly seemed close to tears. "Why didn't my mother find someone like you, instead of the loser she married?"

Gus let out a little laugh. "She almost did."

Lily gave him a questioning look.

"Never mind," he said. "It's too long a story to get into now."

CHAPTER 14

Sheriff Lucas and Max were sitting at a glass-topped table on the brick patio as Gus came out. They both looked up.

"Are you finished in there?" Lucas asked.

"For now. What about you two?"

Lucas patted the chair. "Sit down here for a minute. I want Max to tell you what he's been tellin' me about Derek Abrams."

Gus pulled out a chair and sat. "What've you got on him, Max?"

"Nothing, really. We haven't had any serious problems with him here, but I did have to get after him for coming in late to work last week, and then Dad chewed him out for some sloppy driving out in the field the other day, and Derek lipped off to him."

"He was late last week because he was helping me pull Johnny Birdsong's truck out of the canal," Gus said. "I offered to call your dad and tell him, but Derek wouldn't let me."

"I figured he must've had a good reason for being late, but Dad's a fanatic about squeezing every minute out of anyone who works here. I'll tell him that Derek was helping you get someone out of the canal."

"Did Derek and Morgan ever have a run-in that you know of?" Lucas asked.

Max shook his head. "I don't think Morgan would've known who he was even if he'd seen him."

"Why'd you hire him?" Lucas asked. "You must've known it would upset your dad and Morgan."

Max shrugged. "I never even thought about that. I just figured he'd fit in with the other guys who work here. Most of them know who he is, and like him, even though some of them think he's a little odd sometimes."

"In what way?"

"Oh, just the way he sits out there on the canal bank during his break, staring up at Mount Adams and praying."

"His dad was the same way," Gus said. "He and Derek were very active in the longhouse out at White Swan. I don't know whether he still is or not, but I know his beliefs meant a lot to him growing up, and personally, I don't think he'd jeopardize everything he believes in just to get revenge on Morgan."

"Well, all I know is what the kids here say about him," Max said, "and they all seem to like him."

Gus turned to Lucas. "Did you and Andrew come up with any other suspects?"

Lucas shook his head. "No. Cullen's convinced that Derek's the one who did it. What about your talk with Mrs. Cullen?"

"She admitted that Morgan was responsible for the accident that messed up his leg. She told me he'd taken a bottle of whiskey from their liquor cabinet and went for a joyride and ran into an Indian. She didn't know it was Derek's father until I told her just now."

Max's mouth flew open. "Did Mom actually tell you that Morgan was the one who was drunk?"

"Yes," Gus said. "Everybody who knew Jason Abrams knew he never touched any kind of liquor."

Max shook his head in disgust. "No wonder Dad's always blamed Derek's father for the accident. He's afraid the truth is gonna come out about his perfect son."

"I think it's time we talked to Derek," Lucas said. "Did he come in today?"

Max nodded. "I saw him this morning, and I assume he's still here, but if you need to talk to him, can we wait till the trucks come in just before closing. We've gotta get these hops into the kiln to dry, or they're gonna rot, and there's no telling what'll happen once you talk to Derek."

Gus pushed his chair back, then reached over and shook hands with Max. "I'm sorry for being the one to tell you about your brother killing Derek's dad. I just assumed you knew. Everybody else on the Reservation does."

Max gave a disgusted grunt. "Dad's always treated Morgan like he could do no wrong, so I'm glad to finally hear the truth."

Lucas stood up and shook Max's hand. "Thanks for your help," he said. "Now, if you don't mind, we'll go out to the kiln with you and wait for Abrams to come in."

The blue Ford that Derek drove had just backed in as the three men walked out to the kiln. Derek was still in the cab as Max went over to him. "Sheriff Lucas and Gus wanna talk to you," he said. "Why don't you go on over and see what they want? I'll get one of the other guys to help unload this."

"What do they want with me?"

"They'll tell you," Max said.

Derek got out of the truck and walked over to Gus and Lucas. "Max says you guys wanna talk to me. I'll be glad to answer any questions I can, but let me start by saying that if you think I had anything to do with killing Morgan, I didn't. I'm not sorry he's dead, but I had nothing to do with it."

"No one's accusin' you of killin' him," Lucas said. "We just wanna know why you took this job, considerin' how you feel about the Cullens."

"I needed the money, and I was hoping to clear my father's name."

"And how were you planning to do that?" Gus asked.

"By asking Mr. Cullen to admit to me that his son caused the accident."

"And if he wouldn't?" Gus asked.

"Then I wanted him to know that I was going to ask the Toppenish police to take another look at what happened the night Dad was killed."

Gus let out a surprised laugh. "How were you gonna get them to do that?"

"I wasn't, but Senator Magnuson was one of my fans at WSC, and after I told him what had happened to Dad, he told me he'd be glad to have the case reopened it if I ever wanted him to."

"Are you sure you wanna threaten Cullen with that?" Gus asked.

"Looks like someone's made that unnecessary," Derek replied.

"That 'someone' wouldn't be you, would it?" Lucas asked.

Derek frowned at him. "Do you honestly think I'd have shown up here today if I'd killed him?"

"Might be a clever way to throw suspicion off yourself," Lucas retorted.

"Oh, come on! If I *hadn't* shown up, you'd think I'd taken off for the hills. I can't win with you guys. I'll just have to let the facts clear me." He paused a moment, then gave them a questioning look. "You *are* planning to investigate this, aren't you?"

"Of course we are," Lucas said, "that's why we need to know where you were yesterday afternoon between three and four o'clock."

"I was in my truck out in the field."

"Are there people who can vouch for you?"

"Of course there are, but a lot of people won't stick their neck out if they think it'll get them in trouble with Cullen."

"That's probably true," Lucas said, "but if you've got witnesses as to where you were about the time Morgan was killed, then you'll be in the clear."

"My word isn't enough?"

Lucas looked exasperated. "Look, kid, I'm not accusin' you of lyin'. I'm not accusin' you of anything. I'm just followin' up on every lead, and your name came up several times as someone who wouldn't mind seein' Morgan dead. I'm just tryin' to get to the bottom of this mess."

Derek let out a caustic laugh. "Sheriff, if you're going to investigate everyone who had a grudge against Morgan Cullen, you'd better plan on dedicating the rest of your life to this, but I want to get one thing straight right now: *I didn't kill him.* Now, unless you're planning to arrest me, I'd like to get my truck unloaded."

Derek waited for a response, but when he didn't get one, he turned and walked back to his truck, leaving Lucas with his mouth hanging open. "That's the most arrogant Indian I've ever seen," he said to Gus.

"Would you think he was arrogant if he wasn't an Indian?" Gus asked.

Lucas pulled back with a frown. "I don't like what you're implyin'. If you think I'm after him just because he's an Indian, you're dead wrong. He admitted he wasn't sorry that Morgan was dead, so all I'm tryin' to find out is if he mighta helped him get that way. Does that make me the bad guy?"

Gus gave him a genial pat on the back. "No, it doesn't, and I apologize for jumping on you, but I think he's telling the truth. He's got too much to lose by doing such a stupid thing."

"You'd certainly think so," Lucas said. "Anyway, I'm gonna talk to the guys he was workin' with yesterday and see if he was with someone every minute. Then, if I don't get the answers I want, I'm gonna get a search warrant for his pickup and his house, and see if he has that cane stashed somewhere."

"That's fine with me," Gus said, "but in the meantime, I want to exhaust every possibility of finding it here on the ranch. It's a big place, and your men couldn't have covered it all in one day."

"They've been at it since early this mornin'," Lucas said, then looked at his watch. "They'll be gatherin' at the kiln office pretty soon, so let's go see what ground they've covered."

The two men walked back over to the office, and Lucas debriefed his men, then gave them the schedule for the next day. They all began heading for their cars, and as Gus looked up at the mansion, he saw Lily watching them from her third-story balcony. He waved up at her, and to his surprise, she waved back. He chuckled to himself as he walked on to his pickup. That kid didn't miss a thing from her little perch up there.

He got into his pickup and sat for a moment with his hands propped on the steering wheel as a thought began to nag at him. Laura said Lily spent all her time in her room—or out on her private balcony—and from up there she could see most of the ranch, including the pool. He suddenly felt the hair rise on his arms as he realized that Lily probably saw who killed her brother.

CHAPTER 15

Lily lay in her bed in the darkened room trying to decide what to do with Morgan's cane. One thing was sure; she didn't want it in her room any longer. She got up and pulled it out from under her bed, battling with herself at the ramifications of what she was planning to do with it, but there was no turning back now.

When she'd first looked down at the pool yesterday, and seen Sam in an argument with Morgan, she'd been curious, but not alarmed. Then, as she'd watched their dispute escalate, Morgan got off his lounge chair and took a violent swing at Sam with his cane, and Sam grabbed it from him and clubbed him over the head with it, and pushed him into the pool.

As Morgan thrashed there in the water, too disoriented to find his way to the steps, Sam had hurled the cane into the wisteria vines on top of the pool house. Lily's first instinct had been to scream for help, but something stopped her. If he drowned, she'd no longer have to put up with his abuse, and the realization of that paralyzed her.

She'd continued watching Morgan as he weakened and finally stopped thrashing, and was still looking at him when she saw a girl jump in and drag him over to the steps. Then Sam yelled that someone had been hurt in the pool, and she'd raced down the stairs with her mother and saw Morgan lying there on the pool steps, and she'd been filled with conflicting emotions. That was her own flesh and blood, but he was also the one who'd ruined her life, and if he were dead, she'd never have to fear him again.

With that thought easing her conscience, she'd climbed down to the roof of the pool house late last night and retrieved the cane and stuck it under her bed until she could decide what to do with it. But having watched the two sheriffs' hostile interrogation of Derek earlier today, she knew what she had to do with the cane.

She slipped a robe over her nightgown, and tucked the cane under it. The clock by her bed showed it was three a.m. as she quietly opened her bedroom door and went out. The Persian runner muffled her steps as she crept down the stairs past her parents' and Max's rooms and moved to the door leading from the kitchen into the garage. Four cars were parked side by side, and she went to her dad's silver Cadillac on the far end. Opening the trunk as quietly as she could, she laid the cane beside the leather carrying case containing his shotgun. As she was closing the lid, a light went on at the top of the stairs leading up to Sam's apartment. She knelt down behind the cars and held her breath. Sam appeared sleepily at the top of the stairs.

"Who's down there?" he called. "Is someone there?"

Lily didn't move.

"Is that you, Mr. Andrew?"

She pulled back farther into the shadows as she heard his steps descending the stairs. About halfway down, he paused and called again.

"Mr. Andrew?"

When he got no answer, he shrugged and went back up the stairs. In a moment the light went out and Lily let out a sigh. She waited another few minutes, then quickly retraced her steps to her room. As she shut her bedroom door behind her, she leaned against it, her heart pounding wildly.

Cullen's sleep had been sporadic that night as he grappled with the events of the past two days. His precious Morgan was dead. That sad fact could not be changed, but somebody was going to pay dearly for it, even if he had to take matters into his own hands. Those two bungling sheriffs were too stupid to see the obvious. That Abrams kid had done it. He was the only one who had a reason to hate Morgan, so why hadn't they just gone out and arrested him before he had time to get rid of the cane? This business of needing a search warrant to go into an Indian's house or look in his pickup was ridiculous. Cullen could easily get a look at them without one. The more he stewed about it, the more that seemed like the perfect thing to do. He'd go over to the kid's house first-thing in the morning and rip the place apart until he found the cane.

He tried to get back to sleep, but the more he thought about what Abrams had done, the more he realized that he had to take action before the kid got rid of the cane. He glanced at the clock and saw that it was about five a.m. He got up, quickly dressed, and crept down into the kitchen. Thankfully, none of the help was up yet, so he went into the garage, and quietly raised the garage door behind his car. It screeched as it went up, and he winced.

Quickly moving to his silver Cadillac, he opened the trunk to get his shotgun out, but recoiled as he saw Morgan's cane lying next to it. "My God!" he groaned. "Where did that come from?"

The light at the top of the stairs went on as Sam came out of his room and started down the stairs for the second time that night. This time, his voice sounded worried. "Who's down there? Mr. Andrew? Is that you?"

Cullen shut the trunk lid and whipped around. "What do you want?" he barked up at him.

Sam stiffened at the harsh greeting. "I heard the garage door go up, and I wondered who was going out. You didn't say you were leaving early, that's all. I'm sorry if I startled you."

Cullen quickly collected himself. "I guess we're all a little jumpy. I've got an early appointment. Sorry if I woke you."

"That's okay. I didn't sleep much last night anyway. Were you down here earlier?"

"No. Why?"

"Well, I thought I heard someone in the middle of the night. I came down, but didn't see anyone."

"What time was that?"

"I don't know. Around three, I guess."

"Did the garage door open?"

Sam shook his head. "Not that I heard."

Cullen was too stunned to sort it all out right then, but one thing was sure; he did not want Sam to know that the cane was in the trunk of his car. He took a few steps toward him. "Well, thanks for keeping on top of things, Sam. We've all gotta keep a sharp eye out until this killer's caught. No telling if he might try to come after me, or the rest of my family. You did the right thing in coming down to check, but you can go on back up now. Everything seems to be in order here."

"Let me know if I can help in any way."

"I will."

Sam went back up the stairs, and Cullen returned to his car and stood bewildered in front of the trunk. Someone had gotten into the garage during the night and put that cane in his trunk with the obvious intention of trying to implicate him in Morgan's murder. But that was preposterous! Who would believe he had anything to do with killing his own son? And then it hit him! Derek Abrams must've sneaked into the garage, either yesterday or during the night, and put it in his trunk to draw suspicion off himself. Well, if he wanted to play that kind of game, two of them could play it, but they'd play by *his* rules, not Derek's.

Cullen took a raincoat off a hook on the wall and slipped it on, then opened the trunk again and tucked the cane inside the coat. As he stepped outside, he looked around for the two men Lucas had posted on the grounds, and his own armed guards, but saw none of them as he made his way toward the kiln. Six work trucks were lined up there in front of it, and when he was certain no one was watching, he went to the blue Ford that Derek Abrams drove and quietly opened the door to the cab. He pulled the cane out from under his raincoat and wedged it in behind the driver's seat. He was just starting back to the house when one of the Lucas's guards emerged from around the corner of the kiln.

"Who's there?" the man demanded.

Startled, Cullen wheeled around to face him. "It's Andrew Cullen. I was just checking to see if you guys were on the job. Some cops you are! I could've been in and out of here before you saw a thing."

The man was flustered by Cullen's reproach. "I was just checking out behind the kiln. Sorry if I startled you."

"Where are the other guys that're supposed to be out here?" Cullen demanded.

"I don't know. My partner was over by the pool when I last saw him, and your two guys are wandering around here somewhere. I saw them about a half hour ago out in front of your house."

"Well," Cullen snapped, "if anybody gets onto this property tonight, I'm holding all of you responsible. Is that understood?"

"Don't worry. We're doing our job."

"Well, see to it that you do." With that, Cullen stormed off toward the house. When he got back up to his room, he looked out his window toward the kiln and a slow smile spread across his face. "That should take care of you, Abrams. Your little surprise backfired on you."

CHAPTER 16

Sheriff Lucas had arranged to meet Gus at the Cullen ranch the next morning at nine. They walked out to the kiln office together, and Cullen's secretary, Dorothy, ushered them into his office where he was seated at his desk waiting for them.

"It's about time you guys showed up," Cullen said, motioning them to the two leather chairs in front of his desk. "Sit down and let's get this over with."

Neither man moved toward the chairs. "We'll stand," Lucas said.

"C'mon. Sit down," Cullen chided. "I'm just blowing off steam. I didn't have a very good night worrying about whether that Abrams kid has taken off for the hills."

The two men remained where they were. "Well, has he?" Lucas asked.

"No. As a matter of fact he showed up here this morning. I've gotta hand it to him. He's got nerve."

"Or maybe he's got a clean conscience," Gus said.

Cullen gave Gus a caustic look. "I never figured you for an Indian lover, Gus."

Gus's face reddened slightly. "Let's talk about consciences,

94

Andrew. Is it possible yours might be bothering you over the way you handled Morgan's car accident a few years ago, and that's why you're going after Derek with such a vengeance? There's always been a lot of talk that you bought off Judge Harmon. Any truth to that?"

Cullen lurched forward in his chair. "Who says that? That Indian was responsible for the accident, and everybody knows it."

"They tell it a little different around the station in Toppenish," Lucas put in. "They say they were warned by Judge Harmon not to press charges against Morgan even though everyone knew he was underage and drunk. Now I wonder why Harmon woulda done that?"

Cullen leaned back in his chair. "I'm sure he had his reasons."

"It wouldn't have anything to do with your hefty contributions to his campaigns, would it?" Lucas asked.

Cullen jabbed his finger toward the sheriff. "You're skating on thin ice, Lucas. I'd watch my step if I were you."

"And maybe you need to watch *your* step," Lucas shot back. "The way you're pushin' this Abrams thing is making some people take a second look at what really happened with Morgan's accident."

"I haven't got anything to hide. I just want my boy's killer caught, and if you guys weren't so interested in playing Dick Tracy, you could've arrested him yesterday."

"You don't arrest somebody unless you've got evidence," Lucas said, "and the only evidence that'll convince me that Abrams is involved in this is if we find the cane with his fingerprints on it."

"Well, get out there and start looking then," Cullen said, scooting his chair back. "You said you wanted to search the kiln and the trucks today, so I'll take you out there myself."

The three men left the office and walked over to the kiln. A truck was being unloaded, but Cullen hollered up to Max. "Shut all that stuff off up there, Max. We're gonna do a thorough search of the kiln for Morgan's cane, and when the guys come in, have them pull up in a line over here so we can search their trucks."

"Okay," Max yelled back.

In a few minutes, everything shut down, and Sheriff Lucas and Gus and Max began a systematic search of the kiln. They scrambled up ladders, over scaffoldings and conveyor belts. They peeked into furnaces, poked around in piles of drying hops, and after an hour had pretty well covered the kiln, but there was no sign of the cane. As they came back out to where the trucks were lined up, the drivers and cutters had taken advantage of their unexpected break, and were sitting on the ground, smoking and playing cards. Derek Abrams leaned against the door of his truck cab, his attention focused on Cullen.

"Let's get a look at these trucks now," Lucas said. "Gus, why don't you and Mr. Cullen start here, and Max and I'll start at the other end?"

Gus nodded, and Lucas and Max moved down the line to the last truck. Gus and Cullen walked over to a red Ford, and Gus opened the door to the cab. He poked around under the seat and behind it while Cullen climbed up on the back and made a show of looking under the racks of hops. Neither of them found anything, so they went on to the next truck. It was another red Ford. They went through the same procedure, but found nothing.

They came next to Derek's blue Ford. He was leaning against the door when Gus walked up. "You're wasting your time," Derek said, stepping back. "You won't find it in there."

"For your sake, I hope not," Gus replied. He opened the door and felt all around under the seat and then looked behind the driver's side. He went around to the other side and did the same, then shut the door and came back around. "It's not in there," he said.

Cullen had climbed up on the back of Derek's truck and was making a show of looking for the cane by poking around among the racks of hops, but all his attention was riveted on Gus. When Gus climbed out of the cab empty-handed, Cullen jumped down from the back in a rage. "I know it's in there," he said, yanking the cab door open. He got into the cab and lay on the floor under the steering wheel, feeling all around under the seat. He pulled himself out from under the wheel and turned to Derek. "What did you do with it, Abrams? I know it was in there."

"Is this what you're looking for?" Derek asked, pulling the cane out from under a gunnysack on the back of the truck.

"That's it!" Cullen cried. "That's Morgan's cane! I told you he had it."

Gus walked over to Derek and gingerly took the cane from him. "Where'd you get this, Derek?"

"I found it behind the seat of my truck this morning. Someone put it there last night."

"Do you have any idea who?"

Derek looked over at Cullen, but said nothing.

"And you're sure you didn't put it there yourself?"

"Positive."

Gus hollered at Lucas and Max, and they came running. Lucas grimaced as he looked at the dried blood on the head of the cane. "We were right, Gus. This was the murder weapon. Where was it?"

"Derek says he found it behind the seat of his truck this morning."

Lucas turned to Derek. "And you don't have any idea how it got there?"

"I don't think that would be hard to figure out," he said, glancing at Cullen again.

Cullen exploded. "What's going on here? You think he's gonna tell you the truth? You caught him with the murder weapon. What more proof do you need? I demand that you arrest him right now."

"You don't need to tell me how to do my job," Lucas said. "I know what needs to be done." He motioned with his head to Gus. "Can I talk to you for a minute?"

They moved away from the others. "What do you think?" Lucas asked.

"I think we'd better get Derek outta here before Cullen incites these guys into a lynching. They all saw Derek pull the cane out from the back of his truck, so they know he's involved in some way. One word from Cullen, and they're liable to jump him."

"I was thinkin' the same thing," Lucas said. "I'd better take him and the cane into the station and see if we can get to the bottom of this."

The two men walked back to the others. Gus handed the cane to Lucas and he tucked it under his arm, then turned to Derek. "I need you to come into Toppenish with me," he said.

"Are you arresting me?"

"No, I just wanna get your story down on paper, and I think we can do that better without this audience."

"Can I call my mother first?"

"You can call her from the station. Let's get outta here now. My car's out front."

As they turned to leave, Cullen was nearly beside himself. "Aren't you going to handcuff him?"

Lucas gave him a withering look. "If he'd wanted to run, he's had two days to do it."

"Judge Harmon's gonna have your badge for this!" Cullen yelled after him. He started for his office, then barked at Max. "Get these people back to work. I'm calling Harmon."

Gus hurried and caught up with Lucas and Derek. "Cullen's really got his tail in a knot," he said. "He's calling Harmon right now."

"Oh, great!" Lucas replied. "That's all we need. I'd better get a move on then. Harmon'll probably call the station wantin' my badge before I even get there. I'll call you after Derek and I've talked. I may wanna bring you in on this since you two know each other, but I'll see how our talk goes. I'd like you to stick around here now and see if any of these guys can vouch for Derek's whereabouts Wednesday afternoon." Lucas took Derek by the arm and quickly led him off.

Gus spent the next hour talking to the crew, and was able to determine that, with the exception of a short break between three and three-fifteen, someone had been with Derek all day Wednesday—the day Morgan was killed—and they were willing to swear to that.

It was that fifteen-minute afternoon break that had Gus worried. He didn't know if the coroner had determined the time of death yet, or not, but according to the Hampton girl, she found Morgan between three and three thirty. It would've been almost impossible for Derek to have done it and then gotten back to his truck without being missed by his cutters. It just didn't make sense.

When Derek had first come up as a suspect, Gus had found it difficult to believe he could've been involved in any way. And even the business of his bringing out the cane in the dramatic way he did just now, seemed highly unlikely for someone who was guilty of murder. If he'd hidden it in his truck after using it on Morgan, why produce it at all? Why not just get rid of it? It had been two days since Morgan had been killed, and that was plenty of time for Derek to have tossed it in the canal, or a dozen other places, so why hadn't he?

Gus pulled his cap off and wiped his brow, then angrily plopped it back on. It looked to him like someone was trying to frame Derek, and that ticked him off. It was time to have another talk with Lily—and this time he wasn't going to let her off the hook until he got the answers he was after.

CHAPTER 17

Lily knew very little about Derek Abrams, but from what Max had said about him, and from watching him from her balcony for the past month, she could see that he wasn't like the other jerks who worked for her father. He didn't sit around smoking and gambling during their breaks, but seemed content just sitting in his truck with a book. She was impressed when Max told her that he was an All-American football star at WSC, and a math teacher and coach out at White Swan High School, and she had made a point of watching him every day after that. He obviously marched to his own drum the way he wore his hair in braids, and she liked that independent spirit. She could remember thinking that she and Derek probably had a lot in common, and although she'd never spoken a word to him, she began to feel that he was a kindred spirit.

So she was aghast as she saw Derek pull Morgan's cane from the back of his truck and hand it to Deputy Styvessan. How, in God's name, had Derek gotten the cane? Had he taken it out of the trunk of her father's car? He must know that whoever had it would be a prime suspect in Morgan's murder. She was stunned as she watched what was going on, then suddenly gasped as it hit her. Her father must've found it in his trunk and planted it in Derek's truck. There was no other explanation for it being there.

As she watched Sheriff Lucas lead Derek to his patrol car, she told herself that he would certainly be able to clear himself, and this would all blow over. But if it didn't, she'd have to tell them about her part in all this, and that would finish her with her father, and get Sam thrown in jail.

Thankfully, it was time for lunch, so she went down to the dining room. There were only two places set, and Max was already seated at one. She sat down next to him.

"Where's everybody?" she asked.

"Mom's probably in her room, and Dad's gone up to Yakima to see Judge Harmon. I think we got the guy who killed Morgan."

"Derek Abrams?"

Max raised his brows at her. "How'd you know?"

"I was watching from my balcony when the sheriff took him away. What makes them think he did it?"

"They found Morgan's cane in his truck."

"Did he confess?"

Max shook his head. "No. He says he found it there this morning when he came to work. That's hard to believe, though. Who would do something like that?"

"Oh, come on, Max. I wouldn't put it past half the guys who work here. One of them might've found it somewhere on the ranch and thought they could make some points with Dad if they put the finger on Derek. Everyone knows that he thinks Derek killed Morgan."

Max frowned at her. "That's crazy. You're letting your hate for Dad mess with your head. It's not like you."

Lily gave a sigh. "Maybe you're right. It's just that I hate to see a guy like Derek Abrams take the blame for something he didn't do just because Dad blames his father for laming his precious Morgan."

"Gus Styvessan won't let that happen. He's been around Harrah long enough to know the good guys from the bad ones, and he thinks a lot of Derek."

Lily picked at her food for a bit, then looked over at Max. "Well, I hope nothing bad happens to him," she said. "He seems like a nice guy. I think you and he could've been friends now that you're not going back to school."

"I thought so too, but there's not going to be much chance of that now, unless he can explain how that cane got into his truck."

Lily flinched, thinking about her part in the whole cane business. She struggled with whether to tell Max what she'd done, but decided to let things play out. If it looked like Derek couldn't come up with a reason for it being in his truck, she'd have to tell Sheriff Lucas about finding it and putting it in her dad's car, and that he'd obviously put it in Derek's truck. She hoped it wouldn't come to that. It would cause a whole lot of trouble for her with the sheriff and with her family.

Max rested his elbows on the table and turned to Lily. "I've been wanting to talk to you about what was going on between you and Morgan," he said. "I know you two didn't get along, but it really tears me up to see you filled with so much hate for him. What did he ever do to you?"

Lily took a deep breath and let it out slowly. "You don't wanna know, Max, but I'm free of him now, and that's all that matters."

He reached over and put his hand on hers. "But don't you see, hon, you aren't free of him as long as you still hate him so much. Whatever he did to you, you've gotta forgive him and get on with your life."

Tears began to fill her eyes. "What he did to me is unforgivable, and I meant what I said the other night. I'm glad he's dead."

"For God's sake! What did he do to you?" Max exclaimed, then suddenly pulled back with an apprehensive look. "He didn't mess with you, did he?"

Her tears had turned into sobs, and Max pulled her into his arms. When she finally found her voice, it was so small he could scarcely hear it. "He raped me when I was sixteen," she cried.

"Oh, God!" he moaned. "I was hoping it wasn't that!" He pulled back from her and looked into her stricken face. "Didn't you tell Mom and Dad?"

"I told Mom, and she told Dad, but he said I was lying, and Mom just fell apart. She's tried to keep me away from here as much as she could since then, but Dad made me come home this summer."

"Why didn't you tell me this before? I would've stopped him."

"What could you have done if even Mom and Dad couldn't do anything?"

"Believe me, I would've found a way to stop him," Max said. "Did he try anything this summer?"

"He tried, but I told him I'd kill him if he ever touched me again, and I would've, Max. I really would've." She wiped at her face with her napkin. "So now you see why I can never forgive him. He ruined my life."

Max took her hands in his. "No one can ruin the wonderful spirit that's always made you so special, but if you let this make you bitter, then he's won. You can't let him do that."

"I think he's already done it. I feel so dirty."

"That's ridiculous! You're one of the strongest people I've ever known, and you'll pull through this. You wait and see. You will."

She snuffed back her tears. "I hope you're right."

"I *am* right, and I'll be here for you any time you need me. This is one brother who won't let you down."

They both looked up as Sam came into the dining room and told them Deputy Styvessan was in the sunroom and wanted to speak to Lily.

"Go ahead," Max said. "If you need me, I'll be out at the kiln. Just send Sam out for me."

Lily wiped her eyes with the napkin, then went into the sunroom. Gus stood as she came in.

"You wanted to see me?" she asked.

Gus could see that she'd been crying, and he suddenly wondered whether this was the best time to talk to her, but time was running out for Derek. "Yes, I do," he said. "Something's come up, and I was hoping you could help me out. Can we sit down for a minute?"

"I guess so."

They both sat on the rattan sofa.

Gus shifted awkwardly, his cap dangling loosely in his hands. "You remember the little talk we had yesterday?"

She nodded.

"You remember I asked you if you'd killed your brother, and you told me you hadn't?"

"Right."

"And I told you if that if you had, and someone innocent got blamed for it, that you'd have to own up to what you'd done. Remember?"

"Get to the point, Mr. Styvessan."

He gave his cap a twist. "Okay. I don't think you did it, but I think you saw who did."

She looked startled, then let out a hollow little laugh. "I don't know how you came to that conclusion. I certainly didn't say anything that would lead you to believe that."

"No, you didn't, but something I observed yesterday got me to thinking."

"What?"

"When I started to leave here last night, you were looking down from your balcony at Lucas and me as we went to our trucks. Remember? You waved to me. And since your mother says you spend most of your time on that balcony, I thought you might've seen something you'd want to tell me." He hesitated for just a second. "Did you?"

The smile on Lily's mouth slowly vanished. "I've told you everything I saw, and I'm sorry if that's no help."

"I wish it was, Lily, but Sheriff Lucas just took Derek Abrams in for questioning, and there's a good chance he'll be charged with Morgan's murder. Now, I can't swear to you that he didn't do it, but if you know anything at all about this, you've gotta tell me, or a wonderful young man is gonna have his life ruined. Please, Lily, help me out with this."

She was silent for a long moment, her dilemma obvious, even to Gus. "I wish I could, Mr. Styvessan, but I can't."

"Can't or won't?"

She hesitated for a moment, then said, "Both."

Gus raised his brows. "Okay. But I want you to think about something. If Derek Abrams is convicted of murder and gets a prison sentence—or maybe even the death penalty—you'd better be sure you can live with that the rest of your life. That's all I'm gonna say, except, like I said yesterday, if you decide you want someone to talk to, I'm available."

Lily stood up and stuck out her hand to him. "I appreciate your offer, and if I feel the need to unburden on someone, you'll be the first person I call."

She walked him to the door, and he put his cap on and started down the front steps, then turned and looked back at her for a long moment before continuing down the rest of the steps. She stood in the doorway and watched his pickup disappear down the driveway toward the gate, then suddenly found it difficult to breathe. Surely they couldn't convict Derek Abrams for something he hadn't done. Or could they?

CHAPTER 18

Derek Abrams sat stone-faced in Sheriff Lucas's patrol car, his intense brown eyes riveted on the arid gray hills of the Toppenish Ridge off to his right. Sheriff Lucas tried to engage him in conversation, but Derek remained silent. What was there for him to say? He'd already told Lucas he had no idea how the cane got into his truck, but that hadn't stopped Lucas from taking him in for questioning. He'd felt such poetic justice that Morgan had died the same way his father had—violently and unexpectedly—but it was beginning to dawn on him that he wasn't a simple bystander anymore: someone had set him up to take the blame for Morgan's murder, and he was sure it was Andrew Cullen.

When they arrived at the sheriff's station in Toppenish, Lucas led Derek into the drab stucco building. Several deputies stared at him curiously, then snickered as one of them pulled at imaginary braids when Derek passed by them.

Lucas took Derek into his office, then excused himself and went into the outer office. He dialed the coroner's office for his report, then called Gus and found out that Derek had been seen by his cutters all day, except for their break from three to three thirty.

"Has the coroner determined the time and cause of death?" Gus asked Lucas.

"Yeah. He said the actual cause of death was drowning, not the head wound, and Morgan's watch had stopped at three thirty, so he either stumbled or was pushed into the pool before then."

"Dammit!" Gus muttered. "I was hoping it had happened earlier than that so Derek would be in the clear."

"You really like this kid, don't you?" Lucas said.

"Yes, I do, and I hate to think he could've been driven to do something like this. What's your next step?"

"Well, I guess I'll have to book him, and then call Bob Haskell from the Indian Agency and get him involved. Maybe they can get Derek an attorney. I doubt he can afford one."

"I'm sure he can't. He's only been teaching a couple of years. Doesn't the Agency pay for that kind of thing for Indians?" Gus asked.

"No. They only handle petty stuff like divorce and drunkenness and theft. The Bureau of Indian Affairs handles capital cases, but they only pay for an investigator, and he just works along with an Indian's own attorney."

"Do you know of any Indian attorneys Derek might contact? They'd probably take it for nothing."

"There aren't any on this Reservation," Lucas replied.

"Maybe Haskell knows a white attorney who'd see that Derek got a good defense."

"Maybe," Lucas said, "but I'll have to book him before Haskell can get involved."

"Are you gonna ask the court to set bail?"

"I don't see why not. Do you think he's a flight risk?"

There was a moment's pause, then Gus said, "I don't think so. With his job on the line out there at White Swan, I think he's got too much to lose to run. He says he's innocent, and I think he'll look forward to bringing the whole thing about his father's death back into the spotlight."

"I appreciate your help on all this," Lucas said. "Dealin' with Andrew Cullen isn't gonna be any picnic."

Gus laughed. "Better you than me."

"Don't think you're gettin' outta this," Lucas said. "You know all those people out there, so I'll need your help interviewin' 'em."

"I was afraid you were gonna say that, but you need to know my heart isn't in this. I think Derek's getting railroaded."

"Well, I've got him in my office right now, so maybe I can get to the bottom of this and avoid havin' to arrest him. I'll stay in touch."

When Lucas went back to his office, Derek was standing at the window, staring out at the barren hills of the Toppenish Ridge, and Lucas went over and stood by him for a moment. "Beautiful, aren't they?" Lucas said. "I never get tired of lookin' at those hills."

Derek gave a little nod. "I was just remembering my dad and me chasing down some wild cayuses up there when I was a kid."

"I'm sure those were good times for you," Lucas said, then turned and sat down at his desk and motioned Derek to the chair across from him. "I just talked with Gus and he says that no one can vouch for your whereabouts during your break from around three to three thirty on Friday. The coroner says they found Morgan around three forty-five. Where were you during your break?"

"I was sitting on the bank of the canal praying toward Pahto."

"*Pahto?*"

"You Whites call it Mount Adams, but we've always called it Pahto. It's our sacred mountain."

"Did anyone see you doin' this?"

"I don't know. My concentration was on the mountain."

"Well, if no one saw you out there, then there's no way you can prove it."

"My word isn't enough?"

"I didn't say that," Lucas replied. "I just don't think you realize how much trouble you're in."

Derek gave a derisive laugh. "I may be an Indian, but I'm not stupid. I know what's happening. Another Indian is going to be sacrificed to keep the Whites happy."

"Dammit, Abrams! This isn't some cowboy and Indian movie. The man you blame for your father's death has been murdered, and the murder weapon was found in *your* truck, and you can't verify where you were at the time of the murder. Can all that just be a coincidence?"

"Of course not. Someone obviously set me up."

"And why would someone do that?"

"To throw suspicion off himself, I guess."

"Who else had it in for Morgan, besides you?"

Derek let out a caustic laugh. "How much time have you got, Sheriff?"

"Not enough to listen to any more of this," Lucas said, "so unless you can give me somethin' that at least puts some doubt on your involvement in this, I'm gonna have to book you and let the court decide if you had anything to do with it. You can call your mother now and tell her what's happened, and see if she can get you a lawyer. I'll notify the Bureau of Indian Affairs, and their investigator, Bob Haskell, will probably wanna talk to you right away. He might be able to help you get a lawyer. If not, we've got a public defender who can help you." Lucas paused a moment, almost apologetic. "I'm sorry to have to do this to you, son, but I don't have any other choice. Do you have any questions before I book you?"

Derek had a way of fixing you with a gaze that demanded an honest answer. His dark eyes bore into Lucas now. "Just one, Sheriff. Do you honestly think I'd risk everything I've lived and worked for all my life just to kill someone as inconsequential as Morgan Cullen?"

Lucas forced himself to maintain eye contact. "I honestly don't know. That's somethin' a jury's gonna have to decide, but if you did, it was a terrible price to pay to avenge your father's death. I don't think he'd be very proud of you."

Derek let out a brittle laugh. "You have no idea how proud he *would* be if someone had avenged his death, but it wasn't me."

CHAPTER 19

Derek was fingerprinted and booked, then given the chance to call his mother. She listened quietly to what he had to say, and when he'd finished, she asked him simply, "Did you do it?"

"No, Mother, I swear on my father's grave that I didn't."

"That's good enough for me. I'll get the money somehow for a lawyer."

Derek was taken to a cell, and as the deputy locked it behind him, the reality of what was happening to him began to sink in. He stood with his hands on the bars watching the deputy retreat, then turned and looked at the claustrophobic cell. A bunk bed hung from one wall and a dirty sink and toilet were on another. A small window above his head let in streaks of sunlight through the bars, and a single bulb glared down from the tall ceiling. He took it all in, then went to the bunk and lay down, covering his eyes with his arm.

Caught up in this nightmare, he determined—as his father had taught him—to send his mind to a place of tranquility far away. With his eyes tightly shut, he gradually conjured up the wind on his face as he raced across the hills on his horse. Breathing deeply, he could smell the sage and pine, and hear his father's laughter as he galloped along beside him.

He lay this way for several hours, transported to another time and place, unconscious of his surroundings until a voice startled him. He sat upright at the sound.

A White-man was standing at his cell door beside the deputy. "I'm Bob Haskell from the Bureau of Indian Affairs," the man said. "I'd like to talk to you for a few minutes. Is it okay if the deputy lets me in?"

Derek stood up and came to the door. "What do you want to talk about?"

"I'd like to hear your side of all this. It's my job to see that you Indians get a fair trial, and I'd like to talk this whole thing over with you. Right now you don't have a lot of other options as I see it."

Derek stood back from the door. "I don't know what you can do for me, but you're welcome to come in. Obviously I'm not going anywhere."

Haskell rolled his eyes at the deputy as he opened the cell door and let him in. The deputy locked the door behind him, and Derek sat down on the edge of the bunk.

"Well," Haskell said, "it seems like you've gotten yourself into quite a mess. I talked with Sheriff Lucas and he pretty much told me what happened."

"Well then, you have one version of it."

Haskell raised his brows. "Look, I'm not here to pass judgment on whether you're innocent or guilty. My job is just to make sure that you've got the best possible representation and to assist whatever attorney you get—White or Indian. It's up to a jury of your peers to decide if you're guilty or not."

Derek raised his brows. "A jury of my peers? You must be new around here, Mr. Haskell. When did you ever see an all-Indian jury, or one with even a single Indian on it?"

"By 'your peers,' I mean people who know the problems you Indians face."

Derek let out a caustic laugh. "Doesn't that seem a little ironic to you? Those same people are responsible for most of those problems."

"Well, I'm not going to try to defend our system of justice. It's the best we've got, and we're just going to have to work with it. Now, have you done anything about trying to get an attorney?"

"My mother's working on it, but since you're the authority on Indians, you probably realize that we don't have that kind of money."

Haskell nodded. "Yes, I'm sure that'll be a problem. I'll get in touch with your mother and see what I can do to help. In the meantime, I'll contact the Indian Agency and let them know what's happened and see if they can get you out of here as soon as bail is set."

Derek shrugged. "Whatever."

Haskell was plainly irritated. "Look, young man, I know this is an awful mess you've gotten yourself into, but that kind of attitude isn't going to help you one bit. Whether you or I like it or not, no one feels any sympathy for a smart-aleck Indian."

"Well, I'll try to behave like I'm civilized then, Mr. Haskell. I certainly wouldn't want to offend anyone's sensibilities."

Haskell went to the cell door and called for the deputy. As he was starting to leave, he turned back to Derek. "You've got a real attitude problem. You know that?"

Derek's lips parted in a barely perceptible smile. "Oh, yes," he said. "Far better than you'll ever know."

Two days later, Derek's mother had still not been able to get him a lawyer, but bail had been set for the staggering sum of thirty thousand dollars—Judge Harmon's work.

On the third day of his incarceration, Sheriff Lucas had Derek brought to his office. "Your bail's been posted," he said. "You're free to go, but you'll be arrested if you leave the Reservation. I'll give you another week to get yourself an attorney, but if you can't get one by then, I'll have to have the court appoint you a public defender."

Derek was still reeling from the news that his bail had been posted. He looked around. "Who posted my bail?"

"The young woman is waiting for you outside."

A deputy gave him his watch and wallet, and he walked out the door of the jail into the bright sunlight. He put up his hand to shield his eyes, unsure who might be waiting for him. As his eyes adjusted to the light, he saw Lily Cullen standing by her red Ford convertible.

When she saw him, she came toward him. "I know we've never met," she said, "but I'm Lily Cullen."

"I know who you are. Did your father send you?"

"Are you kidding? My father would have a heart attack if he knew I was here. I paid your bail."

All his senses were suddenly alert. "*You* paid my bail? Why?"

"Because I know you didn't kill my brother."

His eyes narrowed. "And how do you know that?"

"Look," she said testily, "I paid your bail, and I'm here to drive you home. Now you can call someone else to come and get you, or you can let me drive you home and explain why I bailed you out. What do you want to do? It's up to you."

He studied her for a moment, then shrugged, "It's your money. I guess I owe you a half hour of my time."

They got into her car and pulled out of the station heading for the Fort Road. The top was down, and the wind was whipping Lily's long hair into a swirl around her head. "Where do you live?" she asked, brushing the tangle of wheat-colored hair from her face.

Derek kept his eyes straight ahead. "On the Fort Road, near White Swan."

They drove in silence for a few miles. A blistering sun beat down on them, raising beads of sweat on Derek's forehead. He reached up several times and wiped it off. Finally he looked over at Lily. "I still want to know why you bailed me out. You don't know me. How do you know I didn't kill your brother?"

She looked over at him. "Trust me. I know."

He digested that for a moment, then said, "Well, if you know anything about me at all, you know I'm not the least bit sorry he's dead."

A cynical little laugh erupted from her. "Join the crowd."

His brow creased. "You wanted him dead too? Why?"

"Like you, I had my reasons."

Lily slowed down as a truck in front of her turned off onto Lateral A. She pulled around it and continued on.

Derek kept his eyes fixed on the road. "I think you should know I don't have any money to pay you back," he said.

"I don't expect you to."

He was quiet again as he studied her profile. There was a defiant grace to the way she held her head. He had seen her several times at The Oaks, but had never really taken note of her. "What *do* you expect of me then?" he asked. "No one does something like this for nothing. Especially not for an Indian."

She glanced over at him with a frown. "Look, I don't care what you are. I told you I believe you're innocent, and since no one else seems to think so, I just think you deserve a chance to prove it, and you can't do that sitting in jail."

"Does your father know the way you feel?"

"My father doesn't know anything about me. He's as bad as Morgan was—maybe worse."

Derek let out a brittle laugh. "This is really rich. I'm sitting in the car next to the sister of the man I'm supposed to have murdered, and she tells me she hated her dead brother *and* hates her father, who's trying to get me lynched. Doesn't all this strike you as a little bizarre?"

"If you knew my family, that wouldn't surprise you."

"You seem to have some common sense," he said. "Where'd that come from?"

"From my Grandfather Barron. He was a maverick too, so they tell me."

Derek continued studying her, trying to figure out what her angle was. Was she some White 'do-gooder' who saw a chance to help a poor, misguided Indian, or was she trying to make some kind of statement to her father? Or was it possible she knew who had killed her brother, and her conscience was bothering her?

"What's your father going to say when he finds out you paid my bail?"

"He's not going to—unless you tell him. I made Sheriff Lucas swear not to tell anyone who paid it, and he gave me his word he wouldn't."

"Thirty thousand dollars is a lot of money."

"Not to my mother, it isn't."

He gave her a puzzled look. "Your mother gave you the money?"

She hesitated a moment, then said, a little sheepishly, "Well, not exactly. I pawned some of her jewelry."

"You did what?"

"I pawned some of her jewelry. It's no big deal. She never wears it anyway, so she won't miss it. And if she does, she'll just think one of the help stole it, and the insurance will replace it."

He knotted his brows in obvious displeasure. "It looks to me like you're just driving another nail into my coffin. Aren't you afraid your mother will tell your father when she discovers her jewelry's gone?"

"My mother doesn't say two words to him unless she has to. They've hated each other for years."

Derek shook his head. "And to think, people envy you Cullens."

"It's not a pretty picture, is it?"

"No, it isn't. My mother and I don't have much, but at least we love each other, and I wouldn't trade that for all the Cullen money in the world."

"Did your mother remarry after your father died?"

"My father didn't *die*, Miss Cullen. He was *murdered* by your drunken brother."

"My mistake," she said, glancing over at him. "I knew Morgan sneaked liquor from Dad's liquor cabinet from the time he was ten years old. Max told me that."

"Then why wasn't he arrested for killing my father?"

"You know the answer to that: Judge Harmon."

Derek gave a derisive snort. "Your father's own private judge and jury."

"Yes, he is, and that's why I've bailed you out, so you can do something about it."

"What did you have in mind?"

"You need to get a good attorney to start with."

"Mr. Lamont is working on that. My mother works for them."

"Has he had any luck?"

"I don't know. I was only able to talk to her about it once."

"What about your job out at White Swan? Did they fire you?"

He turned his face from her and stared out at the passing scene. The sun had gone down, and a grimy twilight had begun to soften the distant hills. He hadn't let himself think about his job. It was too painful contemplating what his students and the faculty must be thinking about him from what they'd heard and read in the newspaper. He felt that most of them would give him the benefit of the doubt, but there would be a few—like the one who had written him that ugly note—who'd be only too eager to believe the worst.

He looked back at Lily. "I don't know what's happening with

my job. School starts September tenth, so they've probably replaced me by now."

Lily was clearly distraught. "I don't see how they could fire you before you have a trial. That's not fair."

"This has never been about what's fair. It's about who holds the power on this Reservation, and your father is one of those who holds it." He looked up and pointed to the left. "Turn into that next lane up there. That's where I live."

Lily slowed down and turned into a dirt driveway leading to a small clapboard house badly in need of paint. A weeping willow tree was struggling to stay alive in front of it. In an obvious effort to brighten the drab surroundings, someone had planted a border of yellow daisies along the dirt path leading from the driveway to the back door. A weathered old barn and small corral stood off to the left of the house with several horses standing near the railing. Lily pulled up in front of the house and shut off the engine. Derek made no move to get out. "I don't suppose you'd like to meet my mother, would you?" he asked.

Lily looked startled at his offer. "I'd like very much to meet her, if you don't think it would upset her. I'm sure she doesn't think too kindly of my family."

"No, she doesn't, but it would give her *some* comfort to know that not all the Cullens are as depraved as Morgan and your father."

Derek had just gotten out of the car when the door of the house burst open, and Lucy came rushing out. She ran to him and threw her arms around his neck, tears flooding her cheeks, then pulled back and held his face between her hands. "Did they drop the charges?"

He shook his head, then turned to Lily who had just gotten out of the car. "This is Lily Cullen, Mom. She bailed me out."

Lucy stuck out her hand to Lily. "Thank you so much, Miss Cullen. You don't know what it means for me to have Derek back."

Lily shook her hand. "I'm glad I could help, because I believe he's innocent."

"He *is* innocent," she said. "We just have to find a way to prove it."

"Were you able to get an attorney?" Derek asked.

"Mr. Lamont's still working on it."

"He didn't fire you?"

"Heavens, no! He knows you didn't do it, and he's furious that they arrested you."

"Thank God he didn't fire you," Derek said. "That would really have made this unbearable."

Lucy put her hand on Derek's arm and looked up at him gravely. "But I do have some bad news about your job. The superintendent called yesterday, and they're replacing you. I begged him not to, but he said they couldn't afford to wait and see how the trial comes out. They had to get someone lined-up to take your place before school starts. I'm so sorry, honey."

"How can they do that? " Lily exclaimed.

"Did they say whether the replacement is permanent or just till the trial's over?" Derek asked.

"It's permanent for this year. He has no idea how long your trial will take or how it will turn out, and he's worried about the kids. He thinks some of them, and their parents, will always wonder what really happened."

Derek took a deep breath, blinking rapidly, then reached out for Lily's hand and gave it a quick shake. "If you don't mind, I'd like to be alone with my mother now. Thanks for bailing me out, but I'm not sure you did me a favor."

He put his arm around his mother's shoulders, and they walked down the path into the house.

Lily climbed into her car, and the tears she'd been holding back began streaming down her cheeks. She drove home slowly, but could barely see the road. How had things come to this? She'd never dreamed that Derek would be caught in the middle of her personal feud with Morgan, but how could she tell him the truth? How could she tell anyone? She wiped at her eyes. *Things will work out*, she told herself. *He'll get a good attorney, and he'll get him off. There's no way they can convict someone who's completely innocent.* But even as she tried to convince herself with that thought, she knew there was a very real chance he'd be convicted unless she was willing to tell them who killed Morgan, and that was something she simply could not do.

CHAPTER 20

Charlie's Tavern was the closest thing Harrah had to a town hall. Sooner or later in any given day or evening, most of the ranchers would drop in for a beer or a game of pool, the only place in town where either was available. Gus Styvessan closed up the station at nine and walked over to Charlie's. Smoke hung heavy in the air as Gus made his way to the bar and took a seat on one of the battered stools.

"What'll you have, Gus?" Charlie asked.

"Gimme a Rainier draft."

Charlie got down a stein and drew the beer. Gus swiveled around and surveyed the room, which was unusually crowded for this time of night on a weekday. "Looks like you've got a good crowd tonight."

Charlie set the mug in front of him. "Yeah. Everybody's buzzin' about the Cullen murder. We haven't had this much excitement since old Miss Carpenter dropped her bloomers on the street out there in front of Tiny's Cafe. Remember?"

Gus laughed. "Yeah, I remember that. The poor old thing. I don't think she's ever been the same since then."

"It was Colonel Plimpton who rescued her. Remember? He

came along in his big Pierce Arrow, hopped out and scooped her up into the passenger seat, then just as gallant as you please, he reached down and grabbed those bloomers and tossed them in on her lap and drove off without missing a beat. That old fella has class, I tell you. If I hadn't thought so before, I've sure thought so since."

Gus was still chuckling as Charlie gave the counter a swipe with a soiled dishtowel. "We have some real characters in this town. That's for sure," Charlie said. He leaned in to Gus and lowered his voice. "Whaddya really think about this Cullen murder? Did Abrams do it?"

Gus took a drink of his beer, then set the stein back down and wiped his mouth with the back of his hand. "You know I can't talk about it. But I will say that things aren't looking good for him right now."

"I hear Hank Lamont's gotten him a lawyer. He must believe he's innocent."

"He does," Gus said. "He called me this morning and told me he was standing behind him all the way. I was glad to hear that. The boy needs somebody like Hank in his corner."

Charlie nodded. "It seems like the town's pretty divided on what they think. About half the ones who've been in here the last few days think he's guilty, and the other half either think he's innocent or don't give a darn."

"That's about what I expected."

"I've been surprised at how many think Morgan had it comin' to him, though," Charlie said.

"It's because he's thumbed his nose at people around here ever since he was a kid," Gus said. "I never liked him personally—or his old man—but I've gotta try to keep myself neutral in all of this. Mostly for Laura's sake."

"How's she holdin' up?"

"Not too well."

Charlie poked Gus's arm playfully. "You still kinda sweet on her?"

Gus shrugged. "Oh, hell! That's been over for years. You know that. I'm not in the same league as Andrew Cullen."

"Well, you can thank God for that! I don't know how that woman's put up with him all these years, and you really can't blame Morgan for the way he turned out. 'Like father, like son,' my momma always said."

"Well, all is not well in paradise," Gus said. "Take my word for it. Andrew Cullen's gonna get his comeuppance one of these days, and personally, I'll be standing in the middle of town cheering when it happens."

Billy Aimes, one of the ranch hands at The Oaks, came up just then and laid a hand on Gus's shoulder. "Hey, Gus, I been meanin' to tell you, you're a big hero for nabbin' that Injun kid the other day." Billy grabbed Gus's baseball cap and ruffled his hair. "I was really worried about that pretty scalp of yours. I thought he might come at you with his tomahawk and take it off."

Gus grinned good-naturedly, then grabbed his cap from Billy's hand and plopped it back on his head. "He's about as dangerous as your big mouth, Billy."

Everyone's snickers only spurred Billy on.

"Come on, Gus, tell us the truth," Billy goaded. "What would you have done if he'd come at you with a knife? Would you have shot him?"

"Billy Bob, sit down here." Gus patted the seat beside him, and Billy sat down somewhat tentatively. Gus put one hand on the man's shoulder and looked him straight in the eye. "In the first place, I don't own a gun, 'cause if I did, I'd've filled your rear end with buckshot very time you come barreling through town here, three sheets in the wind. And in the second place, Derek Abrams is about as far removed from knives and tomahawks as old Charlie here. He's more likely to be carrying a slide-rule and a football, and I never heard of anybody getting killed with either one of those."

"So you don't think he done it?" Billy asked. "Everybody else in town does."

"Well, this town's got more busybodies than Carter's got liver pills. Derek may not be able to come in here and buy a beer because he's an Indian, but I'd sure hate to see some of you guys come up against him in a battle of wits. He'd win, hands down."

Billy stood up and shrugged Gus's hand off his shoulder. "You ain't goin' soft on us, are ya, Gus? Sounds like this Injun's bamboozled you."

Gus could feel the hairs on his neck starting to bristle. "I tell you what, Billy, I'm buying you one final beer, then I want you to get your butt outta here and get it on home before I have to handcuff you to that old pole out front of my station for making a public nuisance of yourself." He stood up and turned to Charlie. "Give him a beer and put it on my tab, then see that he gets on his way in the next ten minutes. I'm going on home. It's starting to smell a little gamey in here." He turned and stormed out the door of the tavern.

As Gus headed toward his little house behind the station, he stopped in the middle of the intersection under the infamous stoplight and looked up and down the street. In spite of idiots like Billy Aimes, he loved this old town. The main street was only four blocks long, but everything he needed in life was right here. Tiny's Café across the street from his station had the best meatloaf and biscuits ever made, and Marge Bukowski's milkshakes at the drugstore had put ten extra pounds on him over the years. He chuckled when he saw Doc Stevens's medical clinic, remembering the many times Doc had patched him up in his wild youth. Next to Doc's was Colonel Plimpton's bank, dark and imposing at this time of night, but it had kept his station afloat on more than one occasion. He smiled sadly as he saw the elementary school where his beloved Emily had dispensed her wisdom to hundreds of children over the years. And next to it was the Brethren Church where she had faithfully sung in the choir and prayed so hard for him to get saved. She never thought her prayers 'took', but they had. In spite of his many sins—or maybe because of them—he loved her Jesus, and he loved this crazy old town, and wouldn't change a thing about it, even if he could.

He turned and looked back across the intersection to Charlie's. Its red neon sign blinked "Charlie's Tavern" into the hot muggy night and was the only place in town at this hour with cars and pickups parked in front of it. He saw that Billy Aimes's battered old pickup was still there, and he glanced at his watch. Billy still had a couple more minutes to get himself out of Charlie's. If he didn't, Gus supposed he'd have to go back over there and haul him out. He wasn't looking forward to that. There was already enough tension in town.

He glanced up at the stoplight above him and frowned. It looked to him like a big, bloodshot eye, and he suddenly found himself longing for the days when that stoplight had been the biggest controversy in town. People were starting to take sides about this Cullen murder, and that could only spell trouble. If Billy Aimes was any indication of the way people were thinking, he was frankly worried. Derek Abrams's best interests would not be served by an inflamed mob. He glanced over at Charlie's as several men came stumbling out the door, laughing raucously. He saw Billy Aimes stagger over to his pickup and get in. Gus watched as he backed it out and spun off down the road, tires squealing. He stood there shaking his head till Billy was out of sight, then walked on over to his house, telling himself he needed to have a long talk with Billy when he sobered up tomorrow.

CHAPTER 21

Hank Lamont had never gotten caught up in hop fever like so many of his fellow ranchers had. He would have made more money, especially during World War II when there'd been such a demand for beer for the troops, but he still favored cattle and sugar beets. His 600 acres, running along both sides of the Fort Road, had regularly produced high-quality beets, and that, combined with the prime cattle he still kept, and numerous side ventures, had made him a rich man. Just last week he'd bought four Army surplus P-38s and had them flown from Spokane to Seattle where he sold them at a huge profit.

He'd been in the Army in World War II, but had always been sorry his eyesight had kept him out of the Air Corps. He'd have loved to test his flying skills against those German Messerschmitts, but the closest he ever came to aerial combat was trying to dodge a stray cow as he landed his little Cessna on the canal bank that ran along one side of his property. He now had an airstrip and hangar on his ranch, but occasionally still came down on the canal bank just to keep his skills sharp.

He was thinking now, as he sat on the old leather sofa in his study, of the meeting that had taken place earlier in the day between Derek, the BIA investigator, Bob Haskell, and Lawrence Speer, the attorney he'd gotten for Derek. According to Speer, it had not gone well. Derek had been uncooperative and hostile. What was that dumb kid thinking of? Didn't he know the spot he was in? It was costing Hank a lot of money to get Speer to take the case, and he was doing it mainly because Helen was so fond of the boy and his mother, and because she was convinced Derek was innocent. Personally, he didn't know whether he was or not, but he was willing to give him the benefit of the doubt to keep Helen happy.

He looked up as she poked her head into his study.

"Are you busy?" she asked.

He smiled at her and patted the seat beside him. "I'm never too busy for you, Toots. Come in here and sit that gorgeous body of yours down by me. I haven't seen you all day. What've you been up to?"

She gave him a kiss on the cheek and snuggled up next to him on the sofa. "Lucy and Cassie and I just got back from a special prayer meeting at the church."

He smiled down at her. "That took all day? Must've been some heavy-duty praying."

"It was. Pastor Ralph felt we should really pray about this whole thing with Derek and the Cullens."

Hank looked surprised. "The church is getting into this now?"

"A lot of people are taking sides, but he felt our church should stay as neutral as possible and pray for Derek *and* the Cullens."

Hank let out a laugh. "I'll bet that's the first time anyone's ever prayed for Andrew Cullen. That old reprobate! He needs all the prayers he can get, but I think it's probably too late for him."

"Hank!" Helen scolded, "it's never too late to pray for old reprobates. I even said a couple for you."

He clamped his hand on her knee and chuckled. "Good for you, Toots. You keep badgering God about me, and one of these days I might just surprise you and get myself saved."

She cocked one raised brow at him. "And I've got some swamp land in Florida I'd like to sell you."

"I think I already bought that," he laughed.

"I am concerned about Derek though, and Lucy's worried about him too. She thinks he might do something crazy."

Hank pulled back with a frown. "Like what?"

"Like—maybe run off up into the hills."

"Hasn't he got any better sense than that? Nothing could make him look guiltier."

"I guess he's just so upset about losing his job up at the school, and he's sure he won't get a fair trial."

"That's ridiculous. Lawrence Speer is one of the best criminal lawyers in Yakima. He'll see that he gets a fair trial. He'd better. I'm paying him enough."

"I know you are, and Lucy's so grateful for your help, but we were both wondering if you might be willing to have a talk with him. He doesn't have any man he can talk to, but he knows you've always been good to him and his mother." Her eyes pleaded up at him. "Would you talk to him, honey? For my sake?"

He gave a sigh, knowing he couldn't refuse those big, brown eyes. He didn't want to get personally involved in this, but he couldn't turn Helen down. Derek had been one of her little missionary projects ever since his father was killed, and he knew she was especially fond of him. He pondered it for a second, then thought, *Why not, if it could keep the kid from making a stupid mistake?*

"Okay," he said, "but if he's as hostile as Speer says he is, he might not want to talk to anybody."

"I think he'll talk to you, since you're paying for his lawyer." She got up. "I'll tell Lucy now, before she leaves, and she can ask Derek to come by tomorrow. Will you be here?"

"I have to leave for Seattle around noon, but I can see him at ten if he wants to come then. What do you want me to tell him?"

Helen took his face in her hands. "Tell him the things you'd tell your own son if you had one. You'll know what to say." She gave him a long kiss on the mouth. "I love you, sweetheart. I knew I could count on you." She stood up. "I've got to catch Lucy before she leaves, but I'll see you at dinner. We're going to eat in about half an hour."

Hank went over and sat down at his desk after she left. Why had he agreed to do that? He really didn't know the kid that well, and what did he know about talking to kids anyway? He thought about what Helen had said about talking to Derek like he was his own son. She'd never know how much it pained him not being a father. He'd always wanted a son to work beside him and carry on his name, but he'd been pretty sure when he got married that he'd never be able to father a child. And Helen had known it too, but loved him enough to marry him anyway, and that had made him love her all the more.

It had never been easy for him to talk about his feelings or show them to Helen, but she knew the special place she had in his heart. Sometimes, when he was up there flying through the clouds, looking down at the tiny specks of humanity below and feeling very small and insignificant, he'd given thanks to Helen's God for letting a woman like her fall in love with a big, dumb clod like him. Well, he'd talk to the boy tomorrow. He wasn't sure it would do any good, but he'd talk to him like a Dutch uncle, and he'd do it because his Toots wanted him to.

CHAPTER 22

When Lucy asked Derek that night if he would be willing to talk to Hank Lamont the next day, he reluctantly agreed, but told her not to get her hopes up. What he didn't tell her was that he'd already made up his mind as to what he was going to do.

When Derek arrived at the Lamonts the next morning, Lucy smiled hopefully as she let him in. "Listen to what he has to say, honey. He's a very wise man, and he really cares about you and me."

"I told you I'd listen to him, Mom. I just don't want you to get your hopes up that it's going to make any difference in the way things turn out. I think that's pretty well decided."

"Just give him a chance. That's all I'm asking."

"Where is he?"

"In his study. He's waiting for you."

Lucy took Derek to the study and tapped lightly on the door.

"Come in," Hank called.

She opened the door and stuck her head in. "Derek's here."

"Oh, fine," he said, motioning Derek in. He thanked Lucy, then stood up behind his desk and extended his hand across to Derek. Derek reached over and shook it, then took the chair he motioned to in front of his desk.

Hank sat back in his chair and studied Derek for a moment. He'd been remembering him as a tall, scrawny kid, but this was no kid sitting in front of him. This was a full-grown man. Bulging biceps, strong jaw, piercing dark eyes, and those silly braids hanging down both sides of his head.

It took Hank a moment to digest it all, then he said, "Well, you've certainly grown up since I last saw you. I was still thinking of you as one of Mrs. Lamont's Sunday school boys, but obviously you're a full-grown man now—with all the troubles that come with that."

"Yes, I've grown up," Derek said.

When he said nothing more, Hank said somewhat tentatively, "Your mother and my wife seem to think we oughta have a talk. I told them I didn't know if you were in any mood to tell your troubles to a stranger like me, but they seemed to think you might want to. Is there anything I can do to help you, other than paying for your attorney?"

"Can you guarantee that I won't be sent to jail for something I didn't do?"

Hank gave an annoyed little laugh. "Well, no, I can't, but Lawrence Speer will do his best to see that you're given a chance to tell your side of things, and he feels that if you'll cooperate with him, there's a good chance he can get you off."

Derek gave Hank a skeptical look. "Let's don't kid each other, Mr. Lamont. Lawrence Speer could be Clarence Darrow, and he couldn't get me off. People want an Indian lynching, and they're not going to be happy until they get one."

Hank frowned. "That's a pretty big chip you've got on your

shoulder. I don't think folks around here are nearly as prejudiced against Indians as you seem to think. I've lived here all my life, and I've never seen an Indian that didn't get a fair shake when it came to the law."

Derek's brows went up. "You must be kidding! Where were you when my father was run down by Andrew Cullen's drunken son? Did people demand that there be an investigation? Did *you*? No! None of you got stirred up because it was just another Indian getting killed on the Fort Road. If it had been your father, Mr. Lamont—your *white* father—wouldn't you have demanded an investigation? Would you have let Mrs. Lamont go to work cleaning people's dirty toilets so you could put food on the table? And as for the White-man's law giving the Indians justice, what, in God's name, do you call all the broken treaties and promises for the past two hundred years? Certainly not justice by any decent man's standard—White or Indian."

Hank was taken aback at the outburst. What the boy was saying was all too true, but he didn't like his tone or his attitude, and he certainly didn't like being lumped in with all the white bigots on the Reservation. He'd always treated his Indians fairly, and he'd given this boy's mother a job for over ten years. And on top of all that, he'd gone out on a limb and hired one of the best attorneys in Yakima to defend him. No! He didn't like Derek's attitude one bit, and it was fast becoming obvious to him that the kid was filled with enough rage that he *could've* killed Morgan.

Hank leaned forward and looked intently into Derek's brooding eyes, and his voice was stern. "Well, I can tell you one thing, young man, that kind of attitude is not going to endear you to any jury, whether you're innocent or guilty. My advice to you is to get rid of that chip on your shoulder before you walk into that courtroom, or you might as well plead guilty right now and save yourself—and all of us—the headache of a trial. It's costing me a helluva lot of money to try to save your hide, and I'd like to think I'm not just pouring it down a rat hole. Do you understand me?"

Derek stood up, his face expressionless. "I think you've made yourself very clear, and I hope I have too. Thank you for your time and all the expense you've gone to so far. I won't bother you anymore." He turned and started toward the door.

"You're cutting your own throat," Hank called after him.

Derek stopped and turned back. "That's just the point, Mr. Lamont. If my throat is going to be cut, *I'll* be the one to do it, not some bigoted white jury." He opened the door and went out.

Hank pounded the desk angrily. That stupid kid! He *was* going to get himself lynched with that attitude. He'd known a lot of Indians in his time, but this one was the most arrogant one he'd ever encountered. Maybe it was all that education and athletic praise he'd gotten. It must have done something to his head.

He swiveled his chair around and looked out the window. Helen's big Palomino was scampering around in the corral kicking up little wisps of dust. As Hank watched him, he thought about what Derek had said about people's failure to react to the accident that had killed Jason Abrams. He had to admit that Derek was right about that. Hank was one of those who'd kept his mouth shut about his suspicions, and he wondered now why he had. He certainly had no love for Andrew Cullen. They'd done business together through the years, but Hank had never really liked him. No! He hadn't raised a fuss simply because nobody else had. In a place as small as Harrah, it was just easier to let the whole thing blow over.

Obviously, it *hadn't* blown over for Derek. Until this outburst from him, Hank hadn't really thought about how devastating Jason's death must've been to Lucy and her son. What Derek had said was true. He wouldn't have taken it lying down if some drunk kid—White or Indian—had run into his father and killed him. He'd have screamed bloody murder, and now, maybe that was what Derek was doing in his own way. Maybe he *had* killed Morgan, but Hank could see now why he'd have felt justified in doing so.

He turned back to his desk and began gathering some papers he planned to take with him to Seattle. He wasn't feeling very good about the way he'd handled things, especially because he knew Helen was going to be disappointed in him. He looked up as she came into the room, her face eager.

"How'd it go?" she asked.

Hank shook his head. "Not the way you'd hoped. I tried to talk to him, but he just wanted to spill out his guts about how he thinks he's being railroaded because he's an Indian. I don't know, Helen. With his attitude like it is, I don't think he'll find a very sympathetic judge or jury. Personally I think he's in a whole lot of trouble, and I don't know if Speer is gonna be able to do anything for him or not."

The phone rang just then, and Hank picked it up. He listened intently, a frown drawing his brows together. He nodded several times, then thanked the caller and hung up.

"Well, there's another strike against Derek. That was Larry Speer, and he just told me that Judge Harmon's going to try this case personally. He's that District Court judge Andrew Cullen's got in his pocket. Dear God! This thing is getting out of hand. I'm sorry I got involved."

"Don't say that!" Helen pleaded. "We've got to stand behind Derek. He needs us now more than ever. Lucy's going to be devastated by all this."

Hank gathered up the papers on his desk and stuck them in his briefcase. "Well, Toots, you girls are gonna have to hold things together here by yourselves for awhile because I've gotta get to Seattle, and the way things look, I could be gone for a week."

"You're going to miss Morgan's funeral tomorrow! Can't you put off going for another day?"

"I can't. This trip's been planned for months, and guys are flying in from all over the country. You'll have to offer my condolences to Andrew and Laura."

"Andrew's going to take it personally if you're not there. You know how he is."

"He may not be too happy with me anyway, seeing as how I'm paying for Derek's defense, but I'll give him a call when I get back and smooth his ruffled feathers. In the meantime, maybe he'll cool off a little."

"And maybe he'll have some second thoughts about going through with this prosecution," Helen said.

Hank's brows went up skeptically. "And maybe pigs'll fly someday, but I wouldn't count on it. Besides, it's out of his hands now anyway. Derek's gonna have to stand trial, and hopefully

Speer can get him to cooperate, but if my encounter with him today is any indication of the kind of cooperation Speer can expect, it doesn't look too promising."

"Did you talk to him about not jumping bail?"

He shook his head. "We never even got to that. He just came in here and spilled out his guts, then stormed out. I didn't have a chance to ask him what he was planning, but it wouldn't surprise me one bit if he did take off for the hills. He's mad enough."

"Well, I'm just going to keep praying for him. I know he's innocent."

Hank came around the desk and tipped her chin up, looking down into her worried eyes. "He's a lucky kid to have you in his corner. When you sink your teeth into something, you don't let go, and when you start praying for someone, they haven't got a chance!"

He leaned down and gave her a long kiss, and she clung to him almost desperately. He pulled back and looked into her face and saw that tears had filled her eyes. "Hey now, what's this?" he said as he dabbed at them.

"I'm going to miss you, that's all. I just feel like I need your strength right now. We all do."

"I'll only be a phone call away."

"I know, but it's not the same as having you here where I can snuggle up against you at night. I always feel so safe when your arms are around me."

He pulled her into his arms and whispered against her hair, "Funny thing is, sweetheart, that's when I feel the safest too."

CHAPTER 23

In the first few days after Morgan had been killed, Andrew Cullen had been running on sheer adrenalin, focused only on trying to find out who killed his son. But as he thought about the funeral tomorrow in Yakima, the reality that Morgan was actually gone had finally sunk in, and he found himself experiencing a terrible sense of loss. Morgan was the only one in the whole family he truly cared about, and now there was nothing that linked him with the rest of them—not even their grief. Max had gone on about his business like nothing had happened, and Lily—that miserable excuse for a daughter—had actually acted like she was glad her brother was dead.

Then there was Laura. He never knew what she was thinking, not even when he'd stopped by her room earlier tonight, hoping for a little comfort, but she'd told him she was too upset to invite him in. You'd think any woman would want to comfort her husband at a time like this, but not Laura. She was the coldest woman he'd ever known, and he wouldn't have bothered with her at all if he hadn't felt the need for some human touch to ease the ache that gnawed at him.

He got into his pajamas and fell into bed, but thinking about

Morgan's funeral and what it was going to be like, living without him, made it impossible to get to sleep. Outside, a hot wind had begun to rattle the shutters, and he lay in the gloom, awake and utterly alone. He'd turned fifty-two on his last birthday—still a young man by any standards—but with Morgan gone, there was no one left for him to love, and no one left who loved him.

He'd had such dreams for his own life when he was a young, virile cowpoke drifting from one ranch to another in search of his niche. Then, when he'd literally dropped into Laura Barron's bed, those dreams had become a reality far beyond his wildest imagination. That he didn't love her had never entered into the equation. He could put up with anything if it gave him what he wanted, and she had: a son that any man could be proud of—and her father's wealth. But now that son was gone, and the money and power he'd accumulated gave him little comfort in light of that fact.

He tossed and turned for awhile, unable to find a comfortable position, and finally decided he needed a sleeping pill, but didn't want to go all the way downstairs to get one. Laura always had some in her bedroom, but he knew she'd think he had other motives if he went to her room again. Well, that was too bad. If she wouldn't give him what he wanted, at least she could give him something to put him to sleep.

Laura had showered and gotten ready for bed, but was also too distressed to sleep, so she had sat down in an overstuffed chair in her sitting room and picked up an old family album, looking for pictures of Morgan. She smiled as she saw him holding up his first fish when he was six. And there were the three kids on a sled when she and Andrew had taken them up to Sunrise Park at Mount Rainier. Here was one of her and Andrew holding Morgan right after he was born. Had they really been as happy as they looked? It was hard to believe they had. Here was a picture of her in her wedding gown, but Andrew was nowhere to be seen. She flipped the page and smiled down at the picture of her and her parents when she was six years old. She loved that picture; the last one ever taken of her mother. Her parents looked so happy together, and tears always filled her eyes when she saw the joy that two people in love could have for each other.

Her head jerked up from the album as she heard steps in the hall. *Surely that couldn't be Andrew again.* She caught her breath as he tapped on her door and stuck his head in.

"What do you want?" she demanded, her voice sharper than she'd intended.

He was taken aback by her tone. "Well, obviously not what you're thinking. I was just looking for a sleeping pill. Do you have any?"

"Yes," she said tightly.

He pushed the door open and came all the way in. "Laura," he began, "I . . . I . . . Oh forget it!" he said and turned to leave, but her voice stopped him.

"If it's sex you want, I'm too upset for that tonight," she said.

"Don't you think I'm hurting too?"

"I know you are. I know how much Morgan meant to you."

"I doubt that. You always resented the relationship we had."

"That's not true. I was glad you two were close. What I resented was the way you favored him and neglected the other children."

"What did you want me to do? Treat him like nothing had happened to him? He needed special attention after the accident."

"Of course he did, but you didn't need to continually make excuses for his bad behavior. He never learned to accept responsibility for any of his actions, and that turned him into an angry young man with no real friends. I know you didn't mean for him to turn out that way, but he did—and you've only got yourself to blame for that."

"I suppose you're blaming me for him being murdered too."

"In some ways, I am," she said. "He might still be alive if he hadn't caused someone to hate him enough to kill him." She looked down at the album in her lap, and her voice softened. "I was just looking at some of these pictures of him when he was little, and he was such a sweet little boy. It breaks my heart to think what he turned into."

"Can I see?" he asked.

She hesitated a moment, then turned the album toward him as he knelt down beside her chair.

A quick rush of tears glazed his eyes as he pointed to the picture of Morgan holding up a fish. "I remember this," he said. "Morgan's first fish. He was so proud of himself. Not many kids can land a fish that big at his age. God, he was cute." His gaze traveled over the page. "Look at him here on the end of the diving board. He was such a little daredevil." He turned the page. "And look at this one of him on his skis. When was this taken?"

"When he was about twelve. That was the winter you taught Lily how to ski."

"I remember that. It was up at Snoqualmie Pass. Look at that Morgan. Even I wouldn't have tried some of the stunts he pulled on his skis." He smiled sadly as he pointed to another picture. "Look at him in his crazy clown outfit. We took the kids up to Yakima trick-or-treating, and Morgan got sick from too much candy. He was so cute."

"You didn't think it was so cute when he threw up all over you on the way home."

He chuckled softly. "I remember that. I could've strangled him."

He pointed to a picture of Laura when she was about eight months pregnant with Morgan. "Look at that belly of yours. I knew I was going to have my first son."

"*Our* first son, Andrew. You seem to forget that he was my son too."

He looked up at her, and there was an unfamiliar softness in his voice. "What happened to us?"

She eyed him skeptically. "Do you really want me to be honest?"

He sat back on his heels and gave her a look she hadn't seen on his face in years. "I know it's too late for us, but I would like to know if you ever loved me. Did you?"

She closed the album and laid her hands on top of it. "I tried to when we first got married, but I knew you'd only married me because I was Cyrus Barron's daughter. Maybe we would've been happy if Daddy hadn't died so soon. I don't know. I guess none of that matters now. I'm surprised you even care enough to ask."

He reached over and covered her hand with his, and she felt herself recoil inside. His voice thickened. "It's awful hard for me right now. I guess maybe I just wanted to know if anyone ever really loved me, besides that boy."

"Max and Lily love you," she said.

He abruptly withdrew his hand and stood up. "I doubt that. I'm their meal ticket, and that's about it."

"That's not true. You haven't been very kind to Lily, but I know she loves you. And dear Max. He loves everybody, even though he knows you favored Morgan. When he was a little boy, he used to ask me why you liked Morgan better than him, and I always told him you didn't, but he knew even then."

Andrew shoved his hands into the pockets of his robe and stood looking down at her. He seemed to want to talk. "I was thinking tonight about the future," he said, "and what it's going to be like without Morgan. I had so many hopes pinned on that boy."

"You've still got Max, and he loves this ranch much more than Morgan ever did, and he'd love to take some of the responsibility off your shoulders. Why don't you give him a chance? I think you two could be every bit as close as you and Morgan were."

Andrew shook his head. "I don't know. He's never really understood me. But Morgan and I. That was different. Looking at him was like looking at myself twenty-five years ago." He blinked several times, and Laura could tell he was fighting tears. "I'm not looking forward to the funeral tomorrow. I can tell you that," he said.

"Nor am I," she said. "I'm going to miss him so much."

Andrew turned his head from her as tears glazed his eyes. "I will too," he said, starting for the door.

Laura stood up. "Andrew?" she called after him.

He turned back, a hopeful look on his face. "Yes?"

"You forgot the sleeping pills. I'll get them for you."

"That's not what I want from you, and you know it."

"I haven't got anything else to offer you."

He dismissed her words with an angry flick of his hand and went out the door, slamming it behind him.

CHAPTER 24

The McKinley Chapel in Yakima holds over 300 people, and it was packed. Floral arrangements of every size and shape were banked across the front near the open casket, and the fragrance in the air was nearly overpowering. Everyone from Harrah was there, plus numerous dignitaries from Yakima and Seattle. This was—in some macabre way—the social event of the year. People who had only heard the Cullen name came to get a glimpse of these legendary people, and hopefully to gaze on the face of their fallen son.

Laura and Andrew Cullen sat side by side in the front row of the mourner's alcove, veiled from curious eyes by an opaque black curtain. Laura was all in black, with a small black hat and veil drawn tightly over her hair. Lily and Max sat beside them. Max was in his best suit, while Lily had on a bright fuchsia dress, and her blond hair hung long and loose on her shoulders. Behind them sat Elsie, their cook, Sarah, the housekeeper, the two maids, and Sam, their houseman. The four women were in black, and had already begun dabbing at their eyes with handkerchiefs, even though the service had not yet begun.

The Cullens were not churchgoers, so the mortuary had obtained the services of the Unitarian minister in Yakima. His choir soloist was on hand for the music, and the Episcopal church had volunteered their harpist, a young woman who could be found playing in the bar of the Chinook Hotel every evening.

The service opened with a call to prayer.

"Oh, God," the minister intoned, "we come before you this day with heavy hearts to remember this fine young man who was so cruelly cut down in the prime of his youth; a young man loved and revered by his family, a man who was a friend to all who knew him, a son who was a comfort to his parents, Laura and Andrew Cullen, a companion and friend to his brother, Max, and a sterling example of young manhood to his sister, Lily. We beseech you, oh God, to look down on all here today who will forever feel the loss of this servant of Yours. We are comforted to know that he is now with You, never again to know the sorrows and pains of this world. We commit him into Your hands, and ask that Your healing balm will soothe those whose hearts are grieving here today. Amen."

Lily listened in astonishment, then leaned over and whispered to Max, "'A sterling example of young manhood'? Who wrote that crap?"

"Lily!" Max said, giving her a jab with his elbow. "Mom and Dad will hear you."

"What do I care? They know it's all a bunch of lies, especially the part about him being in heaven enjoying eternal bliss. The only bliss he's ever known has been from a bottle."

Just then the soloist began "Beyond the Sunset" in an airy soprano voice. When she finished, the minister read the names of the bereaved family, told a little about Morgan's life—carefully avoiding the subject of how he'd died—discussed the virtues of heaven over earth, and then asked those who wished to view the body to line up and come forward.

The harpist played softy as people eagerly lined up to view Morgan's body. The first person was Gus Styvessan. As he approached the casket, he glanced toward the family curtain. It was obvious to anyone who knew him that he longed to be with Laura in this moment of her grief, but he continued on to the casket and gazed briefly down at Morgan, then moved toward the exit. Behind him were Helen Lamont and her niece, Cassie Hampton.

Following closely behind them were Charlie Anderson, Tiny Shallenburger, Beulah Rasmussen, Doc Stevens, Colonel Plimpton, Marge Bukowski, and the two old-maid Carpenter sisters in wide-brimmed black hats swathed in black veiling, wearing identical, long-sleeved, black dresses, and clutching white handkerchiefs in their black lace gloves. Even Billy Aimes was there in his new cowboy boots, although he was still wearing dirty blue jeans and a black tee shirt with a cheap, imitation turquoise clasp hanging down the front of it.

As the crowd moved slowly past the casket, some mourners stopped and bent over for a closer look, while others, moved by the harp music, dabbed at their eyes. One of the last viewers was a pregnant young woman, and she stopped longer than the others. She leaned over the body and muttered something, then, to the complete shock of those near her, she spit on Morgan's face and ran toward the door. There was an audible gasp from those in line behind her.

Lily had been bored by all of this, and was thankful it was nearly over when she suddenly saw the pregnant girl spit on her brother. At first she was stunned, then a knowing smile turned up the corners of her mouth. Obviously this "virtuous" brother of hers had had his dirty hands on someone else.

Andrew Cullen jumped out of his seat and brushed the curtain aside before Laura could restrain him. He lunged toward where the girl had been in front of the casket, but she had already been swallowed up outside by the crowd of mourners.

"You little bitch!" he yelled after her. "I'll find out who you are, and you'll be sorry you did this." He turned back to the casket, and wiped the spit off Morgan's face with his handkerchief. Laura had come up beside him and took him gently by the arm. The crowd moved back without a word as she led Andrew toward the door.

Gus was already outside, but was quickly informed of what had happened. When he saw Laura and Andrew come out of the mortuary, he hurried to them and took Laura's arm. "I heard what happened in there. Are you alright?"

She nodded. "Yes, thank you. I can't understand what would have made that girl do such a terrible thing."

"I can," Andrew said. "I'm sure she's the one who tried to blackmail Morgan."

"What's this?" Gus asked, turning to Cullen. "Someone was blackmailing Morgan?"

Cullen realized too late what he'd let slip, and he quickly lowered his voice. "Well, she wasn't *exactly* blackmailing him. She claims Morgan got her pregnant, but I had a long talk with him and he adamantly denied it."

Gus looked at him curiously. "How did you find out about her accusation? Did Morgan tell you?"

Cullen hesitated. "I told Lucas about it. It wasn't anything. I got a letter from some attorney her father had hired demanding some money, so, to get him off Morgan's back, I paid him something. That's all."

"How much did you pay him?"

"Well, not what he was asking—I can tell you that—but how much I paid him is none of your business."

"It might be my business if this guy felt he got short-changed. It might've been enough of a reason for him to kill Morgan."

"That's ridiculous!" Cullen said. "Everybody knows Derek Abrams killed him."

"That hasn't been proven," Gus said. "In any case, I'd like to get a look at that letter from the attorney. I want to know who this man is that claims your son got his daughter pregnant."

"Fine. Come by my office tomorrow and I'll give you a copy of it, but you're barking up the wrong tree."

"I'll make that decision after I see the letter," Gus said.

Just then, the pallbearers appeared at the side door of the chapel with the casket, and the crowd stepped back as Max and five others bore the ornate oak casket to the hearse and slid it in the back.

Laura touched Andrew's arm. "The funeral director's motioning to us. They're ready to leave." She turned to Gus. "Are you coming to the cemetery?"

"Yes. I'll see you over there."

Andrew, Laura, Lily, and Max moved toward the black limousine parked behind the hearse, and the crowd parted silently as they passed through. All of a sudden a heavyset man jumped from the crowd and threw himself on Andrew, dragging him to the ground. He began beating on him ferociously—punching his face and tearing at his jacket. Andrew tried to defend himself, but the enraged man seemed to be endowed with superhuman strength as he pummeled away at Cullen's face and body.

"You lousy bastard!" the man screamed. "I'll kill you for what your son did to my daughter."

Max and Lily had already gotten into the limousine when they heard their father's cry for help. Max jumped out and ran to him, grabbing at the man's arm, trying to pull him off. The man kicked out at him, but continued pounding on Cullen.

"Help me, Max!" Cullen cried out. "Help me!"

Gus was already headed toward his car when he heard the commotion. He fought his way back through the crowd that had closed in on the fracas and saw what was happening. He tried to pull Max away from it, but Max shoved at him. "What are you doing? Help me get this guy off Dad!"

"Stay out of it!" Gus said. "Your father can take care of himself."

"Are you crazy? The guy's killing him! Help me!"

Cullen was lying on his back grunting and moaning under the hail of punches, his face smeared with blood. "Max! For God's sake, get him off me!" Cullen cried.

Lily watched with fascination as the three men punched and pulled at one another.

Laura grabbed Gus by the arm. "Help him, Gus. Please!"

Gus looked at her and gave a deep sigh, then took off his jacket, handed it to her, and jumped into the fight. He grabbed at one of the man's flailing arms, and Max got the other one, and together they pulled him off Cullen, who lay bleeding and gasping for breath on the driveway. The man twisted and squirmed, trying to free himself from Gus and Max while they dragged him away from Cullen.

After they got him away from the ruckus, the man finally stopped struggling and appeared to calm down. Gus and Max let go of him, and he pulled his torn jacket back up onto his shoulders.

"What's all this about?" Gus demanded.

"He knows," the man said, pointing to Cullen. "His son raped my daughter and got her pregnant, and refused to accept any responsibility for it. I'd have killed him myself, if someone hadn't beat me to it."

Cullen had struggled to his feet. Blood gushed from his battered nose, and his eyes were beginning to swell shut. The sleeve of his jacket was torn completely from its shoulder seam, and he pulled it free and threw it on the ground, then jabbed his finger toward the man. "You're a liar," Cullen said, "and I'm gonna sue you till you bleed!"

"And I'm suing you for every dime you've got!" the man yelled back at Cullen. "You Cullens think you're so high and mighty that nobody can touch you. Well, this is one man you're not going to push around. If your son was too much of a coward to face what he did to my daughter, then I'll get it out of you!"

The man flung his arm out toward the crowd and raised his voice as he pointed back to Andrew. "I want all of you to know what kind of people these Cullens are. His son raped my daughter, then was too much of a coward to take responsibility for it. Why you'd come to pay respects to this rotten family, God only knows. His son got what he deserved."

Gus took the man firmly by his arm. "I think that's enough," he said. "You've made your point."

"Who are you?" the man demanded.

"Deputy Gus Styvessan."

The man shrugged Gus's hand off his arm. "Well, Deputy, I haven't even started making my point with him, but I'll let it go for now. I think he's gotten an idea what's on my mind."

"Yes, I think you've made yourself very clear, but this really isn't the time or place to settle this. Why don't you give me your name and phone number, and I'll be in touch with you tomorrow, and we'll see if we can't straighten this all out?"

"You'll hear from my lawyer," Cullen yelled through his swollen lips.

"Good!" the man yelled back. "You've already heard from mine, but you can bet you haven't heard the last from him— or me."

The man took out his wallet and handed Gus his card, then turned and pushed his way through the stunned crowd. Gus went over to Cullen. "You'd better get your face looked at, Andrew. It looks like your nose might be broken. I'll ride to the cemetery with your family if you'd like."

Cullen nodded. "Thanks."

"I'll drive Dad to the hospital in our car and then take him home," Max said. He turned to Gus. "Can you bring Mom and Lily home afterwards?"

"Sure," Gus replied.

"Thanks for helping Dad," he said, then took his father by the arm and propelled him toward their car as the crowd stood back and silently let them pass.

Gus took his jacket from Laura and put it on, sighing deeply. "I'm so sorry you had to be put through this," he said. "You sure don't deserve it." He slipped his arm around her shoulders. "C'mon. Let's get in the limousine before we give these people any more of a sideshow. They really got their money's worth today."

Lily leaned back in the seat of the limousine as it made its way slowly down Yakima Avenue at the head of the funeral cortege. There was just the faintest smile on her lips. *There is a God*, she said to herself.

CHAPTER 25

Max glanced over at his father as he drove him home from the hospital in the family's Cadillac. When it was discovered that Andrew's nose was broken, it had taken longer than expected in the emergency room, and Cullen had not spoken since they'd gotten into the car. When the fight had first broken out, and Andrew had cried out to him for help, some deep well of love had broken loose inside Max, and he'd fought like a madman to tear the attacker off his father. He could still feel the anguish he had when—for the first time in his life—he saw his father lying helpless on the ground.

Theirs had always been a complicated relationship. Max had lived in Morgan's shadow for as long as he could remember, never measuring up to his father's expectations. He'd stopped trying in his teens and had just accepted things the way they were, but there had always been a void in his life that he knew could only be filled by his father's love. Looking over at him now, a splint and bandage covering his broken nose, and his eyes nearly swollen shut, Max felt for the first time that maybe there was a chance for them now that Morgan was gone. Even so, the same old fear of his father rejecting any show of love on his part kept him silent as they drove along. After about twenty minutes of awkward silence, Max looked over at him and said, "Are you okay, Dad?"

Cullen made an effort to turn his head, but it was obviously difficult to speak through his swollen lips. "I didn't even get to say a final goodbye to Morgan at the cemetery."

"I didn't either, but we can come up in a few days when you're feeling better."

"I wish I'd been able to smear that guy's face all over the ground," Cullen said.

"What made him do it, Dad? Do you even know him?"

"I've never seen him before, but you heard what he said. He thinks Morgan got his daughter pregnant, but I talked to Morgan about it, and he said he didn't even know the girl." He paused a moment, then said, "Did he ever say anything to you about getting someone pregnant?"

Max shook his head. "No. I know he was seeing some girl in Yakima for months, but I don't even know if that's the same girl."

Cullen was quiet a long moment. "I'd sure like to know if Morgan's the father of that girl's baby."

"What difference could that make now?"

He didn't answer for a minute, and Max looked over at him and saw tears ooze out from the swollen slits of his eyes. "If she's carrying Morgan's son, I want it."

"What?" Max gasped, nearly missing the turnoff down to Harrah. "You must be joking! What would you do with a baby?"

"I'd raise it as my own. It would give me something of Morgan to hang on to."

Max gave him an incredulous glance. "That's the most ridiculous thing I've ever heard you say. Would you expect Mom to help you?"

"If she wanted to. If not, I'd get a nanny."

"Good grief, Dad! You're fifty-two years old, and you've already raised one family. You're ready for grandchildren. What you're saying is insane."

Cullen shrugged. "I know it may sound crazy to you, but the thought of a son of Morgan's existing somewhere, and me not having any part in its life is unthinkable. It's all that's left of Morgan."

"You don't even know if it *is* Morgan's baby, and even if it is, the chances of them letting you have it are zero after what happened today. If you feel that strongly about it, give the girl some money so she can take good care of it. That's what Morgan would've wanted."

Cullen couldn't seem to let it go. "Isn't it possible they could've been in love with each other?" he asked.

"Gosh, I don't know. Morgan never talked to me about things like that, but if I know him, he probably *didn't* love her." He paused a moment, then added with more bitterness than he intended, "I don't think he ever loved anybody but himself—and maybe you."

Cullen did his best to turn his head toward Max again, and there was more hurt than anger in his voice. "That's a rotten thing to say about your brother. He was very loving."

Max started to retort, but thought better of it and merely shrugged. "If you say so."

"He was! Of all you kids, he showed me more love than all of you put together."

Max tried to bite back the words that rushed to his lips, but he couldn't. "Maybe that's because you gave all your love to him and none to the rest of us. I know I personally never felt you loved me."

A caustic laugh erupted from Cullen's throat. "Well, I guess this is my day to be dumped on."

"You're probably not even aware of how much you've neglected all the rest of us. Lily feels it, and I know Mom does, and I sure do. Are you saying we're all wrong?"

"It's hard for me to tell people how I feel. You all know that."

Max felt his throat begin to tighten again. "Well, it wouldn't have hurt you to tell me—*just once in my life*—that you loved me. I can't ever remember you saying those words to me."

"I just assumed you knew."

"Well, I didn't! And you can't even say it now, can you?"

Cullen sat quietly for a moment, then reached over and put his hand on Max's arm. "I'm not very good with this kind of stuff, but I do love you, son."

Cullen's hand lay like a searing brand on his arm, and Max clamped his hand over it. "It's taken you twenty-two years to say it, but I'll settle for that. Thanks."

Cullen's swollen lips took on the shape of a smile. "I'll try not to make it twenty-two years till the next time."

Max let out a whoop and pounded the steering wheel with the heel of his hand. "You don't know how good that makes me feel! I know this should be a sad day with all that's happened, but I feel great. Really great!"

"I'm feeling a little better myself," Cullen said.

CHAPTER 26

The service at the cemetery was short. Only a few people attended—the crowd made even smaller with Max and Andrew gone to the emergency room. Most of the onlookers were still on edge about the fight that had taken place, so they kept their distance, but that was okay with Gus. He wanted this over with so he could get Laura away from these people and their prying eyes.

He reached down and covered her hand with his. "It's almost over. Hang on just a little longer."

She looked up at him with a sad smile.

The minister concluded the graveside service with a prayer, and Laura stood and tossed a white rose onto the casket as it was being lowered. Gus and Lily stood beside her as people began to leave. A few stopped and offered their condolences, and she sadly acknowledged them, then Lily gathered up several bouquets of flowers, and the three of them climbed into the back seat of the limousine.

"I hope Andrew's okay," Gus said, as they were being driven back to the funeral home. "He got a pretty good roughing up."

"He got what he deserved," Lily said.

Laura gave her a reproving look. "No one deserves that kind of unprovoked attack."

"Unprovoked? You heard what the guy said about Morgan raping his daughter, and don't tell me you don't believe it, Mom. We both know what Morgan was capable of."

"Whatever he might have done, your father wasn't responsible for it. Morgan made his own mistakes, and he's obviously paid for them."

"How do you think he got to be like he was? He has Dad to thank for that."

Gus leaned toward her. "Can't all this wait till later? There'll be plenty of time to analyze everyone's fault once the attorneys get involved."

"I'm only telling the truth, and Mom knows it. Dad's been a lousy father, but none of us has ever had the nerve to say it to him—or to one another."

"He wasn't always that way," Laura said. "There was a time when he really tried to be a good father. Just last night we were looking at some pictures of you kids when you were little, and there was a picture of you on skis when you were just learning, and, if you'll remember, it was your father who taught you how to ski. And there was a picture of you kids trick or treating on Halloween, and your father was with us. And another picture of you learning how to ride the pony he bought you on your sixth birthday. Lots of busy fathers never do any of those things with their kids."

"A couple of old photographs can't make up for a lifetime of emotional abuse. You, of all people, should know that, Mother."

"I'm not trying to justify everything he's done, but I am saying that he did try, in the best way he knew how, to do the right thing by you kids when you were little. I know he hasn't been a good father to you or Max in recent years, and I'm sorry for that, but he's really hurting right now, and I think you ought to be a little kinder in your judgment of him. It may be that Morgan's death has finally opened his eyes to what kind of father he's been, and it could change him."

Gus could feel a little knot of dread begin to tighten his stomach. Had Andrew managed to con Laura again?

Lily leaned back against the seat with a defiant air. "Well, you can stick around and find out if you want to, Mom, but I'm taking off as soon as I can."

"Taking off for where?"

"I don't know, but I'm going to start looking for a job in Seattle or New York, or any place far away from here, and as soon as I find one, I'm gone. I hate to leave *you*, but as long as Max is willing to stick around, maybe you'll be okay. In any case, I can't take it any longer. I've got to get out of that house while I still have some sanity left."

"Oh, Lily! Your father and I want you to go to college this fall. Why don't you do that? That'll get you away from the ranch."

"But I'd have to go where *he* wants me to go, and use *his* money to do it, and I don't want to be beholden to him for one more thing. Don't you understand, Mom? That's how he's tied all of us to him all these years. He's used his money like a club to make us do what he's wanted, and I won't let him do that to me anymore, and you shouldn't either. You should get out while you can."

Gus frowned as he leaned toward her. "I think that's a decision your mother needs to make for herself. You have your whole life ahead of you, but she has a lot more to consider. It's not easy to make such a big decision when you're older. You'll see that when you get to be our age."

"Well, I plan to make the right choices now so I won't have to regret them when I get older."

"Ahh, the wisdom of youth," Gus said. "Well, I hope you do make all the right choices, but sometimes those choices aren't in your own hands. Your mother and I know that from experience."

Laura put her hand affectionately on his. "We certainly do."

Lily looked down at their clasped hands, then leaned over and eyed Gus suspiciously. "What's with you two, anyway? You hinted to me a couple of days ago that you and Mom have some kind of history together. Is there something I should know about?"

He let out a little chuckle as he shook his head. "No, there's nothing you should know about."

She gave her mother a questioning look. "Mother, are you and Mr. Styvessan having an affair?"

"Oh, for heaven's sake, Lily! You heard Gus. We've known each other for almost thirty years, and he's been a wonderful comfort to me this past week. That's all there is to it. Nothing more."

Lily leaned back on the seat and gave a little shrug. "Well, I'm sorry to hear that. I think you two would make a great couple, so if you do decide to get together, you have my blessing."

Gus let out a little laugh. "Well, that's nice to know. I'll keep that in mind."

After the limousine dropped them back at the chapel, Gus drove Laura and Lily back to The Oaks in his car. The house was dark as he pulled up to the front steps. Lily gathered up an armload of flowers and got out of the backseat. "I'll go in and see if the coast is clear," she said, with a wink at Gus. "You two kids probably wanna be alone anyway. Good night, Mr. Styvessan."

Gus grinned at her. "Why don't you call me Gus?" he said. "That 'Mister' business makes me feel old."

She grinned back at him. "Okay, *Gus*. Good night."

"I'll be in in a minute," Laura said. "If your Dad's home, tell him I'll be right in."

Lily went up the steps, and Gus put his arm on the seat behind Laura. "She's very perceptive, that little girl of yours."

"And very foolish. I don't know what kind of a job she thinks an eighteen-year-old girl without a college education or any work experience can get that's going to allow her to live like she's been used to."

"Do you have any money you can help her with until she gets on her feet?"

"Yes. Fortunately Dad left me a large trust fund that I've rarely used. Andrew's tried to get his hands on it for years, but the trustees won't let him touch it."

"Good for them," he said. "You're gonna need it if you decide to leave Andrew." He hesitated a moment before adding, "I thought I detected some change of heart about that in the car earlier. Are you having second thoughts?"

She looked down, avoiding his eyes. "Maybe a little. Andrew

and I had a good talk last night, and I got the impression he was reaching out to me."

"So you didn't say anything to him about leaving him?"

She looked up at him. "I was all set to until he broke down in tears over Morgan. It's the first time I've ever seen him cry, and I don't know what it would do to him if I told him I was leaving him now. Maybe I'll give it a little more time and see if he's really had a change of heart. I've invested an awful lot of years in this marriage, Gus, and it's not something I want to throw away lightly if there's any chance it can be saved. I hope you understand that."

Gus swallowed hard. "Of course I do. You won't get any pressure from me. Just make sure any change in him is real and not just some ploy for him to keep the ranch."

"He can have the ranch. I don't want it." She shook her head. "No, if I stay, it'll be because I think he needs me."

"But what about *your* needs? Can he meet those?"

She shook her head. "I don't know what I need anymore."

He took her hands in his. "You need to be loved and cherished. You've given Andrew twenty-six years to do that, and if he can't love a woman like you in that amount of time, he simply isn't capable of it. You have so much to give to the right man, and I think I'm that man. I really do."

"Maybe you are, Gus, but I have to be sure. You don't know how scary it is to think about starting all over again at my age. I can't make another mistake, and I sure don't want to break your heart again."

Gus squeezed her shoulder. "We won't jump into anything. We'll take our time and get to know each other again. I'd like to court you like I used to. I've still got that old picnic basket of my mom's, and it's just hankering to be used again."

"Oh, Gus, that brings back such wonderful memories, but we're not kids anymore. A lot of water has passed under both our bridges since then, and we're not the same people we were back then. You might not even love me if you got to know me today."

"Are you kidding? I've never stopped loving you."

She gave him a knowing look. "You love Laura Barron, not Laura Cullen. You don't even *know* Laura Cullen. I don't think anyone really does, not even me."

"Well, then, I think it's time we did something about that, don't you? What I don't know about you, I'd like to spend the rest of my life finding out, and I'd like to show you what an incredible woman you are through my eyes. Is there anything wrong with wanting that?"

Her smile was close to tears as she gently reached up and touched his cheek. "I don't know what to say to you. I know I wouldn't have made it through these past few weeks without you, but I'm so confused right now about so many things, that I can't make any kind of commitment to you at this point. Please try to understand. I'm not trying to keep you waiting in the wings while I try to revive my marriage. Maybe it can't be done, but if there's even the tiniest glimmer of hope that it can, I've got to give it that chance, and I just have to ask you to be patient if you can."

Gus lapsed into a thoughtful silence. "It's awful hard to be patient when I know you're whipping a dead horse, but don't worry about breaking my heart if you decide to stay with Andrew. If you don't want me, my life will go on just like it has before, and

I'll still wave at you when you drive through town, and we'll still be friends." He took her hands in his. "You're not gonna get any pressure from me, I promise you that, but I'm also warning you not to let Andrew con you again. He's a master at that—as you well know. Just keep your eyes open, and call me any time you need me. Okay? Now, you'd better scoot in, young lady, before I do something foolish. I may not be twenty-one anymore, but there's still a lot of fire in this old body, and it's all focused on you right now."

He got out and came around and opened the door for her, then took her hand and walked her up the steps to the front door. He was reluctant to let her go, not knowing when—or if—he was ever going to have another chance like this, but he had told her he wouldn't pressure her, and he intended to keep that promise. He lingered there at the door, his hand still holding hers, then impulsively bent down and kissed her gently on the lips.

Sam Littlefox smiled from the shadow of the garage. He and the household women had gotten home from the funeral about a half hour earlier, and the women had already gone into the house before Gus had driven up with Laura and Lily. Sam had been waiting in the shadows, hoping to see Cullen's condition when he and Max finally got home from the hospital, but they hadn't arrived yet. Instead, he saw Gus lean down and kiss Laura on the mouth, and a slow smile spread across his weathered face. If *he* couldn't have her, Gus was his next best choice.

CHAPTER 27

Sam climbed the stairs to his room above the garage and went to the cabinet where he kept the whiskey that Morgan used to get for him. Pouring himself a glass, he lifted it in a toast. "Here's to you, Morgan, wherever you are. You had a lovely funeral today; just the kind of brawl you would've loved. An old girlfriend of yours spit on your corpse, and your father got the crap beat out of him by her father. Then, to top off the evening, your mother ended up in the arms of her old lover. It's a fitting end to a wonderful day. Too bad you weren't able to enjoy it with us."

He drank deeply, then wiped his mouth with the back of his hand as he sat down in his comfortable old rocker and closed his eyes. He couldn't get the image of Andrew Cullen's bloody face out of his mind. Oh, how he'd wanted to do the same thing to that face ever since that day so long ago when he saw Cullen remove the burr from under the saddle of the horse that killed Cyrus Barron, the only father Sam had ever known.

Laura was only six years old when Sam had come to live with the Barrons at The Oaks. Happy and inquisitive, she never looked at him and saw the color of his skin. She saw only a shy, thirteen-year-old boy filled with fears about his future.

Despite the fact that he was an Indian, she treated him like an older brother. He remembered the time that her doll's arm had come off, and she brought it to him with tears streaming down her face. No one had ever looked at him with such trust, and he'd labored for a whole day putting that doll back together. Then there was the time that her puppy was run over by one of the first cars her father had, and she had brought the limp little thing to him to make it better, but he hadn't been able to save it, and she had thrown herself into his arms and sobbed her heart out against his chest.

And Mrs. Barron. What a saint that woman had been, opening her home and heart to him, and giving him the only mother's love he'd ever known. As she lay dying from cancer a few years later, he'd waited on her night and day, going to the point of such exhaustion that Mr. Barron had to force him to bed. It had been such a tragic day when death took her, leaving twelve-year-old Laura, Mr. Barron, and him to struggle on as best they could. He had been nineteen then, and Mr. Barron was so immobilized with grief that Sam had taken over running the whole house, and had basically been doing it ever since.

As Laura grew from a young girl into a beautiful young woman, he'd often had fantasies about how one day she'd come to him and tell him she loved him, but he knew in his heart that he could never be anything to her but a friend. That was the unspoken rule on the Reservation: Whites with Whites and Indians with Indians.

During the years when Laura was away at boarding school, she often wrote to him, and he still had those letters hidden away in his room. He was embarrassed now to think about his own skimpy little letters to her, written in his childish handwriting with so many misspelled words, but she never gave the slightest hint that they were anything but treasures from her best friend. From time to time he still took out her letters and read them with tears running down his cheeks.

In the summers, when she was home from school, they would sit and talk for hours, and she would tell him all about her adventures, wanting him to experience them through her. She told him about the boys she'd developed crushes on, and asked his advice about boys in general. It always embarrassed him; he knew so little of the ways of boys with girls. All he knew was that his heart was crushed each time she spoke of some other boy.

Then Andrew Cullen came to The Oaks, and everything changed. Sam saw him for what he was the minute he stepped onto the ranch. He was a sleazy drifter who'd conned his way into Cyrus Barron's employment with a few fancy tricks on some of Barron's horses, then deliberately set out to seduce Laura. Sam had tried to warn her about him, but she was eighteen and inexperienced with men, and was swept off her feet by the handsome, fast-talking cowboy. Their secret affair only lasted about a month before Laura saw him for what he was, but by then he'd gotten her pregnant. Sam would have killed him right then, except for Mr. Barron's insistence that Laura marry the man so as not to bring shame on her mother's memory.

And now, for the past twenty-six years, he had watched Andrew Cullen systematically destroy his family, especially Lily. She was the only one of Laura's children that Sam had really gotten close to. When she was growing up, he had taught her how to fish in the canal, how to ride her pony, and how to plant and tend the flowers in her mother's garden, and she became his shadow. No matter where he was on the ranch, Lily was there, asking him questions and wanting him to show her how to do things.

As she grew into young womanhood, he felt very fatherly toward her. That's why he had seethed inside for years at what Morgan had done to her when she was about fourteen. He'd first suspected something when he'd seen the two of them splashing in the pool, then saw her run to her room in tears, and guessed that Morgan must've tried something with her. He'd struggled with whether to go to Laura with his suspicions, but decided not to burden her. He would keep his eyes open and deal with Morgan if it happened again. It hadn't—that he knew of—until the summer when she was sixteen, and he saw Morgan come out of her room, and heard her sobbing inside. He went to Laura about it the next day, and she confirmed that Morgan had raped Lily, but begged him not to get involved in it. Andrew had said he'd take care of it. But Sam had remained alert, and did his best not to let Lily out of his sight when she was home from school on vacations.

And now Morgan was dead, and Andrew Cullen was suffering the way he deserved. Sam knew his precious Laura was also grieving over her son's death, but after what he'd just seen between her and Gus on the front steps, he knew she'd eventually heal from her grief. But Andrew Cullen would never get over the loss of his son. He would grieve for the rest of his life, and that was as it should be. Maybe then he'd appreciate the pain he'd given to a young Indian boy when he took away the only father he'd ever known with a burr planted under his saddle.

He got up from the chair and walked back over to the cupboard. He took down the whiskey bottle again and poured another glass. He held it up to the light and looked at the amber fluid. Yes, everything was working out fine, except for Derek getting caught in all of it. That had never figured into his plans. He'd known Jason Abrams for years, and there'd been no finer man—Indian or White—on the Reservation, and Derek had turned out the same way. Sam held up his glass in tribute to both of them, and made a silent vow that he would do anything he had to, to see that Derek didn't have to pay for what *he'd* done.

CHAPTER 28

It had been a week since Morgan's funeral, and Gus was shocked to hear from Sheriff Lucas that Derek's trial had been set for August thirtieth, less than a month away.

"Good grief!" he told Lucas when he phoned to tell him. "That means Derek's attorney will only have a few weeks to get his defense ready. What's the big rush?"

"Judge Harmon wants to get this over with before he goes on his annual fishin' trip to Alaska the first week of September."

"That's a terrible way to play with a man's life," Gus said. "Can't Speer get a postponement?"

"He's already tried, but Harmon's playin' hardball. There's no question but that he's out to get Abrams."

"And another fat contribution from Cullen," Gus said. "Who's prosecuting?"

"The Assistant DA, Barry Sanders."

"Oh, boy! He plays hardball too. Kinda makes you wonder, doesn't it? If Derek wasn't an Indian, these guys could never get away with a rush job like this."

"Well, they call the shots, and us peons just do what we're told," Lucas replied.

"That doesn't mean we have to like it."

A car pulled into Gus's station just then, and Gus gave the driver a little wave, then turned back to the phone. "I've got someone who needs gas, so let's wind this up. I've already spent more time than I should've on this whole business. That's what you guys get paid the big bucks for."

"Oh yeah, big bucks," Lucas snorted. "Go take care of your customer. I'll talk to you later."

The phone call depressed Gus. He still hadn't made up his mind about Derek's guilt, but he sure didn't wanna see him get shafted by Judge Harmon. Gus went out and put some gas in Jim Benton's car, then decided to ask Jerry if he'd watch things until he got back. It was time to have one final talk with Lily.

When Lily got Gus's call that he wanted to talk to her, she told him she'd given him all the information she had, but he insisted on seeing her, so she agreed to one final meeting.

Sam let him in at The Oaks and gave him an unexpected smile as he drove past him toward the house. Laura came out onto the front portico as he drove up. There was a worried look on her face.

"Hi," he called up to her as he got out of the car.

"Hi," she called back. "Lily told me you wanted to talk to her again. Has something new come up?"

He walked up the steps toward her. "There's nothing for you to look so worried about. I just had a few more questions I wanted to ask her." He took her hand. "How are you anyway? I haven't seen you for a week, and I've missed you."

She turned toward the open door and lowered her voice. "Andrew's in the house."

"Good! I'll say hello to him before I leave."

Her voice dropped even further. "Something's happened to him, Gus."

Gus looked toward the open door. "What?"

"He's obsessed with finding out if that pregnant girl is carrying Morgan's child."

He gave her a questioning look. "What difference could that make now?"

"He wants to force her to have a blood test to see if Morgan's the father, and if it's a boy, he's going to take them to court to get it."

"Good grief! What would he do with a baby?"

"He wants the two of us to raise it here at The Oaks."

"Oh, dear God! I hope you told him you want no part of that."

"Of course I did, but he says he'll hire a nanny and raise it himself."

"Well, you don't have anything to worry about. He'll never get that baby, even if it is Morgan's. I talked to the girl's father, and they despise all you Cullens."

"I tried to tell him that, but you know how he is when he gets his mind made up about something. And he's actually been very nice to the kids and me this past week. Lily isn't buying it, but Max is like a new person."

"And what about you?" Gus asked. "How are you responding to all this?"

She glanced toward the open door again. "I'm wary. I don't want to get my hopes up."

Gus could feel his throat begin to tighten. "Well, I think you're right not to get too excited just yet. A week isn't very long for a man to change a lifetime of habits, but I am glad to hear he's treating all of you better."

Lily appeared at the door just then, and Gus quickly dropped Laura's hand. "Hi, Lily," he said. "I was just coming in to see you."

"Did you congratulate Mom?"

"For what?"

"She's going to be a new mother."

"That's enough!" Laura snapped. "Your sarcasm is wearing very thin with me."

Lily backed up. "Can't you take a joke?"

"This is nothing to joke about," Laura said. "All you're doing is throwing kerosene on something that's very close to exploding."

"Well, excuse me! I thought it was finally okay to say whatever I wanted in my own home." She turned to Gus. "Let's go in and get this over with, so I can crawl back into my hole."

Gus put his hand on her arm and stopped her. "Wait just a minute," he said. "You're being very unfair to your mother, and you know it. She's just trying to keep things from blowing up around here."

Lily paused a moment, then turned and gave her mother a little hug. "He's right, Mom. I'm sorry. It's just that this business about that baby is the final straw for me. I can't believe Dad would do something so stupid."

"They'll never let him have that child," Laura said, "and besides, he doesn't even know if Morgan's the father. He's just so torn up about his death that he's grasping at straws. I'll be able to talk some sense into him after he's calmed down a little."

"He's never listened to you before. What makes you think he will now?" Lily said.

"We've had some good talks this past week, and believe it or not, he even asked me about your plans for this fall."

Lily gave her a wary look. "Did you tell him I'm not going to college? That I'm going to move out and get a job?"

"Yes, and he thought that was a good idea. He even said he'd speak to some of his friends and see if any of them need help. Now doesn't that sound like he's had a change of heart?"

"It sounds to me like he's telling you what he thinks you want to hear."

"No he's not. He was genuinely glad you want to go out and test your wings. He said he'd never been to college, and it hadn't hurt him."

"Well, I sure don't want to make my fortune the way he made his," she retorted.

Laura started to respond, but Gus took Lily by the arm and steered her toward the door. "Let's go into the sunroom where we can talk," he said. He turned to Laura. "Will you excuse us for a few minutes? I have a couple of things I need to talk to Lily about, but I'll see you before I leave. Okay?"

"I'll be up in my room. Lily can let me know when you're through."

Gus and Lily went into the sunroom and sat down. "That

was quite a performance you just put on," he said. "Do you enjoy hurting your mother?"

"I wasn't trying to hurt her."

"You sure could've fooled me. Your mother's very fragile right now, and you're not helping with the way you're treating her. Can't you just lay off for awhile?"

"I really don't think this is any of your business, Mr. Styvessan."

"It *is* my business, dammit! I've watched her misery for years, and now that she's on the verge of doing something about it, she doesn't need this crap from you."

Lily leaned toward him with renewed interest. "What's she thinking about doing?"

"She'll have to tell you that herself, but when you put your father down like that, it just makes her defensive of him. It's having the opposite effect of what you want."

"Is she planning on leaving him?"

"If she is, it's got to be her decision without coercion from anybody else; not you, and not me."

"Have you been trying to talk her into leaving Dad?"

"Absolutely not! I haven't seen her since the funeral, but if she does decide to leave him, it's gotta be because she feels it's the best course for her and you kids, but it'll be a lot easier for her if you've got your life together."

"Well, she doesn't have to worry about that. I'm gonna stick around here until after Derek's trial, then I'm leaving, but I sure won't take a job with any of Dad's cronies. That's just another way for him to keep his strings on me."

"Well, the trial's set for August thirtieth, so you'd better start looking for a job now if you're planning on leaving then."

Lily gave him a stunned look. "Why so soon?"

"Judge Harmon wants to get it over with before his vacation starts."

"Judge Harmon is handling this?"

"Yes."

"Then Derek doesn't stand a chance. Harmon does anything my father tells him to."

"I know that, and that's what I need to talk to you about." He looked her squarely in the eye. "We both know Derek didn't kill Morgan, but there's a very good chance he's gonna be convicted of it anyway, and that'll be the end of that wonderful young man. Is that what you want to see?"

Lily forced herself to maintain eye contact with him. "Of course not, but I've already told you all I can, so please don't ask me again."

"I'm not asking you, Lily. I'm *begging* you. Tell me what you saw that day."

She stood up, and Gus could tell she was deeply troubled. "This conversation is over. I'm going up to my room now, so I'll tell Mother you're leaving."

Gus shook his head wearily. "Don't bother. I'll talk to her another time. But, Lily . . ."

She held up her hand to stop him. "I've told you all I'm going to, and that's final."

"Okay," he said, "but if Derek spends the rest of his life in prison, I hope your conscience will let you sleep at night."

From the look on her face, Gus could see that his words had struck home, but she turned without a further word and left the room. Gus let himself out, and as Sam opened the gate for him, he was no longer smiling.

CHAPTER 29

Lily tossed and turned all night, thinking about her talk with Gus. He was right about her conscience bothering her. It was eating her alive, but she simply could not tell anyone what she'd seen—and she couldn't let Derek take the blame, either. The plan she'd finally come up with was definitely risky for Derek, but given his alternatives, she at least owed him this chance. It was still dark out, but she got up and quickly dressed, then took the two thousand dollars her mother had given her to live on until she could find a job, and stuffed it in her purse. With that money, Derek could go someplace where they'd never find him.

As she drove up the Fort Road to Derek's house, her apprehension grew. Would he take the money, or would he think it was some trick to get him into more trouble? She'd have to convince him she was sincere. Anything would be better than facing a judge as corrupt as Judge Harmon.

She turned off the Fort Road into his driveway and pulled up beside his pickup. She knew he might not be up yet, but she went to the door and knocked numerous times. She was about to leave when Lucy Abrams opened the front door, and even through the screen, Lily could see that she'd been crying.

"I'm sorry for coming so early, Mrs. Abrams, but I *have* to talk to Derek. It's *very* important."

Lucy dabbed at her eyes with a hankie. "He's not here."

Lily looked over at his truck. "His pickup is."

"I know, but he's not."

Lily was suddenly alert. "Where is he?"

Lucy hesitated a moment, then opened the screen door. "I guess you'd better come in," she said. "I'm sorry about the house-coat, but I've been up most of the night."

A little apprehensive, Lily stepped into the living room.

"Sit down, please," Lucy said, motioning to the sofa.

Lily sat down on the edge of it. "What's going on? Where's Derek?"

"Why did you want to see him?" Lucy asked.

"I need to tell him something very important."

"May I ask what it is?"

"It's about his trial. Judge Harmon is going to be sitting on the bench, and he's one of my dad's personal friends and does anything Dad tells him to. Derek doesn't stand a chance."

"He knows that, and I think that's why he's gone."

Lily's eyes widened. "Gone where?"

Lucy looked down at the handkerchief she was twisting between her fingers. "I don't know if I should tell you or not, but I suppose everyone's going to know pretty soon."

"Know what, Mrs. Abrams? What's happened?"

Lucy's eyes began to tear again. "He took his horse and went up into the hills yesterday morning after I left for work, and he took his bedroll and his rifle and bow and arrows with him."

"Did he say when he'd be back?"

She shook her head. "He left a note saying he was going up to talk to his father about whether to come back at all."

"I thought his father was dead," Lily said.

"He is, but his grave is up on that old Indian burial ground on Spirit Mountain."

Lily's hand flew to her mouth. "I can't believe this! That's what I came here for. I wanted to give him some money so he could get away. I guess he had the same idea."

"He won't need any money if he decides to stay up there. He knows how to live off the land."

"Does anyone else know he's gone?"

"The phone rang all last evening, but I didn't answer it. I'm sure it was either his attorney or the Sheriff checking to make sure he hasn't left the Reservation, but it'll only be a matter of time before they figure out he's not here and go looking for him. His trial starts in three weeks, and he has to be back for that, but that's what has me frightened. He might decide not to come back at all." Her mouth began to quiver. "Someone's got to go up there and convince him to come back. I'd go myself, but I don't ride any more."

Lily leaned toward her. "Do you really want him to come back, Mrs. Abrams? You know what he's in for if he does. Isn't it better to just let him do this thing his way?"

"Absolutely not! It only makes him look guilty. If he comes back in the next day or two, there's still a chance his attorney can prove his innocence, but if he doesn't come back at all, people will always believe he did it." Lucy's tears wouldn't seem to stop. "He's got to come back. I can't bear the thought of never seeing him again. He's all I've got left."

Lily looked at the distraught woman for a long moment, then suddenly stood up. "I think I know someone who can find him and talk him into coming back. I just hope that's the right thing for him to do."

"It is. He'll be running the rest of his life if he doesn't."

Lily started for the door, then stopped and turned back to Lucy. "Don't tell *anyone* he's gone. Please! Just stay home for the next few days and pretend you're too sick to go to work or to answer the phone. I don't want the Sheriff to know he's gone and send a posse after him."

"I'll have to tell Mrs. Lamont if she comes to see why I haven't come to work, but I can trust her. She loves Derek like he was her own son."

"Okay, you can tell her, but beg her not to tell anyone else. Especially not her husband. It's very important that no one finds out he's gone. If my friend can get him back here in a day or two, they can't hold it against him."

Lily jumped into her car and sped back down the Fort Road to The Oaks. Her mind was racing. That cane was the only thing that could tie Derek to the murder, and she, alone, knew that her father must've put it in Derek's truck. Telling the sheriff about the cane would sever any remaining ties she had to her father, and probably land her and Sam in jail, but she simply couldn't let a trigger-happy posse go after Derek. She and Sam would have to find him and tell him what they did, and convince him to come back and go to the sheriff with them. But finding him, and convincing him to come back, wasn't going to be easy. She had to talk to Sam immediately.

Sam was in the kitchen pouring himself a cup of coffee when Lily pulled into her slot in the garage. He looked up as she raced into the kitchen. "Hi, Miss Lily," he said. "I heard you go out around seven and wondered where you were going that early."

"I need to talk to you right now, Sam. Let's go up to your room."

He gave her a puzzled look, then said, "Follow me." They went into the open garage and up the stairs to his room.

Sam pulled out a chair for her, and they both sat down at his small table. "What's this all about?" he asked.

"Morgan's cane."

He stiffened slightly. "What about it?"

"I found it on top of the pool house."

A slight wince tightened his jaw. "Did you see how it got there?"

She nodded.

"Are you gonna tell the police?"

"You know I'd never do that."

He seemed to relax ever so slightly. "How did it get in Derek's truck then? Did you put it there?"

"No! I put it in the trunk of my Dad's car."

His looked at her in shock. "Why would you do that?"

"I know this sounds stupid now, but I wanted the sheriff to find it there and let Dad see what it's like to be accused of something you didn't do."

"Then how did it get into Derek's truck?"

"Dad obviously put it there. He must've thought Derek had put it in his trunk to throw the blame on him."

Sam was quiet for a long moment, then reluctantly asked, "What is it you want me to do?"

She searched his weathered face, and suddenly realized that her childhood friend was an old man. "I want you to help me find Derek and talk him into coming back. His mother told me he's taken off for the hills on his horse and might not come back for his trial."

"When is it?"

"August thirtieth."

"He must know they'll come after him if he isn't here for that."

"I think he'll come back now if we can find him and tell him what we did. That cane is the only thing that connects him to Morgan's death, and I'll tell the sheriff that I found it in the wisteria vines and put it in Dad's car."

"And they're gonna ask you why you didn't just turn it over to them."

"I'll tell them it was in the middle of the night when I found it, and I was too scared to keep it in my room, and scared to wake Dad up, so I took it down to his car and was going to tell him in the morning."

Sam frowned at her. "No one's gonna believe that. Admitting you had it at all will only make you a suspect, and I can't let that happen."

"I'll have to take that chance. We can't let Derek be blamed for this."

Sam suddenly seemed very weary. "How long has he been gone?"

"Since yesterday morning."

He shook his head. "Forget it then. He's had a full day and night head start. We'll never find him. There's a hundred places he could hide up there, and he knows them all."

"His mother thinks he's gone up to Spirit Mountain where his father's buried."

Sam let out a bitter laugh. "They tell me that's where my father's buried too."

She leaned over and grasped his hand. "All the more reason for us to go up there. You can look for your father's grave." She paused, then said, "If you don't take me, I'll have to go by myself."

"You wouldn't know how to get up there. And besides, if by some miracle you did find Derek, he wouldn't be talked into coming back by any Cullen."

Lily pushed back from the table and stood up. "Then you'll just have to take me."

He pulled himself out of the chair with the resignation of one who knows he's been beaten. "The roads up there are nothing but dirt trails. That's rough country."

"We'll take Dad's Jeep."

"And how will you explain that to him?"

"Is he home?" she asked.

He nodded. "Yes, but he's leaving for Spokane around four this afternoon."

"That's our answer then. As soon as he leaves, we'll take the Jeep and go."

"He'll come after us when he gets back," Sam said.

"When's he getting back?"

"He said he'd be gone until Friday afternoon, but his plans might change if he finds out what's going on around here."

"We'll just have to make sure he doesn't find out," Lily said. "Today's Wednesday, so if we leave right after he does, we can get up to the mountain and back by Friday morning, and he won't even know we left. No one knows Derek's gone yet, but I'm sure they will in a day or two. Mrs. Abrams can't keep it a secret much longer."

"And how will you explain all this to your mother and Max?"

"I'll leave them a note and tell them that Derek ran off up into the hills, and you think you can find him and talk him into coming back before a posse goes after him and shoots him." She started for the door. "I'll go write the note right now. Will you gas up the Jeep?"

"It's already full." His words were followed by a reluctant pause. "Are you sure this is really what you wanna do? Maybe we should just go to Deputy Styvessan and tell him what really happened."

She shook her head. "It's all too complicated to try to explain at this point. Let's find Derek first, then we'll all go to the sheriff together. When he hears what Morgan's been doing to me for years, neither one of us should get arrested for what we did."

"I hope you're right." he said.

CHAPTER 30

Cullen did not leave for Spokane until six o'clock that day, so Sam and Lily got a late start for the mountains. A couple of miles up into the foothills, they came to Fort Simcoe off to the left. Sam pointed at it. "That's the old Indian fort over there. Have you ever seen it?"

"No. What is it?"

"It was built by the government about a hundred years ago to make sure the Indians wouldn't start any wars."

"Did it work?"

He frowned over at her. "Of course it worked. The Yakimas didn't want war. They just wanted to be left alone. Anyway, the Army was only here a couple of years and then pulled out and left the place to the Indians. These buildings are what's left after a hundred years of prairie fires and neglect."

"Does anybody stay out here?"

"Just my old friends, Elmer and Sophie Trueblood from the Indian Agency. People come up here now and then to look the fort over and he shows them around and tries to keep things from being vandalized any further."

"Do you think they might've seen Derek?"

"He would've made sure they didn't."

Sam looked over at the fort and saw Sophie scattering feed to some chickens, and she looked up and waved at them, and Sam waved back.

"Don't you want to stop and say hello?" Lily asked.

He shook his head. "They'd wanna know what we're doing up here, and the fewer people who know that, the better. I was just up here a week or so ago, so they won't think it's strange if I don't stop today. We can stop on our way back down tomorrow if we don't find Derek."

The sun was just setting over the Cascade ridge and a gray twilight had descended, draining all color from the sage-covered hills. They'd liked to have gotten an earlier start, but had to wait until Cullen left for Spokane. Lily propped her feet up on the dash now, and looked over at Sam. "Do you think we can get to Spirit Mountain before dark?" she asked.

"I hope so, Miss Lily. I don't like driving up here after dark. These dirt roads are in terrible shape."

Lily frowned over at him. "Don't you think you can stop calling me *Miss* Lily? We've gotten way beyond that stage."

"Your father would fire me on the spot if he heard me call you by your first name."

"You've been part of our family longer than he has, so you can call me whatever you want."

"I've always thought of myself as part of your family, but it's hard to remember sometimes that I'm really not. Your mother's always made me feel like I was, and so did your grandparents, but your dad and Morgan are a different breed. To them I'm just a faceless servant whose only reason for being there is to do whatever they want."

"Well you're not that to me. You've always been my best friend."

He looked a little embarrassed. "It's nice of you to say that. I haven't got many friends."

She reached over and patted his arm. "Don't worry about it. Neither do I." She stared off into the growing twilight. "Do you really think Derek's up at Spirit Mountain?"

Sam nodded. "That's where I'd go if I was in his spot."

"What makes it such a special place?"

"It's an old summer encampment where different tribes used to gather for pow-wows and reunions, and there's an old Indian burial ground on the summit that the Indians think is holy."

"Do the Indians still bury people up there?"

"I don't think so. It's too hard to get to."

"Have you ever been up there?" she asked.

"Once, when I was looking for my father's grave, but they all looked the same to me."

"If we have to go up there, I'll help you find him," Lily said.

Sam shook his head. "I don't care if I do or not. He wasn't a real father to me. He just got my mother pregnant and then took off. Honestly, I never even knew his name."

"Maybe you're lucky. He might've turned out to be someone like my father."

"I'm sure he was," Sam replied.

They were climbing steadily now, and the road was getting rougher as it wound through the scrub brush and up and down dry gullies cut by torrents of water that coursed down from the foothills in the spring rains. Up ahead, wild oaks, sumac, and alders dotted the horizon, and in the dimming light you could just make out rows of tall firs and pine that marked the beginning of Mount Adams' foothills.

They rode along in silence for awhile, then Lily said, "You've never told me much about yourself, Sam. Where did you grow up?"

"I spent the first thirteen years of my life in that orphanage in White Swan that your grandfather rescued me from."

"How did you end up there."

"All I was ever told was that my mother was a fifteen-year-old girl who didn't want me, so she gave me to the nuns at the orphanage and never came to see me once. All I knew was that nobody wanted me until your grandfather came along."

"How did he get you out of there?"

"He got some of us older boys to help bring down some wild horses from the hills up here, and he took a liking to me and made me part of their family." He paused a moment, and his voice took on a bitter tone. "Everything was fine until your father came along."

She cocked her head at him. "What'd he do?"

"Oh, he hustled his way into your grandfather's good graces with a few fancy tricks on a horse, then decided he wanted more, so he went after your mother. She was just an innocent young girl and couldn't see that he was a snake, but I saw through him right away, and your mother and grandfather eventually did, but by then it was too late."

She frowned. "Too late for what?"

"I've said enough."

Lily wasn't about to let it go. "I want to know what my father did that turned all of you against him."

"Your mother would never forgive me if I told you."

"I can keep a secret. You of all people should know that."

"Yes, I guess you can," he said.

"So what did my father do?"

Sam was quiet for a long moment, then said, "He got your mother pregnant."

Lily's mouth dropped open. "With Morgan?"

Sam nodded.

"Oh, my gosh! So *that's* why Morgan's always been Dad's favorite. He was Dad's ticket into our family."

He nodded again. "Your mother didn't wanna marry him, but your grandfather was so worried about tarnishing your grandmother's memory, that he made her marry him. She was in love with Gus Styvessan."

"Gus?"

He nodded again.

Lily leaned back in her seat, and let out a little laugh. "So that's what there is between those two. I could see something was going on, but I had no idea they'd once been in love."

"Your mother tried to make the best of things with your father, but all he was after was The Oaks, and he made sure he got that too."

"How?"

Sam was quiet for a long moment, but there was pure malice in his face as he turned to her. "He killed your grandfather."

"What?" she gasped. "That's not true! My grandfather's death was an accident. A horse bucked him off and broke his neck."

"It was no accident. Your father put a burr under the saddle so it would buck him off. I saw him take it out when he unsaddled the horse."

She gaped in disbelief. "You're not just saying that because you hate him, are you?"

"I saw it with my own eyes."

"Does he know you saw him?"

He shook his head. "I never told anyone. It would just be my word against his, and he would've fired me and there'd have been no one to look after your mother. I've never even told her what happened, but I've never forgotten that he robbed her of her father, and me of the only father I ever had."

Lily was almost too stunned to speak. "You should've told Mom. She needed to know what kind of sleaze she'd married."

Sam shook his head. "I couldn't do that to her. She had a new baby to worry about, and she'd already realized she'd made a terrible mistake, so I decided to keep my eyes open and my mouth shut—and that's what I've been doing for the past twenty-six years."

Sam suddenly slammed on the brakes as the Jeep skidded sideways in the loose dirt. "What's wrong?" Lily cried, bracing herself against the dashboard.

He motioned with his head toward a gully that had been washed out of the narrow road. "Take a look at that. It's too dark to go any farther tonight. If you're determined to go on, we'll have to stop and make camp."

Sam pulled off the road and parked under some oaks. Lily got out the food she'd brought along, while Sam took the flashlight and gathered some wood and stones for a campfire. When the fire was going, Lily handed him a sandwich and the jug of lemonade she'd made, and they sat on a log by the fire.

After they'd eaten, they sat staring at the embers until Lily broke the silence. "Do you want to talk about Morgan?"

Sam kept his eyes fixed on the fire. "I was wondering when you were gonna bring that up."

"If Derek hadn't gotten mixed up in all this, I'd never have said anything to you."

Sam poked at the fire with a stick, then gave a deep sigh. "I don't know how much you saw that day out there at the pool, but I'd gone out to bring him his usual beer, and he made some ugly cracks about you, and I finally told him I didn't like it. And he said nobody gave a damn what I liked, and before I could stop myself, I told him I knew he'd raped you a couple of years ago, and that *really* made him mad, and he got up and took a swing at me with his cane, but I grabbed it from him and bashed him over the head with it, and pushed him into the pool. I could've pulled him out, but I knew if I did, it would be the end for me at The Oaks, so I just let him flop around till he drowned."

Lily's hand had come to her breast. "How did you know he'd raped me?"

"Your mother told me."

"How could she? That was a secret between us."

"Don't be mad at her. She didn't have anybody else to turn to. She'd tried to get your father to deal with him, but he never did, so she asked me to keep an eye on you. And I have been ever since."

"Well then, you know he didn't stop trying. I have to keep my door locked all the time."

"I know. I saw him try the handle many times."

"I don't know why you've stuck around all these years, Sam. Why didn't you get out years ago?"

"Where would I have gone? The Oaks is the only home I've ever had, and besides, I can't leave your mother. She still needs me."

As Lily sat looking at him, it suddenly dawned on her. "You're in love with her, aren't you?"

He frowned over at her. "How could I be in love with her, for God's sake? I'm an Indian."

"Indians fall in love don't they?"

"Not with White women they don't."

"Well, I think people should be allowed to fall in love with anyone they want."

Sam gave a little snort. "I think your mother feels the same way. She's obviously in love with Gus Styvessan."

"And how do you feel about that?" she asked.

He stared silently at the fire for a long moment, then said, "I'd rather it was me she was in love with, but Gus will treat her the way she deserves to be treated, and that's all I want for her."

Lily let out a bitter laugh. "We're really a pair, you know that? For a couple of really nice people, we've sure screwed up our lives."

"We've had plenty of help doing it," he said dryly.

CHAPTER 31

The deer was about a foot high, while the stick-figure brave on its back, with his bow drawn taut, was poised for the kill. Derek leaned forward for a closer look. He knew from memory that the cave walls held more images, but it was too dark to see them tonight. In the morning, he'd scan the entire cave for a better look at these old drawings, but tonight he needed to calm himself and get some sleep.

Finding his way to these caves on Spirit Mountain had been easy. He and his father had often camped up here by the waterfall and explored the sandstone caves that lined the lower part of the mountain. And when he was ten years old, and his father had sent him up here on his Vision Quest, he'd stayed in this very cave, fasting and praying for one whole week before he'd gone to the graveyard on the summit and found the eagle feather that was to become his talisman for life.

He lay back on his blanket beside the fire and pulled his knapsack under his head, suddenly realizing how weary he was from all the pressures of the past few weeks. His heart was especially heavy as he thought about his mother. He hadn't even said goodbye to her, because he knew she'd try to stop him, but he'd *had* to come to this sacred place and try to sort out all of his options. He thought about his students, and wondered if they'd think he'd run because he was guilty. Or would they applaud his courage for not allowing himself to be humiliated for something they all knew he was incapable of doing?

He couldn't help thinking about Mrs. Lamont too. She'd been so kind to him and his mother since his father had been killed, and she probably thought he'd forgotten all the things she'd taught him about her God, but he hadn't. He still believed in Him, but he also believed in the Great Spirit. He hadn't decided yet it they were one and the same, but once he'd settled down in this sacred place, he'd go to the summit and take the time to really think it through.

He glanced over at the pile of huckleberries and breadroot he'd spent the afternoon gathering. After a good night's sleep he'd scout the area tomorrow for a prairie hen or rabbit. He knew it would only be a matter of days before someone came looking for him, but he had no real fear they'd find him. No Whites ever came to Spirit Mountain, and if by chance some Indian did, they'd never betray him.

He stoked the fire, then stripped off his vest, leggings, and breechcloth and pulled his coarse blanket over himself and slept. When he woke at dawn, the fire had burned down, and he lay shivering in the morning light. He threw back his blanket and crawled out of the cave. Zimba was still standing below in the meadow where Derek had tethered him, but he lifted his head and whinnied when he saw him. Derek slid down the worn steps and went over and stroked the horse's dark mane. Zimba nudged him with his head, and Derek reached down and undid his tether. "Eat up," he said. "We've got a big day in front of us."

Derek walked over to the waterfall and looked down at the deep pool beside it, remembering the many times as a dumb kid that he'd jumped down into that pool with no fear. Standing there now, he wondered how he could've been so stupid. Just then, Zimba came up behind him and gave him a playful nudge on his bare butt, and Derek jumped.

His long dark hair was plastered to his face as he surfaced a few seconds later, gasping for air. He brushed the hair out of his face and swam for a few minutes—carefully avoiding the pounding waterfall just feet away. Fully refreshed, he climbed back up the slippery steps chiseled into the granite by his ancestors centuries ago, and sat shivering on the ground, his face upturned in meditation toward his beloved Pahto.

Pahto . . . sacred Mount Adams . . . constantly shaping the lives of her sons and daughters, even as she was now shaping his. He was overcome with deep emotion to realize he was so close to the source of all that he and his people held sacred.

A half hour later, his mind and body refreshed, he climbed back up to the cave and put on his leather jerkin, breechcloth, and leggings and slipped into his moccasins. He moved to the back of the cave and got down on his knees near a small outcropping of rock. There it was! His eagle with the sun grasped in its talons just as he had drawn it so many years ago. He could still feel the emotion of that experience. He was ten years old and had just found the eagle's feather on a burial mound at the summit of Spirit Mountain, and could hardly wait to get home to tell his father. And when he *did* share this wondrous experience with him, his father had wept and told him he had known his son's guardian spirit would be a great one like the eagle.

He sat on his haunches for a long time staring at the drawings, then backed away and ate some berries and breadroot. He pulled his hair into a ponytail, tied it with a leather thong, and, as a final touch, stuck his eagle feather into the knot where it was tied. With his talisman in place, he went down to Zimba in the meadow and pulled himself up onto his back, ready to face whatever the day might bring.

From the moment he'd reached Spirit Mountain yesterday, it was all he could do to keep from making his pilgrimage to the sacred burial grounds on the summit, but he knew it would be dark too soon to spend the time there that he needed, so he'd decided to wait until today. Now, as eager as he was to climb the mountain, he needed to take care of his immediate needs so his mind would be completely free from any worldly concerns when he went up there to pray and seek guidance. To that end, he began searching for birds' nests in the clefts of rocks, and soon had his knapsack full of feathers and bird-down which he would use later to make a fire. He scoured the area for old dried logs, and found them in abundance. He made a travois out of fir branches and piled the logs on them, then he and Zimba dragged them back to his cave where he stacked them inside. That had taken most of the morning, so he ate some berries and drank from the pool below the falls, then spent the afternoon hunting for more food. He brought down a prairie hen with an arrow, and skinned and cleaned it. He would roast it tonight and dine in splendor.

All this had taken longer than he'd planned, so his trip to the burial grounds on the summit would have to wait one more day. He turned Zimba loose to graze, and dangled a fishing line into the pool below the falls, using worms as bait. Within a half hour he had a large rainbow trout, which he scaled and cleaned. He had never doubted for a minute when he undertook this journey that he would be able to feed himself from the bounty of Mother Earth, but her generosity amazed even him.

Later that evening as he sat contentedly before his fire in the cave, he thought about the events of the past few weeks. As a rational man, he realized that he'd undertaken a course of events from which he might never be able to return. It was not like him to run from trouble, but since some Whites on the Reservation were determined to make him the scapegoat for whoever had killed Morgan Cullen, this seemed to be the only course open to him until they found the real killer.

There was a part of him that felt he had every right to be bitter, but a voice, that sounded very much like his father, kept reminding him that even without the injustice that had been done to him, this was where he really belonged, and he might never have had the courage to make this move unless he'd been forced into it.

Still, he couldn't help but wonder who would replace him at the high school if he stayed up here, or if he went back and they sent him to prison. The kids had all become such an important part of his life in his two years with them, and it was heartbreaking to leave them when he'd only begun to help some that no one had ever taken any interest in. He knew some people might believe he was guilty, but most would realize he'd gotten a rotten break, simply because he was an Indian. Either way, he had to discipline himself not to brood over it.

He did wonder what Mrs. Lamont was thinking about him right now, though. She had been so good to him and his mother after his father was killed. She'd given his mother a job, and taken them to her church every Sunday, and always made sure he was invited with all the other neighborhood kids for picnics and parties at her house. She'd even sent him to a Christian camp at Rimrock Lake every summer in an effort to make sure he developed a spiritual foundation. It would make him very sad if she thought he'd killed Morgan.

But her husband was another matter. Hank Lamont was like so many Whites on the Reservation. They paid lip service to the Indians, then took their land, ruined their fishing grounds, cut down their forests, and blamed them for everything that went wrong between the Indians and Whites. No. Hank Lamont was just another White-man who was not to be trusted.

He still hadn't made up his mind whether to go back and stand trial, but he felt he would get that answer after a few days up here. He was scared—no question about that—but whatever he decided to do, this time with his ancestors would prepare him for what was to come. With that thought consoling him, he closed his eyes and slept.

CHAPTER 32

It was late Thursday morning when Helen Lamont heard her husband's Cessna buzz the house. She ran out into the yard and waved up at him, and Hank dipped the wings as he passed over again, heading for his airstrip in the lower field. A half hour later, he pulled his pickup into their garage, exhausted from over a week of high-powered negotiations in Seattle with a half dozen financiers from around the country. All he wanted was a hot bath, a tall gin and tonic, and a little nap before he had to deal with any problems that might've come up while he was gone. He grabbed his briefcase and overnight bag and walked down the long path that led from the garage to the house, breaking into a smile as he saw Helen open the screen door and rush out to greet him.

"Hi, Darlin'," he called, as she hurried toward him. He set his bags down and pulled her into his arms.

"I'm so glad you're home," she said. "I've missed you so much."

"I've missed you too," he said, patting her on the fanny.

He picked up the briefcase and bag and slipped his other arm around her shoulders as they walked down to the house. "I'm really beat. Those were a tough bunch of guys."

"Did you get the financing you were after?"

"Yeah, but it took longer than I'd expected. I'm sorry for being gone those extra days." He set his things on the floor by the kitchen table and took off his flight jacket. "Could you fix me a gin and tonic, honey? I'm thirsty as hell . . . uh, sorry, I mean *heck*."

She cocked one eye at him. "Every time I let you go off with your cronies, it takes me a week to clean up your language when you get back. And if you're really thirsty, why don't I give you some fresh lemonade I just made?"

Hank sat down wearily at the kitchen table and held up his thumb and forefinger about a half-inch apart. "Could you put a smidge of gin in it?" he asked sheepishly.

"Absolutely not! I'm not going to contribute to your delinquency."

Hank gave a deep sigh, then chuckled. "Okay, Boss. I'm too tired to argue."

Helen got the lemonade from the refrigerator and poured each of them a glass.

"How'd things go while I was gone?" Hank asked. "How was Morgan's funeral?"

"Oh, Hank, it was just awful," she said, sitting down beside him with her glass. "Some pregnant girl spit on Morgan's body in the coffin, and then her father jumped Andrew in the parking lot and beat him up. It was a terrible ordeal for them to go through at such a sad time."

"Did anybody find out why the guy did it?"

"He claims Morgan got his daughter pregnant and wouldn't

own up to it, so he took it out on Andrew. I felt so sorry for Laura. She was devastated."

"Is Andrew okay?"

"He was pretty banged up, and it looked like his nose might've been broken. I know you don't care much for him, but that's an awful thing to do to someone at his son's funeral."

Hank took a long drink of lemonade and leaned back in his chair. "Looks like Andrew might be getting a taste of his own medicine. He's not above knocking heads together if things don't go his way. I'm sorry Laura and the kids were put through that, though. She's a nice lady. I'll never know how she ever got mixed up with an old reprobate like Andrew Cullen. They're as different as night and day."

Helen leaned toward him and looked up into his face with a little grin. "That's what a lot of people said about us too. Remember? Mama thought you weren't cultured enough for one of her daughters, and Papa never thought you'd have a dime to your name."

Hank laughed as he reached over and laid his big hand on hers. "Well, I guess we showed 'em, didn't we? But your mama was right, you know. I'm still pretty rough around the edges, but I *have* managed to keep us outta the poorhouse. I guess your papa would've been happy about that."

He finished his drink and stood up wearily. "Thanks for the lemonade, honey. You were right. It did take care of my thirst a lot better than a drink would've. I'm gonna take a hot bath now and lie down for a few minutes. If the phone rings for me, tell them I'll call back later."

"Did Mr. Speer get hold of you in Seattle? He called here twice looking for you."

"I got a message that he'd called yesterday, but I didn't pick it up until last night, and I knew he wouldn't be in the office then, so I called him before I left this morning, and his secretary said he was in court already. I told her I'd call him when I got home today."

Helen looked worried. "I wonder if it's something about Derek?"

"I don't know. He's working on another deal for me, so it might have something to do with that." He looked at his watch. "He's probably in the office now. I'd better call him before I get in the tub."

"I'll run your bath water while you call," Helen said.

"Thanks, honey." He went to the phone and dialed Speer's office. The secretary put him right through.

"I hear you're trying to get hold of me," Hank said. "What's up?"

"I'm not sure, but I think we've got a problem with Derek Abrams."

"What now?" Hank asked wearily.

"I've been trying for a couple of days to reach him, but no one's answering the phone at his house. Do you know where he is?"

A frown creased Hank's forehead. "I've been gone for over a week and just got back. I haven't heard anything. Just a minute, Larry, let me ask my wife if Derek's mother has said anything about him being gone. She works for us." He cupped his hand over the phone and yelled at Helen.

She came in from the bathroom. "Were you calling me?"

"Yeah. Larry says he's been trying to reach Derek, but he hasn't been able to get anyone to answer the phone. Is Lucy here today?"

"Yes. She was off yesterday, but she came in this morning."

"Has she said anything to you about Derek not being at home? Larry hasn't been able to reach him."

She shook her head. "Maybe he's just not in any mood to talk to anyone."

"Could you go get her, honey? I need to ask her what's going on." He turned back to the phone. "Larry, I'm gonna talk to his mother and see what she knows. I'll call you right back."

Hank hung up just as Helen and Lucy came into the kitchen. Lucy was clearly nervous.

"Hello, Mr. Lamont. I hope you had a good trip," she said.

"I did. Thanks. Could you sit down here a minute? I need to talk to you about Derek."

All three sat at the kitchen table. "I just got off the phone with Derek's attorney, and he says he's been trying to reach him for two days, but no one's answering the phone at your place. Is Derek there?"

It was obvious that Lucy was on the verge of tears.

"What is it?" Helen asked

Tears began to fill her eyes. "I didn't want to say anything, but I guess I can't keep it quiet any longer. Derek's gone."

Hank's brows went up. "Gone where?"

"I don't know. He took his horse and went up into the hills Tuesday morning after I came to work. I didn't know he'd gone until I got home Tuesday night and found his note. I haven't wanted to tell anybody, because I'm hoping that once he's had a chance to clear his head, he'll come back and get ready for his trial. He hasn't broken any laws because he hasn't left the Reservation, but the more I've thought about it, the more I think he might not be planning to come back at all."

"Oh, Lucy!" Helen moaned.

The tears were now running down Lucy's cheeks. "He told me in his note that he wasn't going to let them lock him up for something he hadn't done." She looked forlornly at Hank. "He didn't do it, Mr. Lamont. I know my son, and he isn't capable of killing anyone."

"Well, it was stupid for him to take off like that," Hank said. "It sure as hell makes him look guilty."

"Hank!" Helen scolded.

"Well, it does. He ought to have sense enough to know that. As soon as the sheriff finds out he's gone, he'll go after him, and Derek will be in a lot more trouble than he is now. Did he say where he was going?"

Lucy shook her head. "He just said he was going where they wouldn't find him. He spent a lot of time up in those mountains with his dad, so he knows them like the back of his hand."

"Did he take his rifle with him?" Hank asked.

Lucy nodded. "And his bow and arrows."

"Oh, dammit!" Hank exclaimed. "If he's got his rifle with him, he isn't gonna let anyone get near him." He turned to Lucy. "I hate to do it, but I'm gonna have to tell Speer about this."

Helen grabbed his arm. "Can't you give him a few more days

before you let Mr. Speer know? Like Lucy said, maybe he just needs a little time to think this over and he'll come back ready to defend himself. Please, Hank. Don't tell Mr. Speer yet."

"I've got to, honey. The trial's in less than three weeks, so Speer's only got a couple weeks to prepare his defense, and he can't do that with Derek gone. I've gotta let him know, and he can make the decision about whether to call the sheriff or not."

Helen's eyes suddenly brightened, and she reached over and put her hand on his. "Maybe you and Lucy could go up there and look for him. If you two found him, I know you could talk him into coming back, and nobody would even know he'd been gone."

He gave her an incredulous look. "Lucy and me? Neither one of us knows those hills like Derek does, and even if we found him, he'd never come back with me there. He let me know what he thinks of me that day I tried to talk to him." He shook his head decisively. "No. He's made his decision, and now he's gonna have to live with the consequences." Hank stood up. "I'll have to call Speer back. You might as well let the water outta the tub, Helen. It doesn't look like I'm gonna get a bath."

Cassie had not meant to eavesdrop on what she'd just heard, but when it finally sank in that Derek had run off into the hills, she was frantic. How could he have done such a stupid thing? He must know that going *anywhere* would make him look guilty, even if he only planned to be gone for a couple of days. She wondered if anyone at The Oaks knew he was gone yet. She and Max had talked on the phone almost every day since she'd found Morgan in the pool, and she'd even had a milkshake with him at Marge's drugstore last night. She decided to call him and see if he'd be willing to take her up into the hills in his dad's Jeep to look for Derek.

She went into the kitchen and picked up the phone, but her uncle was on the line in his office. She eased the phone back onto the hook and decided to drive over to The Oaks and talk to Max in person. She went looking for her aunt and found her on the living room sofa, praying with Lucy. She waited a moment, then said, "Scuse me, Auntie. I'm sorry to interrupt you, but I have to run into Harrah for a minute. I'll be right back."

Helen looked up. "Do you need any money?"

Cassie shook her head. "No, I'm fine. Thanks."

When Cassie got to The Oaks, she honked at the gate and waited, but no one came to open it. She continued honking, but when she realized that no one was going to come, she decided to drive in at the truck entrance and see if Max was out at the kiln. She pulled up in front of the kiln and walked over to where she knew he worked on the upper level. When he saw her, he gave her a little wave and came bounding down the steps.

"Hi," he said. "What're you doing here?"

She lowered her voice and looked around. "I just heard that Derek Abrams has run off into the hills on his horse, and I was hoping you could take me up there to try to get him back before the Sheriff finds out."

He gave her an incredulous look. "I can't leave here. Besides, Lily and Sam already went up there looking for him."

She looked shocked. "How did they know he'd gone?"

"Somehow Lily found out from his mother and talked Sam into taking her. She left Mom a note telling her they were going."

"Does your Dad know he's gone?"

He shook his head. "He's in Spokane and won't be back until tomorrow night, so I'm hoping that Lily and Sam will get back before then, or they're both gonna be in major trouble with Dad."

Cassie looked frustrated. "Is there any way you could take me up there. I know he'd come back if I could talk to him."

"I can't leave here. I run this place when Dad's gone, and he'd fire me if I wasn't here when he gets home. Besides, Derek's better off up in the hills. He won't get a fair trial with Judge Harmon running the show. Dad 'owns' him." He could see Cassie's disappointment, and put his hand on her shoulder. "Let him do this thing his way, Cassie. He can take care of himself." He drew his face up close to hers, and grinned. "You can take care of me, instead of him. Okay?"

She forced a little smile. "Okay, but if anything happens to him, I'm gonna hold it against you."

He gave her a mischievous grin. "I can hardly wait!"

CHAPTER 33

The sun had been a pink and lavender splash just peeking over the mountain ridge when Derek came out of his cave that second morning. He'd slept longer than he planned, but the dreams had been so sweet, he'd hated to wake up. After a quick plunge into the pool below the falls, he put on his vest, breechcloth, and moccasins, then reached for his bow and rifle, but changed his mind. Those weapons had no place where he was going today.

He untethered Zimba, put the bit in his mouth, and grabbed his mane, easily pulling himself up onto the horse's back. It took about an hour to make the steep climb up the treacherous path that led to the graveyard on top of the mountain. Zimba had stumbled several times on the loose shale, but as if he too had sensed the divine mission they were on, he pulled and grunted his way up until horse and rider stood silhouetted against the sky on the top of Spirit Mountain.

The Valley fell away far below them, and as Derek drank in the grandeur all around him, Mount Adams seemed close enough to reach out and touch. But as he surveyed the sacred mountain, he felt a rush of anger at the broad swath of stumps crisscrossing the lower slopes of the mountain where loggers had raped it of its timber. Even here, in the bosom of Mother Earth, the desecration of the White-man plagued him. He turned to the burial grounds with a renewed sadness.

He'd first visited this sacred place when he was ten years old and his father had sent him up here alone to find his spirit guide. It had been both terrifying and awesome to wander over this sacred burial ground in prayer and meditation waiting for a sign from his spirit guide. When he'd found the eagle feather lying on a mound of stones that marked the grave of one of his ancestors, he'd collapsed on those stones in grateful relief and wept till he had no tears left.

His second visit had been two years later when his father was brought here to be buried after Morgan Cullen had run him down on the Fort Road. There were no words for the grief he had felt then, and still felt. His father's wisdom had been Derek's infallible guide, and he knew his father would tell him now whether to go back and defend himself, or stay here until he joined him in the afterlife.

He found himself trembling as he dismounted from Zimba and began looking for his father's grave. There were no names on any of them, but some were marked with unique formations of stones placed there by loving hands to identify those who rested in the sacred ground. But as he walked, something seemed different from when he'd been here twelve years earlier. Some of the graves had crosses on them formed with small pebbles, and that was not something he had remembered. Had these always been there, or was this a desecration of these sacred graves by

Christians? Had they found this place and tried to turn it into a Christian cemetery, or could some of his ancestors have been followers of Jesus as Kamiakin himself had been in his last years?

As he stood there in bewilderment, a sound that began as a blustery howl of wind suddenly assailed his ears. He cocked his head to one side, listening intently to the eerie wail of cries and laughter as dozens of ethereal beings materialized before his eyes, spinning in a frenetic circle around him. Round and round they whirled on the windswept summit, laughing and wailing and calling his name as they grabbed his hand and pulled him along with them. Spinning out of control, he ricocheted from hand to hand, overcome with the pure exhilaration of their joy, until, one by one, they began to evaporate into the wind, leaving him reaching with outstretched arms toward them, not wanting to be left behind.

As the last of them faded out of sight, he fell to his knees with his arms reaching out to them. "Come back!" he cried. "Don't leave me here alone! Please! Don't leave me!"

But the specter had disappeared, and he was alone. He cast his gaze across the barren summit, but all he saw were the lifeless piles of stone and the dead grass that was their only connection to one another.

He stayed on his knees for at least an hour, too weak to rise. Had the apparition been caused by all the stress he'd been under, or had these been emissaries sent by his father to tell him that he was not alone; that they would gladly draw him into their fellowship if he decided to join them?

He finally rose and began to walk the burial ground, half fearing what he might find on his father's grave. But as he wandered from grave to grave, he could feel the spirits of his ancestors reaching out to him, and he began to feel a peace he hadn't known since his father was alive.

When he found his father's grave, he was not surprised to find a cross on it made of small white pebbles, and he knew now that the apparition had been sent by his father to let him know that he would be waiting for him in heaven. He lay on his father's grave for nearly two hours, pouring out his heart to him, while Zimba grazed nearby.

The wind had picked up considerably by the time he rose, and he turned his tear-streaked face toward Mount Adams, raised his arms to the sky, and let out a heart-wrenching howl that died away in the roar of the wind.

Zimba looked up from his grazing and trotted over to him, nuzzling him with his head. Derek threw his arms around the horse's neck and clung to him while waves of unwanted sobs wracked his body. He finally pulled away and leapt onto Zimba's back. Startled, the horse darted forward as Derek ground his heels into his flanks. The horse and rider raced round and round the perimeter of the burial grounds until both were exhausted, and Derek finally reined him in.

Overcome with emotions he could not understand, he threw himself forward against Zimba's mane and wept again. Being in this sacred place of the dead, he'd come face to face with the reality of what he'd sentenced himself to. These ancient ones had had each other for companionship while they lived, but despite their hardships, they'd had love and laughter and fellowship, and even in death they still had each other, while he had no one, and never would again if he stayed here.

He had not allowed himself to cry like this since his father had been killed. Was it fear of what was going to happen to him if he went back, or fear that the voices of his dead ancestors were calling him to stay here with them on this lonely mountain? He did not know the answer to that, but his heart was telling him that as much as he loved this sacred place, this was not where he belonged. At least not until he went to join his father in the afterlife.

CHAPTER 34

Lily came fully awake at the smell of coffee. She slipped the sleeping bag down from around her shoulders and peered over the back of the Jeep. "Is that coffee I smell?"

Sam looked up at her from where he'd slept near the fire. "I thought we'd need it to thaw us out before we get started. It was colder than hades down here last night."

"It was nice and cozy up here," she said as she climbed down from the back of the Jeep.

Sam moved his shoulders up and down and stretched a couple of times. "I haven't slept on the ground since the last time I took you kids camping, and that's been many moons ago."

Lily poured herself a cup of coffee from the enameled pot sitting on the edge of the coals and sat down to warm herself. "Those trips were fun, weren't they?"

He nodded. "You've got lots of good memories like that. I hope you won't let all the garbage that's happened to you since then make you forget them."

"I'm trying not to."

"There's still gonna be some unpleasant stuff ahead for both of us though," he reminded her. "Even if we find Derek and talk him into coming back, I'll have to admit to clubbing Morgan with his cane, and you'll have to admit to putting it in your dad's trunk, and we'll both probably be arrested."

"We won't be arrested," she said. "I'll tell the judge that I saw Morgan trip and fall into the pool as he was coming at you with his cane."

Sam gave her a dubious look. "*And how did that hole get in your brother's head, Miss Cullen?*"

"*He must've hit his head as he was falling into the pool, your Honor.*"

"*And how did the cane get from the pool to Derek's truck?*"

"*Obviously, someone put it there, Sir.*"

"*And who might that be?*"

"*Someone who wanted to get him into trouble.*"

"*Oh, now I understand, Miss Cullen. Thank you for clearing everything up for me.*"

Sam shook his head at her. "You do know how ridiculous that sounds, don't you?"

She let out a little laugh. "Maybe it does need a little fine-tuning."

"How about this," he said: "An innocent young girl is being molested by her older brother, and no one will do anything about it, so a family friend decides to end the problem once and for all, and they all lived happily ever after."

"Oh, Sam. If only it were that simple."

"It is, but as you said, it needs some work."

"I'm afraid it's past that point," she said. "Besides, if the two of us don't end up in jail, I'm clearing out of here as soon as all this is over. There's nothing left for me here."

"What about your mother?"

"She doesn't need me. She's got Max and you, and it sounds like she's got Gus if she wants him. Besides, I have a feeling she'll be leaving The Oaks herself before long." She looked over at Sam. "What'll you do if she goes? Will you stay?"

He gave a brusque shake of his head. "No way. Besides, I'm sure your dad is gonna fire me once he finds out I brought you up here."

"Do you have any money?"

He shrugged. "Enough. Your granddad left me some that your mother made sure I got, and I've saved most of what I've made on the ranch. I'll get by okay."

Lily set her cup down and reached out to the fire to warm her hands. "I'm so sorry for getting you involved in all this," she said. "If I'd left that stupid cane up in the wisteria, none of this would be happening, but I had to get my revenge against Dad, and now you and I are the ones sitting out here in the cold paying for it."

There was something deeper than sadness in his face as Sam looked across the fire at her. "We couldn't let a good man like Derek keep running the rest of his life for something he didn't do. We've both got too much integrity for that."

They put out the campfire and threw their things back into the Jeep. Within twenty minutes, they came to the old wooden bridge that crossed the Klickitat. Some logs and stumps had jammed against the wooden pilings under the ancient bridge, and the swiftly flowing water was splashing up onto it. Several planks were missing where the bridge sagged in the middle, and a faded sign, hanging from the front railing, read, "Signal Peak - 10 miles". Someone had scrawled on the bottom of it in red paint, "cross at your risk".

"I see they still haven't put in a new bridge," Sam said. "The Agency's been promising us one for twenty years."

Lily stood up in the Jeep and looked at it. "Do we have to cross that thing? It doesn't look safe to me."

Sam shook his head. "We would if we were going up to Signal Peak, but Derek's too smart to go up there. He knows that's the first place they'll look for him." He pointed to the narrow dirt road that led upriver from the bridge. "I think he's up at Spirit Mountain where his father's buried. Very few Whites know anything about it, and those who do, think it's haunted because of the Indian cemetery on the summit. If he's anywhere up here, that's where he'll be."

"Can we get up there?" Lily asked.

"Not with the Jeep, but if you don't mind hiking uphill through a mile or more of the thickest forest you've ever seen, we can."

"Well, we've come this far, so we might as well see it through to the bitter end," she said.

Sam gave a fatalistic shrug and turned the Jeep to the right. They followed a very rustic dirt road along the river for about three miles until it suddenly ended at the edge of a dense forest. "This is as far as we can go in the Jeep," he said. "Hop out. I'm gonna hide this thing over here in case somebody comes looking for us. No sense advertising where we are."

Sam pulled the Jeep off the road into some thick underbrush, and grabbed their backpacks from it.

For the next hour they fought their way steadily uphill through trees that grew down the steep slope to the river's edge. Lily was exhausted as she finally plopped down on a large flat boulder. "How much farther?" she groaned.

Sam sat down beside her and wiped the sweat from his face. "About a half mile, just like this last one, only steeper."

"Why would people carry their dead all the way up here? Couldn't they have found an easier place to bury them?"

"They wanted to get them as close to the Great Spirit as they could, and Spirit Mountain's about as close as humans can get to Him on this earth."

She patted him on the back. "I'm sorry I blackmailed you into coming up here. I know you didn't want to."

He met her eyes with a frank gaze. "No, I didn't. I'd rather have left things just as they were."

"And let Derek keep running for the rest of his life?"

"Look," he said, "I'm sorry he got caught up in all this. I sure didn't expect that to happen, but I think he'd eventually have taken off for these hills anyway. This is where his heart is."

"I didn't think you knew him that well."

"I haven't been around him much since he's grown up, but when he was a kid, I used to help him and his dad bring down horses from up in the Horse Heaven Hills, and I knew then that he was gonna have trouble trying to fit into life on the Reservation. His dad filled his head with all the old Indian traditions and legends, and Derek swallowed it all, and I admire him for that. There aren't many on the Reservation who still care about all that stuff." Sam paused a moment, suddenly a little embarrassed, then

223

said, "So if you want the honest truth, Lily, I hope we don't find him. I don't wanna see a nice kid like that face the White-man's justice, especially when your dad owns the judge."

"Hank Lamont isn't going to let that happen," Lily said. "I hear he's hired the best attorney in Yakima to represent him."

"Well, he's gonna need it—especially after this little side-trip of his—so if you're still set on finding him, we'd better keep moving. It's gonna be at least another hour before we get up to the old campground where the caves are, and then another hour to get up to the graveyard on the summit. And if he's not there, it'll take us a couple hours to get back down to the Jeep, and another couple to get back to The Oaks. I just hope that we get there before your dad does, or we're both gonna be in *big* trouble."

CHAPTER 35

The ground rose steadily, and the forest became denser as Sam and Lily fought their way up through the trees to Spirit Mountain. The Klickitat River now rushed down a gorge to the left of them, cascading noisily over huge boulders that jutted out of the water. So far they'd seen no sign of anyone's having been this way recently—no footprints, no hoof tracks, no broken branches or crushed plants; no sign of any humans.

They could hear the roar of the waterfall before they saw it, and Sam stuck his arm out to hold her back. "If he's up here, he'll be in one of those caves over there. Can you see them?"

Lily squinted across a large flat meadow toward the open mouths of two large caves. "How are we gonna let him know we're here? Are we just gonna go over there and start looking in the caves?"

Sam shook his head. "If he's here, he's gonna be spooked when he sees that someone's found him, so I'll go over and take a look first. He won't be as threatened if he sees me alone."

She put her hand on his arm. "Be careful of that waterfall. It looks very close to the caves."

"Don't worry. I've been up here before."

He motioned for her to stay down as he slipped out onto the broad campground and slowly walked across it, his eyes fastened on the caves. As he approached the waterfall, he stopped and looked down at the pool below, remembering the many times he and his friends had jumped into it when they were kids. After a moment he backed away from the rim and was just starting for the first cave when he saw a hoof print in the soft dirt. He knelt down and looked at it carefully, then saw several more near by.

Someone on a horse had been here very recently, and it was probably Derek. He became wary as he pulled himself up to the ledge where the caves were. As he recalled, there were two on this lower part of the mountain, and he remembered the first one. When he was about twelve, one of the Indian teachers at the orphanage had brought all the kids up here to see the cave drawings, then took them up to the summit to look at the graves. Near the mouth of the first cave, he stopped and sniffed. A faint smell of smoke still lingered in the air, and he knew that someone had been in there recently.

He moved closer and called Derek's name. There was no answer, so he called it again. When he still got no response, he called out, "Derek, it's Sam Littlefox. I'm alone and unarmed, and I'm coming in. Okay?"

He cautiously entered the cave, his arms held away from his sides not knowing what to expect. As his eyes adjusted to the dim light, he could see there was no one inside. But someone had been, and very recently, judging from the lingering smell of smoke. He looked around and saw the dimly lit drawings on the wall, remembering the first time he'd seen them. If Derek was up here, this is where he'd be. He moved deeper into the cave and saw a blanket and a leather knapsack shoved behind a pile of logs. Lying next to them were a bow and quiver of arrows, and a rifle. A frown creased his brow. It was obvious Derek wasn't out hunting. Perhaps he'd seen them and was hiding nearby, or maybe he was up on the summit.

It was nearing three in the afternoon, and Sam knew they needed to start back soon if they hoped to have enough light to find their way down to the Jeep, but it was unlikely Derek would show himself if he knew they were there. They hadn't thought to bring something to leave him a note with, but he was sure Lily would never go for that anyway. Whatever her reason, she was determined to talk to him face to face.

He raced across the campground to where she was hiding in the trees, and she stepped out. "Is he there?"

"No, but his things are in that first cave, so he must be up at the graveyard. What do you wanna do? We've only got a few hours to get back to the Jeep before dark, and it'll be midnight before we get back to The Oaks. Your dad isn't supposed to get home until tomorrow, but he could come back tonight. We don't wanna be gone when he gets there."

Lily was adamant. "There's no way I'm going back until we've talked to Derek. His whole future depends on our telling him what really happened that day at the pool."

Sam shook his head in frustration. "There's no telling if he'll show himself at all if he knows someone's here, and when your father finds out that we're up here looking for him, you know he'll come after us."

"He doesn't know how to get to Spirit Mountain. You said yourself that very few Whites even know about this place."

"Yes, but he can bribe some old Indian to bring him up here, and the longer we stay, the more chance there is that we'll run into him on our way back down—or run into the sheriff on his way up here. I'm sure he knows by now that Derek's taken off, and he's probably getting a posse together to come up here and look for him, and once they find the Jeep, they'll know *we* think he's up at Spirit Mountain too." Sam took her by the arm. "We need to get outta here, Lily. We're in way over our heads."

Lily was adamant. "We've gotta stay until we can talk to him. Otherwise he'll have to keep running the rest of his life."

Sam was clearly frustrated. "We can go to the sheriff and tell him the whole story, and that'll clear Derek."

"They won't dismiss the charges just because we tell them he didn't do it, and even if they did give up the search, Derek wouldn't know it, and he'd always be afraid to come back. Don't you see, Sam? The whole reason we're up here is so he can stop running."

Sam let out a sigh of resignation. "What do you wanna do then?"

"I want to stay here till he comes back. If he sees that we're being very open about being here, he'll realize we don't mean him any harm."

"Where do you plan to wait for him? In the cave?"

"Yes," she nodded. "I think we should just go up there and get a fire going so he can see that we're not trying to hide our being here."

"I suppose you'd like to have a three-course meal waiting for him too," Sam quipped.

Lily's eyes lit up playfully. "That's a great idea! Can you throw a line in the river and get us a salmon?"

Sam rolled his eyes upward. "Dear God," he said, "what've I gotten myself into?"

Lily grabbed his hand as they raced across the campground toward the caves.

CHAPTER 36

Gus Styvessan put the receiver back on the hook and swore. What was that stupid kid thinking of, taking off like that? All that did was make him look guilty. And now Lucas wanted him to go up into the mountains with him tomorrow morning to look for him. Gus had tried to talk him out of it, but when Lucas told him Judge Harmon had threatened to send a full posse to look for him, Gus decided he'd better go up with Lucas and see if the two of them could find him first.

He glanced at his watch and saw it was only seven p.m. He usually kept the station open until nine, but things had been slow all day, so he decided to close up early. If anybody was desperate for gas, they could come around back and get him, but he needed his sleep tonight. Lucas was going to be there at five o'clock in the morning with a couple of horses, and wanted them to be up at the fort by six, which meant Gus would need to get up by four-thirty. He hadn't been on a horse for a couple of years, and he could already feel the saddle sores he was going to get from riding around in those hills.

He wondered if Cullen had heard about Derek taking off. He could just picture that. Knowing Cullen, he'd have his own posse up there tonight shooting at anything that moved. The more he thought about that as he went about closing up the station, the more it worried him. He needed to give Andrew a call and feel him out. If he'd heard that Derek had taken off, he'd be more than willing to gloat that he'd been right about him all along.

Gus flipped off the outside lights and went through to his house in the back. It wasn't a large place, only one bedroom with a combination living room and kitchen, but it was cozy. Emily had seen to that with her antiques and lace doilies and country wallpaper with matching curtains. The old braided rug that covered most of the floor had been his mother's prized possession, and it had a lifetime of memories for him etched into it: wrestling with his dad in the evenings, years of school books and papers strewn across it, sprawling in front of the radio listening to *I Love a Mystery* and *Amos and Andy*, and romping with his old dog, Geronimo, just to name a few. He smiled as he remembered the time he and Emily had even made love on it right after they were first married. And then there was the last time Emily had ever seen it, the day he carried her across it to the ambulance. His eyes blurred as he remembered her last words to him, "Take care of our beautiful rug."

He poured himself a Scotch and water and went into the bedroom and sat on the edge of Emily's old antique bed that had come down in her family. He kicked off his shoes and took a sip of the Scotch. It burned as it went down, but felt good. He wasn't much of a drinker, but tonight he needed something to ease all the tension building up in him.

He decided a good hot shower would help, and then he'd settle down in bed and get back to his Louis L'Amour novel. The good guys always came out on top in Louis' books, and that was comforting to think about tonight. He took off his clothes and tossed them in the hamper for his housekeeper, Mrs. Patterson, then stepped into the shower and let the hot water pound out some of the day's tension. As he toweled off and put on his pajama bottoms, he took another sip of Scotch.

His stomach was gnawing under the onslaught of the whiskey, so he went into the kitchen and rummaged through the refrigerator, finally deciding on a peanut butter and jelly sandwich. He slathered a glob of peanut butter on a piece of bread, then covered it with some of Emily's blackberry jam that he'd been doling out sparingly since he was getting down to the end of her canned jams and fruit. He stuffed his mouth with a big bite, then sat down and turned the radio on while he finished the sandwich.

He knew that these were simply stalling tactics to keep from calling Andrew Cullen. Under the best of circumstances, that wasn't something he'd enjoy, but it had to be done, so he washed down the rest of his sandwich with a gulp of whisky and picked up the phone and dialed. It rang eight or nine times, and he was just about to hang up when Laura answered. Her voice immediately alarmed him. "What's wrong?" he asked.

"Oh, Gus, thank God it's you! I thought it might be Andrew again. I've been on the verge of calling you all evening, but I just wasn't sure I should get you involved."

"Involved in what? What's Andrew done now?"

"It's not Andrew. It's Lily and Sam. They took our Jeep and went up into the hills yesterday to look for that Indian boy who killed Morgan, and they're not back yet."

"How did they know Derek was gone?"

"I don't know. Lily left me a note saying Derek had gone up into the hills, and she and Sam were going after him to try to get him to come back, and she'd tell me all about it when they got home. I'm worried sick about them."

Gus could feel his pulse beginning to race. "Does Andrew know that Derek's gone?"

"Yes. He called here a few hours ago to tell me he'd decided to come home tonight, instead of tomorrow, and I ended up telling him the whole thing."

"What was his reaction?"

"He was furious. He blamed me for letting them go. He said if I'd been any kind of mother at all, I could've stopped them, and he's going to fire Sam. It was just awful. Like something in him snapped."

"Did he say what time he was getting home?"

"He's leaving after his meeting tonight and should be here around one or two in the morning. I don't want to be here alone when he gets home. I'm too scared of what he might do to me for letting Lily and Sam go."

"Is Max there?"

"No. He went to a movie in Yakima with some friends, and they were going to an old classmate's house afterwards."

"I'm coming over," Gus said. "Andrew won't do anything with me there."

"I hate to ask you to, but I don't know who else to turn to."

"I'll be right there."

He bolted down the rest of his Scotch and threw on some

clothes. When he got to The Oaks, he saw that the gate was unlocked, and he got out and pushed it opened and drove up to the house. Laura came out the front door as he was getting out of his pickup and ran down the steps toward him. Startled, he pulled her into his arms and heard her muffled sobs against his chest. After a moment, he gently held her away from him and looked down into her stricken face. "Oh, sweetheart," he said, "everything's gonna be okay. I'm here now."

"Am I being punished for my sins, Gus?"

"What sins? You've never committed any sins."

"My sin of marrying Andrew. God must be punishing me for that. I can't think of any other reason why all this is happening."

"Let's go into the house where we can talk," he said.

She gave a quick glance up the steps. "I don't want to go back in there. I don't want to be here when Andrew gets home." She looked up at him. "Take me to your place, Gus. Please."

He wasn't sure he'd heard right. "Andrew will be furious if you're not here when he gets home."

Her eyes pleaded with him. "I've got to get away from this house—just for a little while—or I'm going to lose what's left of my sanity. Please, Gus. I've spent my whole life being here for everyone else, and it's all falling down around me. I need you tonight. Please!"

He swallowed hard. "Well, of course we can go to my place, if that's what you want. Come on." He put his arm around her shoulders and led her to the pickup. "I hope you don't mind this old pickup. It's not what you're used to."

She smiled up at him as he opened the door for her. "It looks like a golden chariot to me."

Gus got in behind the wheel and Laura scooted over and leaned against him. He slipped his arm around her shoulders, but neither spoke during the short drive to Gus's house. He wished now he hadn't had the Scotch because his head felt light, and confusing thoughts were bombarding his mind. *Was Laura just upset and afraid to be alone, or had she decided she was going to leave Andrew and come to him?* He hardly dared to hope.

Normally, he just parked his pickup truck out in front of his station, but as he pulled up to the house, he decided he'd better pull into the garage beside his car so Laura could get out without being seen. There were too many prying eyes in Harrah. He wasn't worried about *his* reputation, but Laura could be badly hurt by wagging tongues.

The door from the garage opened directly into his house, and as Laura stepped into the living room she said, "Oh, Gus, this is charming. I've often wondered how you lived."

He gave the room an appraising look. "It's not very fancy, but Emily had a real homey touch."

Laura looked up at him. "You still miss her, don't you?"

He nodded. "She was a wonderful lady and a good wife, and sure didn't deserve all the pain she had to live with her last couple of years."

"She was lucky she had you to look after her," Laura said. "She was *so* lucky. I hope she knew that."

"She did. She never asked much of me our whole marriage. She was just content to take whatever I gave her. I think she knew she wasn't my first choice, but she taught me an awful lot about unconditional love. The thing that made her the saddest, though, was that we didn't have any kids. That really broke her heart, but as *you* know, kids can be a blessing and a heartache, and you've gotta be ready for both."

Laura had picked up a picture of Gus and Emily that sat on the antique pine buffet, but she nodded up at him as she set the picture back down. "I don't know what I'd do without my children," she said. "They're all I have to live for, and now, with Morgan gone, if anything happens to Max or Lily, I couldn't stand it. I really couldn't."

A warm flood of love passed through him, and he came up behind her and wrapped his arms around her, pressing his face against the back of her hair. "Nothing's gonna happen to them. I'm going up there with Sheriff Lucas in the morning to look for Derek, and we'll find Lily and Sam and get them back home. Don't worry about it. You've got enough to worry about without that."

She turned and put her arms around his neck. "What would I do without you? Why have I wasted all these years?"

"Nothing's ever wasted. You're more beautiful now than you were when I first laid eyes on you. Don't you know that?"

Her eyes began to tear. "No man has said I was beautiful for twenty-six years. You're the last one who ever said that to me. I can't remember Andrew ever saying it."

"Then he's a blind fool. He has no idea what a jewel he's got. When I think about how he's tried to destroy you all these years, I could strangle him. I just hope you're finally through with all that. I know I said I wouldn't push you about it, but even if you don't want to come to me, I hope you've decided to get away from him. Have you?"

She nodded. "That's why I'm here with you right now. I've made my choice . . . " Her voice fell to a whisper, "if you still want me."

He threw back his head and let out a roar. "Still want you? Are you kidding?" Then he suddenly sobered and took her by the shoulders, looking squarely into her face. "But are you sure? You said you were gonna give Andrew another chance."

"I tried. I really did, but the way he talked to me on the phone today made me realize he's too bitter to ever change. I'm through with all his abuse. I don't want any more of it."

"But are you sure it's *me* you want? There can't be any turning back for me. I've waited too long for you."

"I'm sure."

He scooped her up in his arms and carried her into his bedroom. As he laid her on Emily's crocheted bedspread, he looked up and whispered, "Thanks, Emmy."

"Did you say something?" Laura asked.

"I was just giving thanks," he said as he lay down beside her and drew her into his arms.

CHAPTER 37

It was late in the day as Derek and Zimba stood there on the summit of Spirit Mountain. Derek was finding it hard to understand how he could be having such doubts about where he was supposed to be. Only this morning he'd awakened in the cave, so full of joy at being here in this sacred place, but now he found himself bombarded with questions that seemed to have no answers. Why had there been a cross on his father's grave? Had he been a secret follower of Jesus? If so, why hadn't he told him? Maybe he'd been killed before he could, but if he *had* been a Christian, surely his mother would have known. Unless he hadn't told even her.

Derek's mind was flooded with questions as Zimba began to pick his way carefully back down the steep, rocky path. He pulled back firmly on the reins while Zimba chose his footing. The light was beginning to fade, and about a hundred feet down from the summit, he eased Zimba onto a ledge and took one final look out across the Valley. His gaze followed the meandering line of the Klickitat River as it wound its way out of sight on its race toward the Columbia River far to the south. When—if ever—would he see this sight again?

The sun finally dipped behind the Mount Adams, and a harvest moon began peaking up over the ridge behind him—full and unusually bright as he carefully urged Zimba down the narrow path. He should have gotten an earlier start, but he'd hated to pull himself away from his father and beloved ancestors.

When he finally made it down to the campground below the caves, he immediately smelled smoke, but it was too dark to see where it came from. Surely, anyone looking for him would know better than to give their presence away with a campfire.

He quickly spurred Zimba into the forest across from the caves, and tied his reins to the branch of a tree, then made a dash across the darkened campground. He pulled himself up onto the ledge and cautiously approached the mouth of his cave. He instantly recognized Sam's voice, but then heard a woman's voice. He'd only heard that voice on a couple of occasions, but knew it was Lily Cullen. What was she doing up here with Sam? Was her father here too, or had he sent her with Sam, thinking she could talk him into coming back? He listened for several minutes, but did not hear Andrew Cullen's voice.

Derek pressed himself against the side of the mountain, trying to decide what to do. If Cullen was up here, he'd be armed, and with only his knife for protection, Derek would have no chance if he tried to get his things from the cave. He could wait till morning and hope they'd get discouraged and leave, but in the daylight he'd lose any advantage of surprise, and if Cullen *was* here, the chances were slim that he'd leave until he got Derek—one way or another. He could sneak back down and get Zimba and leave, but without his rifle and bow, he'd be forced to go back down to the

Valley, and he hadn't yet decided if that was what he was meant to do. He had to think of a way to get them out of the cave so he could get his things and flee higher into the mountains.

As he grappled with the problem, the answer came. It would be risky, but it was a chance he'd have to take. He had seen earlier that the caves vented through their ceilings, so if he could get to the ledge above his cave and plug the vent, he might be able to smoke them out. He carefully pulled himself to the upper ledge and crawled along until he saw the smoke coming from the vent of his cave directly below. He began digging into the moist earth with his knife and pushing it into the hole until he'd completely plugged it.

A few minutes later, he heard coughing from below. Not daring to look over the ledge for fear of being seen, he waited to see what they would do. There was no way they could stay in the cave with that smoke, so they'd have to come out and wait till it cleared, giving him time to slip in and get his things.

Derek huddled there until he no longer heard their voices, then started crawling back to where he'd climbed up onto the ledge. Just as he reached the steps, Sam poked his head up over the rim of the ledge.

"Derek!" Sam exclaimed. "It's me, Sam."

"You traitor!" Derek cried as he sprang toward him.

Sam threw up his arms to ward him off, but the two of them fell to the ledge below. They grappled on the slippery shale until Derek was able to pin the older man to the ground. Sam finally stopped struggling and gasped, "For God's sake, Derek!. . . Get off me!. . . I'm here to *help* you."

Derek eased up a little, but continued holding him down. "Is Andrew Cullen with you?"

"No! It's only Lily and me."

"Do you swear on this holy mountain that Andrew Cullen isn't here? "

Sam was still out of breath, but had managed to sit up. "Yes!" he panted. "We came up here to tell you who killed Morgan . . . so you can come back."

Derek gave him a wary look. "Who killed him?"

"I did," he said. "I didn't plan to, but I got into an argument with him out at the pool . . . and he said he was gonna have his dad fire me . . . and I just lost it, and hit him over the head with his cane . . . and pushed him into the pool . . . I could've pulled him out, but I figured we'd all be better off if I just let him drown."

Derek didn't know whether to laugh or cry, but he pulled Sam to his feet and flung his arm around his shoulder. "I should've known you wouldn't let me take the blame."

"I was tempted to," he said, "but Lily wouldn't let me. She said we had to come up here and find you and tell you what happened, so here we are. You can stay up here for the rest of your life, or come back with us and hope the judge will believe our story. It's not a great one, but it's the truth."

Just then, Lily came out of the darkness. "He's coming back with us, and we're all three going to the judge and tell him what happened."

Derek had only seen Lily up close once, the day she had bailed him out of jail, and he had not thought she was especially attractive then, but now, with the moon shining down on her long blond hair, he could see that she was actually quite beautiful. "Why are you sticking your neck out for me again?" he asked her. "You don't even know me."

"No, but Sam does, and he says you're one of the best Indians on the Reservation, so I'm taking his word for it."

"Are you willing to testify at my trial?"

"There won't be a trial once I tell the judge what Morgan's been doing to me. Dad would never let that information get out to the public, but there is a good chance he'll fire Sam."

Sam shrugged. "I don't care. I was ready to retire anyway. I'm just sorry you two got mixed up in all this."

Lily threw her arms around Sam's neck. "You don't have to apologize to me. You're the only person who's ever cared what happened to me, and anything you do is okay in my book."

Sam took her arms from around his neck. "I'd like to spend the rest of the night hearing how wonderful I am, but it's been a long time since I've been up here, and I'd like to hike up to the summit and talk all this over with my ancestors. They'll let me know what I should do. "

"Don't you want to wait till morning?" Derek said. "That path up there is pretty treacherous."

Sam shook his head as he picked up his backpack. "I need to get this off my chest tonight. I'll be back in the morning and we can go down and turn ourselves in together."

Lily's heart was heavy as she watched him disappear into the darkness, and she suddenly had a premonition that she might never see him again, but she shook it off and turned to Derek. "Can we see if the smoke's cleared out of the cave yet? I'm freezing out here."

"I'll go up and clear the vent," he said. "You stay here by the entrance till I get back."

Derek climbed to the ledge above and cleared out the vent, and as he made his way back down to the cave, he realized just how cold it really was and didn't envy Sam's journey up the mountain.

Derek and Lily waited about fifteen minutes for the smoke to clear, then they entered the cave, and Derek motioned for her to sit down by the fire. He put some more wood on it and handed her his blanket. "You'll need this tonight," he said.

"What will you use?"

"I'm an Indian. Remember? This is our kind of weather."

She managed a faint smile. "You're very proud of being an Indian, aren't you?"

"Yes. Aren't you proud of your heritage?"

"The Cullens?" she snorted. "From what I've heard, they were all a bunch of losers. But I am proud of my Barron ancestors. I never knew any of them, but mom has told me lots of stories about them. I just wish I'd had a father like hers, instead of the one I got."

Derek leaned over and poked at the fire. "My father was the most incredible man who ever lived, but I didn't have nearly enough time with him. I'm not a vindictive person, but I'm glad Sam did what he did to Morgan. Someone needed to stop him from hurting anyone again."

Lily pulled the blanket closer around her shoulders. "I don't want to talk about him anymore," she said. "He's hurt all of us for the last time, and if there is a hell, he's paying for it right now, and I'd like to go to sleep thinking about that. We can talk more tomorrow when Sam gets back. I'm sure he'll have plenty to tell us that will lift our spirits."

She curled up into a little ball, trying to get comfortable, and Derek soon heard the steady rhythm of her breathing. As he sat there, looking at her face that was finally at peace, he whispered softly, "Sam is very lucky to have you for a friend, Lily Cullen. You have the heart of an Indian."

CHAPTER 38

It was about two in the morning when Andrew Cullen pulled into his garage. He jumped out of the car and raced into the kitchen, angrily calling Laura's name.

She was not asleep. In fact, she'd only been home from Gus's for about an hour, giving her just enough time to shower and fix a pot of chamomile tea—her mother's age-old remedy for stress. She was in her robe in her sitting room when she heard Andrew bellow her name as he came stomping up the stairs, but decided not to answer him. She was through jumping to his beck and call. He could come to her door and knock if he wanted to talk to her.

She heard him yell her name again, and as much as she dreaded the scene that was sure to unfold, there was a deep satisfaction in finally having the courage to defy him. A smile crept across her face as she thought back to the few hours she had just shared with Gus. She had never experienced such tenderness from a man— had not even dreamed that men and women could share such love. When he'd first carried her to his bedroom, she felt like a schoolgirl on her first date. And then when he'd laid her on his bed and begun to undress her, she'd been surprised at how shy she felt, and to her astonishment, he had begun to cry softly as he kissed her naked body and quivering mouth. Then *she* began to cry as they lay entwined in each others' arms, sobbing out their pain and loneliness and love.

Fortified with these memories, she was ready when Andrew burst into her sitting room. He stood looking down at her, his eyes blazing. Laura looked up, but the ridiculous sight of him towering above her with his nose still swollen and his face mottled with yellow and purple bruises dispelled her fear, and she gave him a little smile. "Hello, Andrew," she said pleasantly.

"Didn't you hear me calling?" he demanded.

"Yes, I heard you."

"Then why didn't you answer?"

"Because I'm through jumping through hoops like one of your trained dogs. I decided if you wanted to talk to me, you could come to my room like any civilized person and start by asking how I am, since you haven't seen me for several days."

Her response caught him off guard, and his scowl deepened. "You've been drinking, haven't you? What's in that cup?"

She gave another little laugh and held it up for him to smell. "It's only tea. My mother always drank chamomile tea when she needed to calm her nerves, but she very seldom needed to, because she had a wonderful husband who loved her, and a daughter who worshiped the ground she walked on, and she never had to sit in her room alone at night wondering whether anyone cared if she lived or died. Surely you remember me telling you these things about my mother, don't you? It's a shame you never got to know her. You might've seen what a woman can be when she's loved by her husband."

"You *have* been drinking!" he sneered. "Let me smell that." He took the cup out of her hand and sniffed it, then set it down on the end table. "How can you sit here feeling sorry for yourself when your daughter is running around up in the hills exposed to a killer? I called Max this morning, and he told me about Sam and Lily going up there to look for that Indian, and that's why I came home early. Somebody has to look out for our daughter."

"Oh, Andrew," she laughed, "you're such a fraud. You don't give two hoots about Lily. You never have, and the only reason you're concerned about her now is because she's done something you can't control. You're a pathetic human being, you know that? You gambled everything on Morgan's love, and in the end, who knows if even *he* loved you? And now he's dead, and your other children aren't afraid of you anymore—and neither am I. We've all declared our emancipation from Andrew Cullen."

He had turned to leave, but her words stopped him, and he turned back to her. "You talk about pathetic? What do you think you are? You want a husband who wants to come home to you every night? Then take a look in the mirror and see why you've got one that *doesn't*. I can find a warmer body in any Indian shack on the Fort Road, and believe me, I have—many times."

"Well, I'd like to make that easier for you," she said. "I'm divorcing you."

There was a look of absolute incredulity on his face. "What did you say?"

"I'm divorcing you. I should've done it years ago."

"You're bluffing."

"Oh no I'm not."

"Well, good riddance, then. The sooner you clear out of here, the better. But don't get any ideas about trying to take this ranch away from me. That'll never happen."

Laura's lips suddenly tightened as she looked up at him. "You know something? I'm glad we've had this little talk. I was seriously considering letting you have the ranch if you'd been willing to give me a divorce without any hassle, but your arrogance has changed my mind. You don't deserve any consideration after the way you've treated the children and me all these years. Besides, my father would turn over in his grave if I gave this place to you. He saw what you were the day you walked onto it—even if it did take me a little longer—and as far as getting a divorce is concerned, I'll have no problem with that. There's half a dozen of my friends that you've committed adultery with, and I'm sure my attorneys will have no trouble getting them to testify against you. I wanted to avoid that kind of scandal for the children's sake, but you'll leave me no choice if you contest this divorce."

"Now, wait a minute, Laura," he said, his tone considerably subdued. "You're just talking nonsense because you're all shaken up by Morgan's death. You don't want a divorce. What would you do with this ranch? You can't run it."

"No, but Max can, and he's just itching for the chance."

"He couldn't run this place without me—and he wouldn't do it anyway. You can't turn him against me."

"You've turned him against you all by yourself by the way you've always favored Morgan. He'll jump at the chance to show what he can do with this ranch, and with a little practice he'll be very good at it. If you'll remember, you weren't much older than him when you started running it."

He took a step toward her, and his eyes narrowed menacingly. "You think you've got this all figured out, don't you? Well, we'll see about you trying to take this place away from me. I don't care whose name is on the deed, or how many women you drag in to testify against me. I've got twenty-five years of my sweat invested out there, and no judge in the world will discount that. We'll just let the courts decide who owns what around here."

"Another little hatchet job for your friend, Judge Harmon?" she asked.

"You bet it is!"

"It won't work, Andrew. Remember, I know the truth about the deal you made with him after Morgan's accident." Laura watched him closely to see how he would react to what she was saying. "And thanks to a little investigation I've had done since then, I also know about the money you've been paying him for years to keep his mouth shut. I don't think either of you would want that information to get into the wrong hands, would you?"

He made a threatening move toward her. "You wouldn't dare."

She sat without flinching. "Oh, yes I would, unless you plan to shut me up too. That's how you deal with people who cross you, isn't it? You shut them up, one way or the other, and you don't care who gets hurt just so long as you get what you want."

He drew his hand back and struck her across the face, slamming her head back against the chair. He stood over her, ready to strike again. "I oughta kill you," he said.

Laura put her hand to her cheek, then looked up at him, her eyes cold as ice. "Is that what happened with Morgan? Did he have something on you, and you shut him up?" Her voice was rising as her words took on a life of their own. "Tell me, Andrew, did you kill our son to keep him from exposing some rotten thing you'd done? Did you? Answer me!"

He stood above her, his arm raised to strike her again, then suddenly slumped to his knees in front of her as sobs began to wrack his body. "How can you accuse me of such a thing? I loved that boy more than my own life, and you know that. He *was* my life."

Laura had pulled back into the chair, her arm held up to protect herself from another blow, but seeing him on his knees, a heavy remorse for her angry words suddenly stirred her, and she bent over and lifted his head. "Please, Andrew," she begged. "Don't cry like this. I know you didn't kill him."

"How could you even *think* I might've done it? You know how much I loved him, and now you're telling me he didn't love me? How much can a man take?"

"I didn't mean that. Of course he loved you."

"But *you* don't, do you? You want to throw me out of here with nothing." He gripped her hands in his. "Won't you give me another chance? I'll make it up to you. I promise."

"Oh, Andrew, don't ask that of me. You know you're as miserable as I am. Let's let each other go, and both find some happiness while we've still got time."

He reached up and frantically put his arms around her neck. "I don't want to let you go. I'll change. I promise. I don't want to lose you after everything else I've lost. Please. I need you, Laura."

He pulled her face to his and began kissing her hungrily. She struggled to free herself as he picked her up from the chair and carried her to her bed. There a small moment in which she could have struggled from his grasp and fled, but she chose to remain and let him fill his need one last time.

He fell asleep almost instantly afterward, and she lay there with him cradled like a child against her breast, and wept as she thought about her beloved Gus.

CHAPTER 39

Elmer Trueblood woke with a start and sat upright in bed. He thought Sophie's snoring had awakened him again until he climbed out of bed and went to the window. Someone was unloading two horses from the back of a truck out on the grounds of the fort, and it was only six o'clock in the morning. He quickly pulled on some pants and a shirt and went out onto his front porch. He saw Gus Styvessan and called out to him, "What's goin' on, Gus?"

"Sorry to get you up so early," Gus called back, "but Sheriff Lucas and I are gonna look around up here for Derek Abrams. You haven't seen him, have you? He's on a tan cayuse with a dark mane."

Elmer stepped off the porch and walked toward Gus. "I know Derek real well. He and his dad used to come up and play chess with me when Jason was alive, but I haven't seen Derek lately. Why are you lookin' for him?"

"I guess you haven't heard, but he's been charged with killing Andrew Cullen's kid."

"I heard that, but I don't believe it. "

"A lot of us don't, but he's gonna have to let the courts decide. We're looking for Sam Littlefox and Cullen's daughter,

Lily, too. By any chance did you see them come up this way in Cullen's Jeep?"

"Sophie saw 'em yesterday. She waved at 'em, but they didn't stop. What're they doin' up here?"

"They're hoping to find Derek and talk him into coming back to stand trial."

"What makes everyone think he's up here?" Elmer asked.

"He told his mother he wanted to talk things over with his father, and he's buried up on Spirit Mountain, so we figure that's where he's gone. He's got every right to be up here since his trial doesn't start 'till the end of the month, but Judge Harmon wants him back down on the flat where he can keep an eye on him."

Elmer frowned. "Can a judge do that?"

"He can if he's in Andrew Cullen's pocket."

"Do you think Derek killed the Cullen kid?"

Gus shook his head. "Of course not, but he's been charged with it, so we've gotta bring him back and let a jury sort it all out."

Lucas had finished saddling his horse and rode over to them. He leaned down and shook Elmer's hand. "Sorry to get you up so early," he told Elmer. "Okay if I leave my truck where it is? We'll be back before dark."

"Sure," he said. "Is there anything I can do to help you guys?"

"Just keep an eye on my truck, and if you should see Derek, don't try to stop him. Just take note of where he's headed, and let us know when we get back. It won't be hard to spot him. According to his mother, he's decked out in full Indian garb."

"Wait a minute," Elmer said, "I think Sophie mighta seen him a couple days ago. It like to scared her to death. She was out pickin' berries when she saw an Indian in full buckskin with a bow and rifle slung over his back."

Lucas's eyes lit up. "Where?"

Elmer pointed. "Off there in the sagebrush a couple of miles."

"Did he say anything to her?"

He shook his head. "She doesn't think he even saw her."

"Which way was he headed?" Lucas asked.

Elmer pointed again. "Up towards Spirit Mountain."

"Does this road out here go all the way up there?" Gus asked, pointing to the rough dirt road that ran by the fort.

"It goes part of the way."

Lucas dismounted and reached into his jacket pocket and took out a map. He opened it up and showed it to Gus and Elmer. He had marked the Klickitat River, as well as Signal Peak and Spirit Mountain. "I hope you're not planning on us covering all that," Gus said. "We'll be here for a month."

"I know there's a lotta ground to cover," Lucas replied, "but we can come back tomorrow if we have to." He scowled at Gus's incredulous look, then added, "Hey, I didn't say this was gonna be a picnic. It'll take some work to flush him out, and there's a good chance we never will, but we gotta be able to tell Judge Harmon we tried, or we're both gonna have our butts in a sling."

"Not mine," Gus said. "I'm just a lowly deputy who got drafted into this."

Lucas gave him an impatient wave of his hand. "Okay! Okay! I know your heart's not in this, but you're here, and I need you, so don't gimme a hard time. I got enough to worry about just tryin' to make sure Derek doesn't leave the Reservation."

"He won't," Gus said. "He knows he can't be arrested as long as he stays here and gets back in time for the trial. Can't we just wait and see if he comes back on his own, and if he doesn't, then come looking for him?"

"Judge Harmon wants him outta these hills, and he's the one calling the shots," Lucas said.

"Well, where do you wanna start looking then?"

Elmer had been listening to their conversation and finally spoke up. "If you don't mind me buttin' in, from where Derek was when my wife saw him, I think he was headed for Spirit Mountain. Do you know how to get up there?"

Both men shook their heads.

"Can I take a look at that map?" Elmer asked. "It's easier if I just show you."

Lucas held the map out, and Elmer pointed to a thin green line running through the center of it. "This is the Klickitat River," he said. "It's about twelve miles up here, but when you get to the bridge, don't cross it. Stay on this side of the river and go upstream about three miles till the road gives out." He let out a little laugh. "And then the fun begins. You gotta climb on foot about a mile up through the thickest forest you've ever seen in order to get to Spirit Mountain. I think that's the reason the Indians abandoned that place years ago. It was just too hard to get to."

Gus was frowning down at the map. "Is there a shorter way to get there from here?"

Elmer pointed off into the sagebrush. "You can cut off three or four miles by going out through the sagebrush there, but there's no trail. You just gotta keep Mount Saint Helens on your left and

Spirit Mountain on your right. You'll know when you're getting close to the mountain, 'cuz the ground rises pretty fast and the trees get a lot thicker."

Lucas was getting antsy at the delay. "We can stand here yappin' about it all day, but we need to get goin'." He folded the map and stuck it back in his jacket pocket, then mounted his horse.

Gus reached out and shook Elmer's hand, then mounted. "Apologize to Sophie for us getting you up so early," he said.

Elmer patted the leather gun case slung to Gus's saddle. "Is that shotgun really necessary?"

Gus leaned down and lowered his voice. "Just between you and me, I don't even own a shotgun. I had to borrow this one just to make Lucas happy. I don't even have any shells with me."

Elmer winked up at him. "Good for you. The idea of someone gunnin' down Derek Abrams isn't somethin' I wanna think about."

Gus lowered his voice again. "There's not a bit of evidence that he had anything to do with the Cullen murder. This whole thing is just another way for everyone on this Reservation to suck up to Andrew Cullen. I'm sick of it, myself."

Gus looked up as Lucas called to him. He gave Elmer a wink, then rode over to Lucas, and they began moving off through the sagebrush on the shortcut Elmer had pointed out.

"What are we gonna do if we run into Derek?" Gus asked as they cantered along.

"Try to convince him to come back peacefully."

"And if he won't?"

"Then he needs to know we're authorized to bring him in any way we have to."

"I won't draw on him," Gus said.

"I won't either, unless he draws first. It's all up to him how much force we have to use. I'd like to get this whole thing over peaceful-like, but we gotta bring him in. You know that."

Gus nodded. "I wouldn't be here if I didn't agree, but I do worry about Lily Cullen and Sam being up here. I don't want either of them getting hurt."

"It was a dumb thing for them to get involved in this, and I mean to put the fear of God into both of 'em when I see 'em," Lucas said, then frowned over at Gus. "Those Cullens are a strange bunch if you ask me. The day we questioned 'em, you coulda cut the tension between 'em with a knife."

"They've got their problems," Gus said.

"Those kinda problems I don't need," Lucas retorted.

"Me, neither," Gus said, then lapsed into silence as they rode along. He was thinking back to last night with Laura. It was everything he'd dreamed it would be. He hadn't even showered this morning, because he didn't want to lose her scent from his body. That she still loved him and wanted to spend the rest of her life with him, was only now beginning to sink in. How could he be so lucky after all these years? There were still a lot of problems they were gonna have to work out before she could come to him, but she'd made up her mind to leave Andrew, and that was where it had to start.

They were both under no illusions that Andrew would let her go without a fight. He never gave in gracefully to anybody, and he had it in his power to make life hell for both of them. But Laura had already decided that he could have The Oaks, and she would take what furnishings had belonged to her parents and move in with Gus. When she'd told him that last night, he'd thought it was a great idea. But thinking about it now—in the sober light of day—he realized that his little place behind the station was no place for her, or those elegant things of hers. It simply wouldn't be right for him to expect her to move in with him where he lived now.

The more he thought about it as he rode along, the more he realized that there would have to be a lot of changes in his life if he and Laura were going to be together. He could hardly continue running the gas station with her sitting in the back waiting for him to come in with grease and sweat all over him. No, he'd have to sell it, and they'd have to move into a bigger place, or move out of Harrah altogether. But what could he do if he sold the station? At fifty-two, he was too young to retire, and he had no intention of living on her money. But he wouldn't have enough of his own—even with the sale of the station—to let her live the way she was used to. The thought of all this suddenly depressed him. What if he was simply too old to start all over again with another woman in another place?

CHAPTER 40

The morning air was cold as Derek stood looking down at the waterfall, thinking about the events of the last few days. Sam had not yet returned from the summit, and Derek hoped he was finding some peace in that sacred place. It had certainly brought a new depth into his own life, and now, armed with what they had told him last night about Morgan's death, he was ready to go back down and tell Speer that he would stand trial—if he was still willing to represent him. At the most, he had simply set back the preparation of his defense by a few days, but with what Lily was prepared to reveal about how Morgan's cane had gotten into his truck, Speer's defense should be an easy matter.

He was feeling better about his situation this morning, but was still puzzled about Lily Cullen. He had watched her while she slept during the night—only catching snatches of sleep himself so the fire wouldn't go out—but he could not understand why she had come all the way up here to help him. She could easily have let him keep running, thinking the law was after him, but instead she was risking her relationship with her father in order for him to be able to go back and prove his innocence. By *his* creed, that was a sacred act that would bind him to her forever. Whether she understood it or not, he was now her blood brother, and the thought of that was more than a little unsettling.

Derek took Zimba's tether off and watched him scamper across the campground, then filled his backpack with huckleberries from some bushes at the edge of the forest. It wasn't much of a breakfast, but it would hold them until Sam got back down from the summit, and they could get to Derek's house.

Lily was still curled up in a little ball under his blanket when he went back into the cave, and he looked down at her with a sense of wonder. He'd always wanted a sister, and now he was going to have one.

He put some wood on the fire and was suddenly conscious that Lily's eyes were following his every move. "I hope you got some sleep," he said.

She sat up slowly, pulling the blanket closer around her. "I've had better nights."

He held some berries out to her. "I picked these this morning. It's not much, but we can get more on the way down the mountain."

She reached out and took them. "Does that mean you're coming back with Sam and me?"

He nodded.

"I'm glad," she said. "Is he back?"

"Not yet. That place up there is where people go to speak to God, and it's not something you can hurry."

"Maybe I should go up there," she said. "I don't think I've ever had a conversation with God."

"You don't have to go up there to talk to Him, but somehow He does feel a lot closer up there."

Lily stood up and stretched, then yawned. "I don't see how you people can sleep on the ground like this."

"I assume by '*you people*' that you're referring to Indians?"

She gave him a questioning look. "Did I say something wrong? You are Indians, aren't you?"

"That's what the Pilgrims called us when they landed at Plymouth Rock and thought they were in the West Indies, but most of us prefer to be called by our tribal names, or simply, Native Americans."

"Well, there you go," she said with a little laugh. "I learn something new every day."

"It's no big deal with me," he said. "I've been called much worse."

This time she let out a hearty laugh. "So have I, but being a lady, I won't repeat it." She looked around. "Is there some place I can wash my face and take care of some *personal* needs?"

Derek gave her a little grin. "I'll get some water while you go into the cave next to ours and take care of your *personal* needs."

He emptied out his knapsack and made his way down the steps to the pool below, while Lily went next door. They met just as Derek climbed up from the watering hole with his knapsack leaking water from every seam, and he rushed to her just in time for her to get a quick drink. She jumped back as water ran down her face and soaked the front of her shirt and pants.

"Sorry," he laughed. "You probably didn't want a bath too."

"It's okay. I'm sure I could use one." She gave him a quizzical look. "By the way, how did all those Indian women you see in magazines always look so beautiful, living in such a primitive way?"

He did his best to suppress a grin. "That's simple. Their beauty came from the inside."

She raised a brow at him. "Spoken like a typical man."

He laughed. "That's the first time I've been called a 'typical man', and it sounds good."

She grinned. "Well you certainly aren't typical, but you are a man, and that's good enough for me." She suddenly realized what she'd said, and quickly added, "I didn't mean 'good enough for *me*', I just meant 'good enough." She started to laugh. "Just forget it. You know what I mean."

It had been a long time since Derek had done this kind of bantering with a girl, and it gave him the courage to ask her if she'd like to see something special.

"What is it?" she asked.

"It's some old cave drawings. Some of them have been up here for hundreds of years. There's even one I put here when I was ten years old."

"I'd love to see them," she said. "Where are they?"

"In the back of the cave. I'll show you."

She followed him into the cave, and he motioned for her to come closer as he pointed out the crudely drawn figures on the wall of the cave. When he got to his own drawing of an eagle with a branch in it's talons, he became animated as he told her about coming up here when he was ten years old and finding the eagle feather on the grave on the summit, and how his father had told him that the eagle would always be his spirit guide.

When he'd finished with his story, she leaned back and gave

him an appraising look. "I think it's going to be good for me having a friend like you. You're a very unusual man."

He let out a little laugh. "You make it sound like I'm some kind of freak."

"That's not what I meant, and you know it. I just meant that you're not what I expected you to be."

"What were you expecting?"

"Someone a little more worldly and not so spiritual."

He laughed. "I've lived both ways, and I seem to have better luck with the spiritual."

Lily wasn't equipped to discuss that with him, so she changed the subject. "How long do you think Sam will be up on the mountain?"

"That's hard to say. Once you get up there, it's easy to lose track of time."

"How long should we wait for him?"

"I should get back before anyone else comes looking for me. The next people might not be as friendly as you and Sam."

"Why don't we wait until noon," Lily said, "and if he hasn't come back by then, you go back down, and I'll wait for him."

He shook his head. "I won't leave you up here alone. Sam might decide to spend several days up there, and you can't stay here by yourself. I assume you came up in your dad's Jeep."

She nodded.

"Does Sam have the keys with him?"

"He must have. He didn't give them to me. Why?"

Derek was thoughtful a moment, then said, "There's no telling how much time Sam will need on the mountain. It's easy to lose yourself in all that tranquility. Maybe you should come back down with me and let Sam take as much time as he needs up there. Then when he's ready to come down, he can find his way back to the Jeep. What do think?"

She paused a moment. "I don't want him to think we just abandoned him."

"He won't. I think he'll appreciate the extra time, but he knows it's urgent for me to get back before someone else comes looking for me."

"Is there some way to let him know that we've gone back on our own, and no one's forced us to?"

"I'll leave a pair of crossed arrows in the cave. That's the Indian sign for friendship and peace. He'll know that."

"He's an old man. He may not remember all that Indian stuff."

"He'll remember," Derek said. "There are some things an Indian never forgets."

When Derek had laid the crossed arrows on the floor of the cave and gathered up his things, he asked Lily if she'd wait for him down on the campground. After she went out, he stood looking at the cave drawings for a long time, then ran his hand across his own drawing. "Thank you," he whispered to his eagle, then slung his bow and quiver and knapsack over one arm and his blanket and rifle under the other, and took one last look at the drawings, knowing his eyes might never again see this sacred part of his past.

CHAPTER 41

When Andrew Cullen awoke, he realized he was in bed with a woman, but for the life of him he couldn't remember who it was. He shifted slightly to get a glimpse of her, and it all came back. It was Laura, and she was leaving him and taking his ranch from him. He lay very still, remembering their words of the night before. It seemed incomprehensible to him now that he could have broken down like he did in front of her. How she must despise his weakness. Well, that would be shortlived, because he was anything but weak, as she was soon going to find out. He carefully pushed the covers back and slipped out of the bed. He found his pants and shoes and let himself out her bedroom door.

He didn't even take time to shower and shave, but picked up the phone, glancing at his watch as he did so. It was five in the morning, and Billy Aimes was probably still asleep, but he'd come alive when he heard what Cullen had in store for him. He let Billy's phone ring a dozen times before a sleepy voice finally answered.

"Who's this?" Billy grumbled.

"It's Andrew Cullen."

"Mr. Cullen! Sorry, boss, I couldn't imagine who'd be callin' me this early. Is somethin' wrong?"

"That Indian that killed my boy has run off into the hills, and I need your help going after him. You know those hills above the fort, don't you?"

"Yeah, pretty good, but you're talkin' about a big area. It'll be tough to track him down unless you got some idea where he went. When did he leave?"

"On Tuesday morning. I've been out of town for two days and just got back last night, and for some stupid reason, Sam and my daughter took my Jeep and went up looking for the Indian, and my pickup's getting a new transmission, so I haven't got any wheels. Can you take me up there in your pickup? I'll make it worth your while."

"Well, yeah, sure, boss. I ain't got no use for that Injun myself. Let me get some clothes on, and I'll be right there."

"Thanks, Billy. I'll be out at the kiln. And bring your rifle. We might just bag us an Indian."

"Sure thing!" Billy exclaimed.

Andrew hung up and went downstairs to the garage. He got his shotgun out of the trunk of his car, and grabbed a box of shells from a shelf, then went out to his office in the kiln. No one was there yet, so he left a note to his secretary to tell Max to wait in the house for him until he got back. Boy, was that kid gonna get an earful! The very idea of him thinking he could take over this ranch. Well, he'd see about that!

Thirty minutes had gone by since Cullen had called Billy, so he dialed him again. There was no answer, so he figured he was on his way. When another thirty minutes had gone by and he still wasn't there, Cullen was furious. He rang him again and this time Billy answered.

"What's going on?" Cullen fumed. "It's been an hour since I called you. Where are you?"

"Sorry, boss," Billy sputtered. "I had a flat tire, and didn't have a spare, but I borrowed one from my neighbor, so it shouldn't be but a few more minutes. I'm really sorry, boss. I know you're anxious to get goin', and so am I. Don't call nobody else. I really wanna be in on this with you."

It was close to eight o'clock when Billy finally drove up, and Cullen was beside himself. "You'll be late for your own funeral," he growled as he opened the door and got in. He propped his shotgun between his legs. "Let's get going."

"Sorry I'm late," Billy said, "but the tire I borrowed was the wrong size, and I had to wake up another neighbor and get one of his. I'm really sorry, boss, but we're all set now."

Billy reeked of stale beer and cigarettes, and Cullen sniffed at him a couple of times. "You smell like a sewer," he said.

"Sorry, boss."

"I don't care what you do on your own time as long as it doesn't affect me, but Max has complained about you being hungover on the job more than once, so you better get your act together if you wanna keep your job."

"Oh, I do, boss. I sure do."

"Well, let's get out of here then. Abrams has probably dug in somewhere up there in one of his holes, and it's gonna take some work flushing him out."

Billy turned the pickup around and drove out onto the Harrah Road, heading toward the Fort Road.

"How'd you find out the Injun was gone?" Billy asked.

"My daughter left my wife a note telling her that he'd taken off for the hills, and she and Sam were gonna go up and try to find him and talk him into coming back."

Billy looked over in surprise. "Whadda they want with him?"

"Who knows? Lily's always hated Morgan, so maybe she wants to congratulate the Indian for killing him, but she's gonna be plenty sorry when I get my hands on her. And Sam's gonna find his butt out on the Fort Road. I've had enough of his disloyalty. I've only kept him on for Mrs. Cullen's sake, but I'm through with the whole bunch of 'em."

Billy glanced over at Cullen with a puzzled look, but seemed to know better than to ask any more questions.

It was nearly nine o'clock by the time they got to the fort. "Pull in there," Cullen said. "I wanna see if the caretaker's seen anything of my Jeep."

Billy pulled off the dirt road and drove up to the caretaker's cottage. Cullen was just getting out of Billy's truck when Elmer Trueblood came out onto his porch. Cullen stormed over to him. "I'm Andrew Cullen, and I want to know if my daughter and our houseman came by here in my Jeep in the last day or two."

Elmer stuck out his hand, but Cullen ignored it, so he pulled it back and said, "I'm Elmer Trueblood, the caretaker here at the fort, and your Jeep did go by a couple days ago."

"Which way was it headed?" Cullen demanded.

"Up toward the Klickitat."

"Did you see it come back down?"

Elmer gave a little shrug. "No, but I'm not outside all the time either."

Cullen pointed to Lucas's truck. "Is that yours?"

"No," Elmer replied.

"Well, whose is it?" he demanded.

"It belongs to the Toppenish sheriff."

"Is he looking for the Indian that killed my son?"

"I'm not sure he'd want me tellin' anyone what he's doin' up here."

Cullen was livid. "You'd better tell *me*, or I'll see that this is last job you ever have on this Reservation."

Elmer's face flushed, but he kept his voice civil. "They're lookin' for Derek Abrams, but they didn't say why."

"Where are they looking?" Cullen demanded.

"I don't know, but I'm sure they'll be back before dark if you wanna ask 'em about it."

Cullen was seething. "Look, mister, you're supposed to know everything that goes on up here in these hills, and I'll make sure your supervisor knows what a crappy job you're doing." He turned to Billy. "Let's get out of here and go look for them ourselves."

They got back into Billy's pickup and took off up the road toward the Klickitat. Elmer stood on the porch of his house with a grin on his face.

CHAPTER 42

Gus Styvessan and Sheriff Lucas had been in the saddle for nearly two hours. Gus hadn't done any serious riding for years, and his rear-end was really feeling it. He finally reined his horse to a stop and slid off.

"What're you doin'?" Lucas asked.

"I've gotta stop for a few minutes, or I'm gonna have saddle sores in places I'd still like to use before I die."

Lucas laughed and dismounted beside him. "Well, we can't have that. You're still a young fella with a lotta livin' and lovin' to do."

Gus grunted and did a couple of bowlegged struts trying to get out the kinks in his legs. He stretched both arms into the air, then bent over to touch the ground, but his fingers dangled about six inches above it.

The grin on Lucas's face broadened. "You're outta shape, kid. I'm gonna have to get you on horseback more often."

"Please," Gus pleaded, straightening up with some effort. "My spirit's willing, but my poor old flesh isn't."

"That's a cop-out, and you know it. How old are you anyway?"

"Fifty-two, going on eighty."

"Why, you're just a kid. I'll be sixty-six my next birthday, and I'm still goin' strong. Look at this." Lucas did a couple of waist bends and easily touched the ground.

"Okay! Okay! You've made your point, but you gotta remember your life's a whole lot more exciting than mine. I sit on my butt all day counting flies on the gas pump, although I must say, these last few weeks have certainly livened things up." He patted his horse on the rump, then turned to Lucas. "I've been doing a lot of thinking about all this, and I just don't think Derek had anything to do with Morgan's murder. Too many things don't add up. That cane business for instance. He wouldn't have hidden that in his truck and pulled it out the way he did, unless he's got some kinda death wish. And I've also been thinking about Cullen's reaction when I couldn't find it in Derek's cab that day. Remember? He said, '*I know it's in there*', then nearly busted a gut trying to find it. I think he knew it was in there, because he *put* it there."

Lucas frowned. "But how would he have gotten it?"

"I don't know, unless he's the one who used it on Morgan."

"Aw, come on, Gus. You don't think he'd kill his own son, do you?"

"I think he's *capable* of it. Maybe Morgan did something that threatened him in some way, and they got in a fight over it, and it all got outta hand. And there's something else I haven't told you," Gus added. "I think Lily Cullen saw him do it."

Lucas raised his brows. "Did she tell you that?

"No, but I know she spends most of her time out on her balcony, and it looks right down on the pool. When I asked her if she'd seen who did it, she got very agitated and said she hadn't been out on her balcony that day, but I know she was, because her mother told me she was out there."

Lucas shook his head. "I dunno, Gus. That's pretty farfetched. A man doesn't kill his son if he's mad at him. He just cuts off his allowance or takes his car away." Lucas shook his head again. "No, you're barkin' up the wrong tree. Abrams is still our best bet. Just the fact that he ran is evidence of that."

"Not necessarily. He could've run because he knew he was being railroaded for something he didn't do. You've gotta admit that Cullen pointed the finger at him right from the start, and what better way to throw suspicion off himself. Huh? Think about it. Did any of us ask him where *he* was from three to three-thirty that day? I didn't."

Lucas pursed his mouth thoughtfully. "I didn't either, but you know what I just remembered? One of my guys told me that he came across Cullen out by the trucks about five o'clock in the mornin' the day we found the cane in Derek's truck. He asked Cullen what he was doin' out there, and Cullen told him he was just makin' sure all the guys were doin' their job. He gave my man a hard time, and then walked back to the mansion. You don't suppose he was out there plantin' that cane in Derek's truck, do you?"

"It wouldn't surprise me one bit," Gus said. "What better way to throw the blame on him? I'm more than ever interested in knowing where Cullen was between three and four o'clock the day of the murder."

"I'm sure he's worked out an alibi by now," Lucas retorted.

"Oh, I'm sure he has."

Lucas added, "I'd also like to get a set of Cullen's prints and see if they match any of those on the cane. I know he'll pitch a fit if we ask him for 'em, but I still wanna get 'em."

"I don't care how much of a fit he pitches," Gus said. "If he had anything to do with this, I'd sure rather see him answer for it than have Derek spend the next thirty years in prison for something he didn't do."

Lucas frowned over at Gus. "I know you're fond of the kid, but he's gonna have to let the court decide whether he's innocent or guilty. Harmon won't let him get outta that, but if what we're thinkin' has any possibility of bein' true, and we can get somethin' to back it up, then Derek'll be off the hook."

Gus pulled himself back up into the saddle. "I don't know why that doesn't make me feel any better. With everybody blaming him, I've got a bad feeling that somebody might try to win some points with Cullen by bagging himself an Indian."

"That's why we gotta get him back," Lucas said as he mounted. He paused a moment, then looked over at Gus. "I do wanna get one thing straight with you, though, then I'll drop it. When I asked you to come up here with me, you made it sound like I was out to get Derek because he's an Indian, but if that's what you're thinkin', you're dead wrong. I'd be doin' the same thing if he was white."

"I know you would," Gus said. "I've just got a bone stuck in my craw about this whole Indian thing, and I don't often say much about it, but it bothers me the way people have been so quick to put the finger on Derek. He's just the kind of Indian this Reservation needs, and I think he's getting a raw deal."

"Well, let's hope we can find him and talk him into comin' back with us. If he will, this little escapade isn't gonna count for much. But if we can't find him, Cullen and Harmon won't rest until he's hunted down, and then you *will* see an Indian lynchin'."

CHAPTER 43

When Max came down to breakfast Friday morning, he stopped abruptly when he saw his mother's eye. "What happened to you?" he exclaimed.

She brought her hand up in an effort to cover her eye and cheek. "It's nothing," she said.

He drew her hand down and gasped. "This isn't '*nothing*'! Who did this to you?"

"Your father and I had a little argument last night, and he hit me."

"Why?"

"I told him I was leaving him."

"What!" he exclaimed.

"I'll tell you all about it later, but right now I need to know where your father is. He's not in his room, and Dorothy says he's not in his office."

"Did you check the garage for his car?"

She nodded. "It's here, but Lily and Sam are still gone with the Jeep, so I don't know if he's somewhere out on the ranch, or left here with someone."

"Did you tell him that Lily and Sam have gone up looking for Derek?"

She pointed at her eye and nodded. "He was *very* upset about that, among other things."

Max stood up. "Let me ask around the kiln and see if anyone's seen him."

"Aren't you working today?"

"I was supposed to, but when I went out there this morning, Dorothy said Dad had left a note telling her that he wanted me to stay in the house until he gets back, because he has some things he wants to settle with me."

"Did he tell her what it was?" she asked.

"No, but now I'm sure it's about you leaving him. He probably wants to know if I'm on his side or yours."

"I'm sorry you kids have to get caught in the middle of this, but it's been building up for years. Neither of us has been happy—I'm sure you kids have known that—and now with Morgan gone, and you and Lily old enough to be on your own, there's no reason for us to prolong our misery."

"But where would you go?"

"I wouldn't go anywhere. I told your father I want him to move out."

Max's brows shot up. "How did he react to that?"

She pointed to her eye. "Just what you'd expect. He seems to have forgotten that my father left this place to *me,* not him. I've never interfered with his running of it, but I'm the legal owner—no matter how he rants and raves to the contrary. When Dad set up my trust, he specifically excluded your father from any ownership of The Oaks because he never did trust him."

"Then why did he let you marry him?"

Laura gave a reluctant sigh. "Because I was pregnant with Morgan."

"Oh, Mom!" he moaned. "How could I have been so dense? That accounts for why Dad's always favored him. He used him to get this ranch, didn't he?"

She nodded.

"Did Morgan know?"

"I think he suspected it, and maybe that's why he always felt like he wasn't really a part of the family. I just don't know. It doesn't make any difference now, but I did love him with all my heart."

"Why didn't you ever tell me any of this before?"

"What good would that have done? There wasn't anything you could do about it."

"Maybe not, but at least I would've understood the undercurrent that's been in this family all these years. Does Lily know any of this?"

She shook her head. "I've never told her. She's had enough of a burden to bear as it is."

"You mean with Morgan?"

Laura looked startled. "How did you know about that?"

"She told me last week. I could never understand why she seemed to hate him so much until she finally told me what he'd been doing to her. Couldn't you and Dad have stopped him?"

"I tried to, but your father said he'd take care of it."

Max let out a disgusted snort. "Yeah, like he took care of everything with Morgan—'buy him this, buy him that'. The whole thing makes me sick. In fact, Dad makes me sick. I thought maybe he and I might get close now that Morgan's gone, but I don't think I want to get close to someone like him. It might rub off on me like it did on Morgan."

"Don't be bitter, darling. Please! That'll only make you like the two of them, and I couldn't bear to see that happen to you. You've always been the one bright light in this family. Don't let this change that. For your sake and mine."

"I won't, but I'm not gonna be Dad's little lapdog anymore either. That's for sure. I've begged for crumbs long enough from him."

"I told your father that I wanted you to take over the ranch after he leaves," Laura said.

Max let out a surprised laugh. "I bet he just loved that."

"Naturally he doesn't think you can do it, but I do. Do you feel like you're ready?"

Max's brow furrowed. "Gosh, I don't know. I suppose I could. I'd have to get some help with the business end of it, but you know that running this ranch has always been my dream. I just didn't think it would come so soon."

He pulled back and looked at her. "But you honestly don't think Dad will just walk away without a fight, do you? He'll use every dirty trick he knows to keep this place."

Laura gave him a strained little smile. "I've got a few dirty tricks of my own."

"What?"

She shook her head. "It's better you don't know, but I imagine this whole thing is what he wants to talk to you about. I'm sure he thinks you and I cooked this up together. He never was a graceful loser, but I guess where he came from those kinds of things didn't matter."

"Well, I'm on your side, Mom, so don't worry about him trying to turn me against you. That could never happen."

"I know that, but I'm sure he's going to fire Sam as soon as he gets back He's always thought Sam considered himself superior to him since your grandfather treated him more like a son than he ever did your father." Her eyes began to mist. "No one can know what Sam has meant in my life though. If it hadn't been for him, I would've lost my sanity long ago, but he's always encouraged me to hold on and be brave, and promised me things would get better. He's been such a good friend to me; much more than your father ever has. There's only been one other man who ever loved me like that."

"Who?"

"Gus Styvessan."

"Gus?" Max exclaimed. "That's the first I've ever heard of that. When did you two know each other?"

"When we were young. I broke his heart by marrying your father instead of him, but there wasn't anything we could do about it then. Now there is."

He gave her a questioning look. "What do you mean?"

"Gus and I have found each other again, and he wants me to marry him."

Max brought his hand to his heart. "I'm not sure how much more I can take. You and Gus? You guys are so different. I mean, somehow I just can't see the two of you together." He held up his hand to ward off her response. "Don't get me wrong, Mom. I think he's a great guy, but I just never thought about him with you. Have you told Dad you're going to divorce him?"

She shook her head. "No. My leaving your father has nothing to do with Gus. I would've left him anyway, but being around Gus again these past few weeks has stirred something in me that I thought was dead, and then when he told me he'd never stopped loving me, I just told myself I'd be a fool to let that kind of love go. I might never find it again. I know Gus and I seem different in many ways, but inside we both look at things the same way, and that's what really counts with someone you love. I hope you'll be happy for us, honey."

Max leaned down and put his arms around her. "Of course I will. If you love him and he loves you, that makes him okay in my book."

Laura pulled back from him and searched his face. "Thanks, honey. Your approval means everything to me, and it will to Gus too."

CHAPTER 44

Derek and Lily carefully made their way down the mountain. It was tricky, especially with Derek leading Zimba by his reins and trying to guide Lily with the other arm. The forest was so thick that the sun barely penetrated it.

It was funny, but the curious bond Lily had first felt with this complex man as she had watched him from her balcony at the ranch had grown deeper in the hours they had spent together in the cave. Although many of his actions up till now had mystified her, as they talked last night and again this morning on the way down the mountain, she had seen a depth in him that made her know she could trust him. He'd even told her a little bit about his experience up on the summit, and asked her if she ever prayed about things. The question had surprised her, because her family never attended church, and she couldn't remember if she'd ever actually prayed about anything. Considering the burdens she lived with, she could have used some help from a higher power, but no one had ever told her anything about a God who cared about her personally. It surprised her that he would ask such a personal question.

As the forest began to thin, and they saw the road up ahead,

Lily pointed to a thick cluster of sumac. "The Jeep's hidden over there behind those bushes."

Derek went over to where she was pointing and took a look. "It doesn't look like anyone's messed with it, so it'll be here when Sam comes down."

"I hope that's soon, or my dad will have a fit. His whole identity is tied up with that Jeep. He thinks he's the incarnation of General Patton."

Derek looked around for any tire tracks, but the only ones he found were the Jeep tracks. "It doesn't look like anyone's been up here looking for us, but that doesn't mean they won't be. If your dad's back from Spokane, there's a good chance he'll come up here himself."

Derek went back to Zimba and strapped his backpack and rifle across the horse's neck with a leather thong, then lifted his bow and quiver over his head and slung them across his shoulder and pulled himself up onto Zimba's back. He beckoned to Lily. "Get up here behind me."

"And just how am I supposed to do that?"

He held his hand down to her. "Take my hand and I'll pull you up."

"I can't get up there that way."

He pointed to some large boulders. "Get up on those then, and I'll bring Zimba alongside."

"Why don't I just walk?"

"Because we need to get out of here. C'mon. I'll help you get on."

She let out an exasperated sigh, but climbed up onto the

tallest boulder. Derek nudged Zimba in the flanks, and he side-stepped until he was next to the rock. Lily grabbed Derek's hand and threw one leg over the horse. Startled by the sudden pressure of two riders, Zimba pranced nervously, and Lily let out a little cry as she threw both arms around Derek's waist and pulled herself up against his back.

She had never been behind someone on a horse before, and it was unsettling to suddenly find her face pressed up against his soft leather vest with her arms wrapped around his waist. It was not an unpleasant feeling, but it was unnerving. Regardless of how they'd come to this point, something was obviously happening between the two of them, and she sensed that he felt it too.

They were about a mile from the Klickitat bridge when Derek saw the dust being kicked up by someone coming toward them. He reined Zimba back so abruptly that Lily dug her nails into the flesh of his stomach.

"What's wrong?" she exclaimed.

"Someone's coming!" His eyes darted around for some place to take cover, but there were only occasional oaks and sumac to their left and the river on their right. He jerked Zimba's head around hard. "I can't take any chances on it being somebody looking for me. We've got to get back to the tree-line. Hang on tight. We're going to have to make a run for it."

Before Lily could object, Derek kicked Zimba in the flanks, and the horse tore back up the trail in the direction of Spirit Mountain.

CHAPTER 45

Cullen saw Derek and Lilly at the same time they saw him. He jerked forward in his seat and pointed toward them. "It's him, Billy! It's that renegade Indian!"

"It looks like there's two of 'em on the horse. You think he's got your daughter?"

"I'm sure of it! Kick this thing into gear. We gotta catch them before they get back to the trees."

Billy shifted into low gear and the truck surged forward, kicking up a trail of dust behind it. Cullen tried to load his shotgun, but each time he was about to insert a shell, the truck hit a rut, and he dropped several shells before managing to get one in each barrel.

Billy had closed the gap by more than half when Cullen hung out the window with his shotgun. Billy looked over and gasped. "You'll hit your daughter if you shoot now!"

"No, I won't. I've got a clear bead on the Indian. Just get this thing closer!"

Billy stepped down hard on the accelerator, and the truck slowly gained on the riders. It was only a hundred yards from them when Cullen fired. For one terrible moment, Lilly seemed to float upward, her back arched, her arms flung out above her head, then she fell to the ground and lay still.

When Derek realized that Lily had fallen, he pulled Zimba to a halt, and looked back at her lying in the road with her father running toward her. He was filled with such blinding rage, that he grabbed his rifle and dug his heels into Zimba's flanks and raced back toward them.

Cullen looked up at the charging rider and fired wildly at him. The shot missed, but Derek's shot caught Cullen squarely in his chest, and he flew backwards, dropping his shotgun in the dust. Derek ground Zimba to a halt and jumped down beside Lily and felt her pulse. She was still alive, but bleeding badly. Just then, he caught Billy Aimes bending down to pick up Cullen's shotgun, and Derek swung his rifle toward him. "You touch that, and you're dead too."

Billy held up both hands as he stumbled backward. "Okay! Okay! Don't kill me! I didn't shoot her. He did. I swear!"

Derek leaned down and picked up Cullen's shotgun by the barrel and flung it into the underbrush beside the road. He turned back to Billy and motioned toward Cullen with the barrel of it his rifle. "Check him and see if he's dead."

Billy knelt down beside Cullen, grimacing at the blood slowly spreading over the front of his jacket. He felt for a pulse, but could find none. Billy's face was a mask of terror as he looked up at Derek. "He's dead!"

"Good. Now you sit down right over here where I can see you, and put your hands on top of your head. And if you move, I'll kill you too."

"Okay! Okay!" Billy cried, quickly moving to where Derek pointed. He put his hands on his head and sat down, shaking in terror.

Derek knelt down to Lily again and saw that her eyes were open. He slipped his hand under her head and gently lifted it a few inches. "Lily, it's Derek. Talk to me," he pleaded.

She stared up at him and moved her mouth, but no words came out. Her eyes were glazed with pain. "That's okay. Don't try to talk. Your father shot you, but he's not going to hurt you again. I promise."

Derek glared murderously at Billy. "If she dies, I'll kill you too, even if it takes the rest of my life."

"I didn't have nothin' to do with it!" Billy cried. "I told him he'd hit her if he fired, but no one can tell him nothin'. You know that! He wanted you so bad that he was willin' to risk hittin' his own daughter."

"But you brought him up here in your truck, so you're just as guilty as he is."

"How did I know he was gonna shoot his own kid? I was just helpin' him look for her."

"For *her* or for me?"

"Well . . . for you," Billy admitted, "but Gus Styvessan and the Toppenish sheriff are up here lookin' for you too, so we were just helpin' 'em out."

Derek's eyes bore into him. "How do you know they're up here?"

"We stopped at the fort and the caretaker told us."

Derek thought for a moment, then motioned to Billy. "Get the passenger door of your truck open."

Derek set his rifle on the ground and gently picked Lily up and followed Billy to his truck, laying her on the front seat. He went around to the driver's side and got Billy's rifle from the rack behind the seat and flung it into the river, then turned to Billy and held out his hand, "Give me the keys," he demanded.

"They're in the truck."

"Come with me," Derek said, grabbing him by the arm.

"Whaddya gonna do with me?" he cried. "I told you, this was all Cullen's idea. I didn't have nothin' to do with it."

"Shut up!" Derek ordered.

He shoved Billy in front of him back to where Zimba stood, and picked up his rifle from the ground. Pointing it at Billy, he took his bow and quiver and knapsack from where he'd tied them to the horse's neck, then slipped the bridle off and slapped Zimba on the rump. The horse reluctantly took off through the woods. Derek kept his rifle on Billy as he threw all his gear into the back of Billy's truck.

"Take off your jacket and cap," Derek ordered.

"Whaddya want with them?" Billy exclaimed.

"Just do what I say."

"Okay! Okay!" Billy said. He quickly stripped off his jacket and baseball cap and handed them to Derek. He pulled the jacket on, then put the cap on his head and tucked his ponytail up under it.

"Now your pants," Derek said.

Billy's face twisted in horror. "My pants?"

"Pull them off, or I'll pull them off you myself—and you won't enjoy that."

Billy pulled off his boots, then reluctantly took off his jeans. He had no underwear on, only a sleeveless undershirt, but he held the jeans out to Derek while he tried to pull the undershirt down to cover his private parts.

"Now your boots," Derek said.

"Not my boots!" Billy wailed. "I just got 'em. They're brand new."

Derek grabbed them and the jeans and backed up to the river and tossed them in, while Billy squealed in horror.

"Now, you sit down here by your boss, and don't move until I'm out of sight. You hear me? If you so much as twitch an eyebrow, I'll come back and kill you."

"I won't move," Billy blubbered. "I promise."

Derek leaned his rifle against the dashboard where he could get at it in a hurry, then climbed behind the steering wheel and gently lifted Lily's head onto his lap. She moaned softly, and he looked down in anguish at her pale face. What had he done to this innocent girl? She had done nothing but try to help him, and now she was lying next to him, dying because of him—even after he had pledged to himself on the mountain that he would be her protector for the rest of her life. He cursed himself for being the cause of so much sorrow to so many people.

With a final look of hatred toward Billy, he started the pickup and turned it around. As fast as he could, he raced down the bumpy dirt road toward the fort. It took him about thirty minutes to get there, and when it finally came into sight, Derek saw the truck parked in front of the caretaker's cottage, and knew that Billy had been telling the truth about Lucas and Gus being up here looking for him.

Lily groaned as he sped past the fort. "Hang on, little sister," he said. "I won't let you die. I promise it on my father's grave."

But he was not at all sure she would live. She had taken a direct hit in her back, and it was bleeding profusely. Her blood had soaked him and the seat of the pickup, and her breath was coming in short gasps.

Derek was sick at heart watching the life ebb out of her as he raced down the Fort Road, and it dawned on him, as he held her limp body on the seat with his right arm, that she had become more to him than just a sister. If he lost her now, part of him would die with her, and the thought brought hot tears to his eyes. Somewhere in the back of his mind, he also realized that if she died, Sam would be the only one who could verify his innocence in Morgan's death, and who knew whether Sam was even going to come back from Spirit Mountain. But those were issues he'd have to deal with later. Right now he had to make the decision where to take Lily. The closest hospital was Toppenish, but that was another half hour away. When he came to the Harrah Road, he made a split second decision to take her in to Doc Stevens' clinic. He could call an ambulance, and take care of her until it got there.

The tires of the pickup squealed as he turned off the Fort Road toward Harrah. In three minutes, he pulled up in front of the clinic and lifted the unconscious girl out of the truck. Doc was standing behind the receptionist's desk with his nurse, as Derek burst through the door with Lily in his arms. Doc took one look at her and pushed open the door to his examining room. Derek carried Lily in and laid her on the table.

"What happened?" Doc asked.

"Her father shot her in the back," Derek said.

"My God! Where and when?"

"Up in the hills above the fort about an hour and a half ago. I got here as fast as I could. I didn't think I'd have time to get her to Toppenish."

"Let's get a look at her," Doc said.

Ruth cut Lily's bloody shirt off, and she and Doc turned her on her stomach. Doc grimaced as he saw a half-dozen holes in her back. "I'm going to get her on oxygen, then I've got to get some X-rays to see what kind of damage those pellets have done." He turned to Ruth. "Get that tank over here and get her hooked up."

Ruth rolled the portable oxygen tank over to the table and strapped the mouthpiece over Lily's mouth and nose, then got some antiseptic and wiped as much blood as she could from her back. Doc rolled his large X-ray machine to the table, and Ruth slipped a blank X-ray into a slot in the table.

"Step back," Doc said to Derek.

Derek did not want to leave Lily's side, but he stepped back a few paces as Ruth took X-rays from several angles. When she'd finished, she went to develop them, and Doc turned to Derek. "Okay, son, tell me what happened. Why did her father shoot her?"

"He was aiming at me. He just didn't care that she was in the way."

"I want the whole story, Derek. What were all of you doing up in the hills in the first place?"

"It's a long story, and it won't help Lily by telling it now. I just don't want her to die. Can you save her?"

"I hope so. If the pellets haven't pierced any vital organs, I probably can, but I'm not going to be satisfied until you tell me how this happened. I'm required to report any gunshot wounds I treat, so I have to ask some questions. Why was Andrew shooting at you?"

"He's the only one who can answer that, but that won't be possible. He's dead."

Doc's mouth flew open. "Andrew's dead? How?"

"He fired at me and missed, and I returned his fire—and *didn't.*"

"Where is he now?"

"Up along the Klickitat River about two miles north of the old bridge. Billy Aimes is with him."

"Is he dead too?"

Derek shook his head. "No. He brought Cullen up there in his pickup to look for me, so I left him there with Cullen while I brought Lily down here in his pickup."

They stopped talking as Ruth came in with the X-rays in her hand. She handed them to Doc, and he slipped them into a lighted panel on the wall and peered at them carefully. He sucked in his breath. "Oh, boy! One of these pellets has entered her spine. She'll need a specialist to get that out, but I can get these others out." He closely scrutinized the X-rays again. "It doesn't look like any vital organs have been hit, thank God." He looked up at Ruth. "Let's get her ready for surgery." Turning to Derek, he said, "You'll have to wait in the lobby, son. I can't have any distractions here. I strongly suggest that you go over to Gus's station and tell him what happened."

"How long will it take to get the pellets out?" Derek asked.

"A couple of hours, but Ruth will call an ambulance from Yakima right now to be here to pick her up the minute I'm through. I want a specialist to deal with that pellet in her spine. That's the one that's got me worried."

"Can that kill her?"

"It could, but more likely it could paralyze her."

"Not that!" Derek moaned. "Please! You can't let that happen."

Doc laid his hand on Derek's shoulder. "I'll do the best I can for her, then we'll get her up to Mercy Hospital in Yakima. They'll take good care of her." He patted Derek on the back. "You go on over to Gus's now. You can check back here in a couple of hours. We won't be through before then, but I think you'd better tell your story to Gus as soon as possible. Once word gets out that you shot Andrew Cullen, there's a lot of folks who aren't gonna feel very charitable toward you, seeing's how he signs their paychecks. You just tell the whole thing to Gus, and he'll know what to do. Okay? You go on now. We'll take care of Lily."

Derek reluctantly left the office and got into Billy's pickup. The sight of Lily's blood on the seat brought fresh tears to his eyes, and he crossed his arms on the steering wheel and laid his head on them. Try as he might, he could not hold back the tears, and he sat there quietly sobbing.

CHAPTER 46

Gus and Lucas were in a thick stand of trees about three miles west of Spirit Mountain when they heard a shotgun blast—then another blast a minute later, followed by the crisper sound of a rifle.

"That's two shotgun blasts and a rifle," Lucas exclaimed. "We need to check that out."

Thirty minutes later, they broke out of the trees and came onto the dirt road next to the river. They looked in both directions, but saw no one.

"Which way should we look?" Lucas asked.

Gus looked down at the road. "There's a lot of fresh tire tracks here, but I don't know whether they were headed upstream or down." He paused a moment, then said, "Let's go up toward Spirit Mountain and see if it mighta been someone looking for Derek. If we don't find anyone, we can head back to the fort and see if anyone's showed up there."

They got back on their horses and galloped toward Spirit Mountain about a mile away. It was Gus who spotted the body in the road and yelled back to Lucas, "Someone's up there in the road!"

They raced up to the body, and Gus let out a gasp, "My God! It's Andrew Cullen!"

He and Lucas both slid off their horses and knelt down beside him. Gus picked up his limp hand and felt for a pulse. "He's dead. Looks like he was shot through the heart with a rifle." He looked around. "Who could've done this?"

"Didn't you tell me Derek's mother said he had his rifle with him?" Lucas asked.

Gus nodded. "Yes, but if he used it on Cullen, where's the shotgun we heard?"

Lucas stood up and began looking around for it, then beckoned to Gus. "Take a look over here. Isn't this blood?"

Gus went over to him, and both men knelt down and looked at some bark covered with drops of dried blood. "It sure is, but if Cullen is over there, whose blood is this over here?"

"Maybe Cullen got off a shot at Derek," Lucas said.

"Then where's Cullen's gun? It's gotta be around here, unless Derek took it with him."

They began scouring the area, and it was Lucas who found the shotgun in a thicket of sagebrush. He held it up and let out a yell, and Gus came running.

Gus took the gun from him. It was a twenty-gauge double-barrel shotgun. "This is Cullen's gun alright. His initials are on the stock." He held it up for Lucas to see. Gus broke the gun open and saw two spent casings in the barrel. He took them out and smelled them, then handed the gun to Lucas. "This is the shotgun we heard. Both shells were recently fired."

Lucas took the gun and smelled the end of the barrel. "How'd it get into the bushes?"

"Derek must've thrown it there," Gus said. He looked

thoughtful for a minute. "I have a feeling that blood over on the bark might be Derek's, not Cullen's. Cullen must've got him with his shotgun before Derek fired back with his rifle."

"Well, we can't do anything for Cullen," Lucas said, "so let's get back to the fort and get my truck and come back up here and get him. If that blood is Derek's, he isn't gonna get far. We can get Elmer to come back up here with us to look for him."

"I suppose that's the best we can do," Gus said. He looked toward the grove of trees. "I just hate to think of that boy wandering out there alone, bleeding to death."

"If he did this to Cullen, we know he's a damn good shot. I wouldn't wanna go into those woods after him, and even though you consider him a friend, I think you'd be crazy if you try to track him on your own. Let's just get back to the fort, and I'll call Toppenish to get some officers up here to look for him."

"I guess you're right," Gus said. "Okay, let's go."

Both men mounted, and Gus looked down at the surprised expression on Cullen's dead face. "Well, Andrew, you finally got yourself into a mess you couldn't buy—or bully—your way out of, didn't you?"

Lucas looked back at him. "You say somethin' to me?"

Gus shook his head. "No, I was just saying my goodbyes to Andrew."

The two men took off down the dirt road toward the fort. They'd only gotten a couple of miles from the bridge when they saw someone up ahead in the middle of the road frantically waving them down. As they got closer, Gus saw that it was Billy Aimes. He was barefoot and naked, with his undershirt tied around his waist like an apron, covering his private parts. Sweat was pouring down his face as he limped up to Gus and grabbed his horse's bridle.

"Billy! What're you doing up here half-naked?" Gus asked.

"Am I ever glad to see you guys!" he panted. "Mr. Cullen's been killed! He's up there a couple miles north of the bridge. That Injun shot him."

"How do you know that?" Lucas asked.

"I was with Cullen. I brought him up here in my truck to look for his daughter, and that Injun came ridin' toward us with her on the horse behind him, and when he saw us, he fired at Cullen, then him and the girl took off back up the trail. The boss got a shot off at him, but hit his daughter, and she fell off the horse. Then the Injun came chargin' back at us and got Cullen right through the heart. I just left him about an hour ago, and I been runnin' like hell to get help."

Lucas looked astonished. "What was Lily Cullen doing on a horse with Derek? I thought she came up here with Sam in Cullen's Jeep."

Billy shook his head. "I didn't see no sign of Sam or Cullen's Jeep."

"You say Cullen got a shot off at Derek? Did he hit him?" Gus asked.

"He sure didn't act like he'd been hit. He shoved me around and made me take my clothes and boots off, then laid the girl in the seat of my pickup, and took off in it."

"Was the girl dead?"

"I don't know, but she looked like she was hurt real bad. I told

Cullen he'd hit her if he didn't get a clear shot at the Injun, but he was hell-bent on gettin' him. He was like a crazy man."

"This is important," Gus said, "and you'd better tell us the truth. When you came onto Derek and Lily on the horse, who fired first, Derek or Cullen?"

Billy hesitated a second, then mumbled, "Derek did."

"Did Cullen have his gun up?" Lucas asked.

"I don't think so, but everything happened so fast, all I can remember is that Injun chargin' at us with his rifle blazin'. I thought we was both gonna get it."

"Did he fire at you, or just at Cullen?"

"Just at Cullen, but after he killed him, he told me he'd kill me too if I didn't do exactly what he said. He made me take off my jacket and baseball cap, and he put 'em on. I told him you and Gus was up here lookin' for him, so I think he was tryin' to disguise hisself. Anyway, he took off in my truck with Cullen's daughter bleedin' all over the seat, and I want my truck back. Can you guys get it for me?"

"We'll do our best," Gus said. He reached his hand down to Billy. "Get up here behind me, and we'll take you to the fort."

Billy stuck his foot in Gus's stirrup and pulled himself up behind the deputy. They galloped down the road toward the fort with Billy's bare butt bouncing up and down behind Gus's saddle. When they got to the fort, they all dismounted and ran up to Elmer's house. Gus pounded on the door, and Elmer opened it. He looked surprised to see them. "What're you guys doin' back so soon? Did you find Derek?"

"No, but we found Billy and Andrew Cullen. Cullen's been shot," Lucas said.

"Good God!" Elmer exclaimed. "Is he dead?"

Lucas nodded. "Can I use your phone to call the station?"

"Of course. Come on in." Elmer stepped aside as the three men entered. Lucas headed for the phone, but Billy tried to hide himself behind an overstuffed chair.

"Cullen stopped by here just this morning," Elmer said. "What happened?"

Gus volunteered what he knew. "From what Billy says, he brought Cullen up here to look for his daughter, and they ran into Derek and the girl coming down from Spirit Mountain on Derek's horse, and Derek took a shot at 'em. I guess the kids tried to make a run for it, but Cullen got a shot off at them and hit his daughter instead of Derek, and she fell off. Billy says Derek came charging back and shot Cullen right through the heart."

Sophie's hand went to her mouth. "Is the girl dead too?"

"No, but I guess she's hurt pretty bad. Derek took off with her in Billy's pickup, so I hope to God he's taken her to the hospital in Toppenish."

"Did you see anything of Sam?" Sophie asked. "I saw him and Cullen's daughter go by yesterday, and he waved at me. I wondered why he didn't stop, but he was just up here a week or so ago, so I figured he planned to stop on the way back down."

Gus shook his head. "We didn't see them or Cullen's Jeep, but once we found Cullen's body, we headed down here to get someone to go up and get him."

Elmer frowned. "I wonder where Sam is?"

"At this point, that's anybody's guess," Gus replied.

Elmer couldn't take his eyes off Billy. "What happened to your clothes, Billy? You don't usually go around dressed like that, do you?"

Billy was doing his best to keep himself covered. "Derek threw my clothes in the river so I couldn't go after him."

Elmer turned to Sophie with a wry grin. "See if you can get him somethin' of mine to put on. We can't have him flashin' us like that."

Sophie took Billy into their bedroom and got a pair of Elmer's pajama bottoms and slippers, and Billy pulled them on. "Thanks," he said sheepishly.

Lucas came back from the telephone in the hallway. "The Cullen girl wasn't at the hospital in Toppenish, so I called Doc Stevens in Harrah and found out she's there. Derek's the one who brought her in, but Doc sent him over to see you, Gus. I told Doc you were still up here at the Fort, so he has no idea where Derek went."

Elmer motioned for Sophie to take Billy into the kitchen, so she took him by the arm and told him she needed some help getting coffee ready for everyone. Elmer sidled up to Gus and Lucas and lowered his voice. "Can I talk to you two outside?"

Gus nodded, and the three men walked out onto the front porch. "I need to tell you guys somethin' very important," Elmer said. "A little over a week ago, Sam came up here to unburden himself about what happened at the Oaks, and he told us that *he* was the one who killed Morgan. Derek had nothin' to do with it—just like he's been sayin' all along."

Gus looked stunned. "Did Sophie hear him say this too?"

Elmer nodded. "We don't wanna get Sam in any trouble, but we thought you oughta know what he told us."

"Did he swear you to secrecy?" Gus asked.

Elmer shook his head.

"Then he musta wanted the truth to come out," Lucas said.

"That's what we thought too, so that's why I'm tellin' you guys."

The three stopped talking as Sophie and Billy came out with some cups of coffee.

"Can I use your phone?" Gus asked. "I wanna call Doc Stevens again and see if Lily's still there." He got the operator, and she put him through to Doc's office. The phone rang numerous times, but Ruth finally came on the line.

"Ruth, this is Gus. Is the Cullen girl still there?"

"Yes, but I don't have time to talk now. I've gotta get back to Doc."

"Just a quick question. Is she gonna make it?"

"We think so. Doc's got an ambulance coming from Yakima to get her, and it should be here any minute. There's one piece of shot in her spine that he doesn't want to touch."

"Is Derek still there?"

"He was, but Doc sent him over to see you at your station. Aren't you there?"

"No. I'm up at the fort. Is there any way you can go over and see if Derek's still there?"

"I can't leave right now, Gus."

"Has anyone notified Mrs. Cullen?"

"We haven't had time."

"Good. I don't want you or Doc to say anything to her or anyone else about this. Please! I'm coming down right now, and I'll tell Mrs. Cullen myself. Not a word to anyone, Ruth. Harrah is a powder keg, and all it needs is a spark like this to blow it sky high. Tell Doc I'll be in there as soon as I can."

Gus hung up and stood there with his head down for a moment, then looked up at the others. He let out a deep sigh. "Lily's still at Doc Stevens's office, and she's in pretty bad shape, but they think she's gonna make it. There's an ambulance coming to take her up to Yakima as soon as Doc's finished with her. Doc sent Derek over to my station to wait for me, so I'd better hightail it down there before he changes his mind and bolts." He turned to Elmer. "Can I use your pickup?"

Elmer gave a wave of his hand. "Take it. I'm sure Sheriff Lucas will let us use his truck to go get Cullen."

"You need to get your hands on Derek as soon as you can," Lucas told Gus. "I'll call you after we've gotten Cullen into the mortuary in Toppenish. Don't let Abrams get away. He's got a lot to answer for."

"I won't. I want him as bad as you do." Gus motioned to Billy. "Come on, Billy. You can ride down with me. I'm sure we'll run into Derek eventually, and get your pickup back."

Sophie was fighting tears as she, Elmer, and Lucas stood on the porch and watched Gus and Billy drive away. Lucas turned to Elmer with a weary expression. "Sorry you folks got put out like this," he said, "but I haven't had anything to eat all day. Is there any way I can get somethin' before we go pick up Cullen? He's not goin' anywhere, that's for sure."

CHAPTER 47

Derek sat in Billy's pickup in front of Doc's office, too devastated to know just what to do. He didn't want to leave Lily, but there was nothing more he could do for her. And then, suddenly, he wanted very much to see his mother. She only worked half-days on Friday, so she'd be home.

He pulled out of the side street in front of Doc Stevens's office and followed a series of back roads until he got to his ranch near White Swan. As he drove into the yard and saw his old pickup sitting there, a lump came into his throat.

He pulled up in front of the house and got out just as the front door opened. When Lucy saw who it was, she pushed open the screen and ran into his arms. "You're home," she cried. "I knew you'd come back."

"Yes, I'm home, Mom, but I don't know for how long."

She pulled back and saw his bloody outfit. "Have you been hurt?"

"It's a long story, and you're the only one who'll believe me, so I need to tell you before they come to get me."

"Who's coming to get you?"

"Probably the Toppenish sheriff and Gus Styvessan."

"Why?"

"I'll tell you when we get inside."

After Derek told her everything that had happened, her eyes were filled with so much pain that it was all he could do to keep from taking her in his arms and telling her that everything was going to be all right. But everything wasn't going to be, and he knew it.

"So you finally got your revenge on Andrew Cullen," she said. "Do you feel vindicated now?"

He shook his head. "I never wanted it to end like this. Cullen brought it on himself, but if I've gotten Lily killed, I'll never forgive myself."

She took his hands in hers. "You aren't responsible for what happened to her. Her father is the one who shot her."

"But I promised myself up on the mountain that I'd take care of her, and I didn't."

Lucy gave him a quizzical look. "Did something happen between the two of you up there?"

He hesitated a moment, then said, "I think so."

"Have you fallen in love with her?"

"I don't know, but she trusted me, and I let her down." He took Lucy's hands in his. "Will you pray for her, Mom? I tried to, but I don't know how to pray."

"Of course I will, just like I pray for you and your dad every day."

He drew back with a puzzled look. "Why are you praying for Dad? He was a very spiritual man."

"I know that, but just before he died, he asked me to pray that he would go to heaven, and I told him I would."

"Did he believe in Jesus?"

"I don't know. He'd been talking about Him a lot in the weeks before he died, but he died before he could tell me if he'd actually become a believer, so I've just kept praying that he did."

Derek began to nod his head. "That must be why there's a cross on his grave up on the mountain. Did you put it there?"

She looked stunned, then let out a little laugh. "No, I didn't, but God must've had somebody put it there so we'd know that Dad was in heaven."

"Well now you can pray for me," Derek said. "I'm going to need it."

"Oh, honey. I've been praying for you ever since Mrs. Lamont taught me how to pray."

"What should I do now, Mom? Should I call Mr. Lamont and tell him what happened?"

"Yes, and if he's still willing to pay for your defense, then he and Mr. Speer can tell you what to do. But whatever you do, you must do it before word of Mr. Cullen's death gets out. Too many people will think you killed him on purpose if the truth doesn't come out quickly."

"Even if Mr. Lamont decides not to help me, I'm going to fight this."

"It's not going to be easy," she said, "but you've always been able to do anything you set your mind to, so you can do this. Now, you call Mr. Lamont and tell him what's happened. He's a good man, and I know you can make him understand why you did what you did."

He rang the Lamont's number and Helen answered. "Mrs. Lamont, this is Derek Abrams. Is your husband there?"

"Derek!" she exclaimed. "Oh, I'm so glad to hear from you. Are you okay?"

"I hope I will be once I speak to your husband. Is he home?"

"Yes. I'll get him right now."

She left the phone, and moments later, Hank Lamont came on the line. "Where are you?" he growled.

"I'm at my mother's, but I'd like very much to tell you in person what's happened. Can I come over there right now?"

There was a pause on Hank's end, then he said, "I can give you fifteen minutes. Does Cullen know you're back?"

"That's one of the things I need to talk to you about. I'll see you in twenty minutes." Derek started to hang up, but quickly added, "I know I don't deserve a second chance with you, but you'll never have reason to regret helping me. I promise you that."

Hank was obviously taken aback by this. "As a matter of fact, you were a real horse's ass the last time we talked, and I swore I was gonna wash my hands of you. But I'm interested in hearing what you have to say, so come on over. I'll be waiting."

Derek hung up and turned to his mother. "He said he'd see me."

"That's wonderful!" she exclaimed, "but can I ask you to do just one thing for me before you go?"

"What?"

"Will you please shower and change into something else?"

Derek looked down at his bloody outfit and gave a little laugh. "I guess this would be a bit much, even for Hank Lamont."

He went to his room and paused in the doorway. Everything was just as it had been: a White Swan High School pennant hanging on the wall; several football trophies sitting on a shelf next to a football signed by all the players on his championship team at Washington State College; his collection of poetry books by his favorites, Frost, Sandburg, Nash, and others; and an assortment of math books. As he took it all in, his mind suddenly went back to those hours he'd spent with his father on top of Spirit Mountain, and for one brief moment, a wave of regret swept over him, but he shook it off. He took a quick shower, changed into some jeans and a tee shirt and came back out into the living room. Lucy was in the kitchen, and he called to her as he started to leave.

"I'll see you later, Mom."

She came in from the kitchen, wiping her hands on a towel, and smiled at him. "Those are the sweetest words a mother could ever hope to hear."

He took her in his arms again, then quickly left before she could see his tears.

CHAPTER 48

Hank Lamont sat quietly listening to everything Derek told him, occasionally interrupting to clarify a point. Derek had not tried to paint himself without fault. He told Hank about having shot Andrew Cullen, and Hank was aghast to hear that Andrew was dead. But from the way Derek told it, Cullen had shot first, and Derek had just been defending himself and Lily.

When Derek finished with the story, Hank leaned back in his desk chair and looked him straight in the eye. "You've told me the straight truth, Derek? No lies? No bullshit?"

Derek met his gaze without flinching. "Everything I've told you is the truth. I swear it on my father's grave."

Hank reached over and picked up the phone. He got Speer on the line and told him what Derek had just said, and after some heavy arm-twisting on Hank's part, Speer finally agreed to continue with the case and take on the new charge that Cullen's death would add. Even though the next day was Saturday, Speer agreed to meet Derek in his office in Yakima to get things started. It was only two and a half weeks until the trial.

After the call, Hank propped his elbows on his desk and folded his big hands together as he fixed his gaze on Derek. "I'll tell you what you need to do right now. You need to get yourself into Toppenish to the sheriff's office and wait for Lucas to get down from the fort. That way, nobody can say you're trying to hide what you did to Cullen. They might put you in jail overnight, but we'll get you out in time to meet with Speer tomorrow." Hank stood up. "Okay?"

Derek stood up too, and reached for Hank's hand. "I'll do it," he said, "but first I want to go by Doc Stevens's office to see about Lily."

"Don't you go anywhere near Harrah!" Hank ordered. "That town's a powder keg right now. You can call Doc Stevens from the sheriff's office and find out about Lily. You hear me? If you want my help, you get yourself to Toppenish right now."

"Okay," Derek reluctantly said. "I know I don't deserve a second chance with you, but I promise you won't ever have reason to regret helping me, and I'll pay every penny back to you and Mr. Speer, even if it takes the rest of my life."

"If that's what you wanna do, that's fine. Just don't let your mother and Mrs. Lamont down again, or you'll have to deal with me personally. Those are two very special ladies, and they believe in you with all their hearts, and—I must admit—I'm starting to, as well."

Derek thanked him again and left the office. Cassie was standing there beaming when he came out. "I'm so glad you're back," she said. "We were all so worried about you. I couldn't imagine being up at the school without you next year."

"We'll have to wait and see whether I'll be back, or in jail, but if I do come back, it'll be nice having you there. You've always stuck up for me, and I won't forget it."

Cassie stood there blushing as Derek headed for the front door.

Helen caught up to him before he went out and slipped a package into his hands.

"What's this?" Derek asked.

"Just a little something to let you know how happy I am that you're back. You're very special to me. I hope you know that."

Derek seemed embarrassed. "You didn't need to do this."

"You need a little encouragement right now, and you need to know that a lot of people love you and believe you're innocent—especially me."

He wanted to hug her, but his old reticence gripped him, and he merely took her hand in his. "I'd like to say something, if I may," he said.

"Of course."

"While I was up in the mountains, I did a lot of thinking, and one of the people who came to my mind was you. You always treated me like all the other kids you help, and you never let it bother you that I'm an Indian, and I just wanted you to know how much that means to me. You're a wonderful example of your Christian faith, and I'm very happy that I can call you my friend."

Helen impulsively stood on tiptoe and gave him a hug. "If I had a son, I'd want him to be just like you."

Derek could feel tears very close to the surface as he pulled back. "I'd better get going before I make a big fool of myself, but thanks again for the gift."

Derek went out to his truck and sat there a few moments thinking about the Lamonts. How could he ever have thought that Hank Lamont was a bigot? They were both wonderful examples of what they believed, and he hoped their God would become as real to him some day, as He was to them. He looked down at the gift in his hands and unwrapped it. It was a small, leather-bound book of famous Bible quotations. He looked inside the cover, and Mrs. Lamont had written in her dainty handwriting the words of St. Peter: "God's love covers a multitude of sins."

He read the words over several times, then closed the cover and held the book against his heart. "Covering all my sins will keep God busy for a very long time," he said.

CHAPTER 49

As Gus drove Billy Aimes down from the fort in Elmer's pickup, he looked over at Billy, measuring him carefully. He was a miserable excuse for a human being—lazy, bigoted, and a drunk—but he held Derek's fate in his hands, and Gus knew he had to handle him with kid gloves.

"So, tell me, Billy, how'd you get mixed up in all this? I didn't know you and Andrew Cullen were so thick."

Billy gave Gus a sour look. "We weren't. I just worked for the guy, and I was shocked when he called me this mornin' and asked me to take him up to look for that Injun. I didn't have nothin' personal against the kid. I hope you're not thinkin' I did."

"Well, I think people are gonna wonder about your involvement in all this when they hear about Cullen shooting his own daughter in the back from the window of *your* truck. You've been shooting your mouth off about Derek ever since the murder. Everybody at Charlie's knows you wanted to see him hang."

The look on Billy's face suddenly changed to fear. "Now wait just a minute, Gus! You can't pin none-a-this on me. I was just doin' what Cullen ordered me to do."

"Cullen didn't have any authority to go looking for Derek,

and you knew that. Neither one of you had any business going up there, and Cullen sure as hell wasn't authorized to shoot anyone—yet you didn't try to stop him. That clearly makes you an accessory to attempted murder—and real murder if the Cullen girl dies."

Billy exploded. "No it don't! Cullen's the one who done all the shootin'. My gun was still on the rack in the back window of my truck. That Injun can tell you that. I didn't have nothin' to do with that girl gettin' shot."

"But just driving Cullen up there in your truck, when you knew he was planning to kill Derek, makes this premeditated murder if Lily dies. Cullen may have done the actual shooting, but you were sure in on the premeditated part."

Billy's fear was clearly mounting. "But I told you! He *forced* me to chase 'em! You know what he's like when he gets fired up about somethin'. You can't stop him."

"I know that, and that's why I can't believe he'd let Derek get off the first shot."

"Well, he did, because I saw it."

Gus shook his head. "It doesn't wash, Billy. Lucas and I heard three shots, and the first two were a shotgun—not a rifle—so Cullen musta taken the first two shots."

Sweat was beginning to bead up on Billy's upper lip, and Gus pursued his advantage. "You know something, Billy, if the judge knew that Cullen shot twice at Derek before he ever returned fire, that might get you off the hook as an accessory to murder."

Caught in his lie, Billy was extremely flustered. "I see what you mean, Gus. I . . . I was just confused before, but now I remember. Cullen *did* shoot first and got his daughter in the back, and she fell off the horse. Then Derek came chargin' back, and Cullen got off another shot at him, but missed, and the Injun returned fire and got Cullen in the heart."

"So Derek was just defending himself. Is that the way you see it?"

Billy nodded eagerly. "Yeah, that's right. He was just defendin' hisself."

"And you're willing to testify to that?"

"I sure am."

"And you're sure your memory won't fail you again?"

Billy gave his head a vigorous shake. "No, sir. It won't. That's just the way it happened. I swear to God."

Gus kept his eyes on the road ahead, but a tiny smile turned up the corners of his mouth. "Well, then, I don't see how any judge could hold you as an accessory to murder. There wasn't anything you could do to stop Cullen. He ordered you to take him up there to look for Derek, and you were scared you'd lose your job if you said no. Then the two of you found Derek and Lily on horseback heading down from the mountain to give themselves up, and Cullen ordered you to chase them so he could get a shot at Derek. Isn't that about right?"

Billy nodded vigorously, but quickly added, "And don't forget, I told him not to shoot, 'cause he might hit his daughter, but he was hell-bent on stoppin' that Injun and didn't pay no attention to what I said."

"Then the whole thing was Cullen's own doing. Right?"

"It sure was, but you'll have to back me up, Gus. You'll have to tell the judge how Cullen was always bullyin' people into doin' what he wanted."

Gus's head slowly turned toward Billy, and the look in his eyes was deadly. "I'll back you up if you tell the truth about who shot first, but I'll *bury* you if you lie about it again. You understand me?"

"I sure do, Gus. It all happened so fast, I just couldn't remember before, but thanks for helpin' me get it straight."

"Okay, it's a deal then. You tell the truth, and I'll back you up. That's all I'm asking."

Gus pulled up in front of his service station, and he and Billy climbed out of Elmer's pickup. He glanced around for Billy's pickup, but it wasn't there.

Jerry had been lounging in Gus's old chrome chair, but got up when Gus drove in.

"Hi, Gus," Jerry called out. "I didn't expect you back before dark. I guess you called off the search, huh?"

"Why would you think that?" Gus asked.

Jerry gave him a puzzled look. "Well, Derek Abrams came in here a couple hours ago in Billy's truck lookin' for you, but I told him you were up in the mountains lookin' for *him*, so he took off, and I ain't seen him since. What's goin' on?"

Gus gave Jerry a friendly pat on the back. "It's a long story, my friend. I'll tell you all about it later." He glanced over at Billy, who was looking around for his truck. "I'm going over to Doc Stevens's," Gus said. "I'll be back in a few minutes."

"But what about my truck?" Billy wailed. "When am I gonna get it back?"

"All in good time," Gus said. "You can wait here and keep Jerry company till Derek shows up with it, or you can go on over to Charlie's and have a beer on me, if you don't mind being seen in Elmer's pajamas and slippers."

Billy looked down at himself, then cursed. "I forgot I had these on. I can't go over there lookin' like this. Those guys'll laugh me outta there, and what'll I tell 'em?"

Gus gripped his arm. "You can tell them whatever you want, but if Charlie tells me you say *one word* about anything that happened up on that mountain, our deal is off with the judge. You got it?"

Billy nodded. "I won't say nothin'. I promise." He started across the street, then sheepishly turned back to Gus. "Can I put *two* beers on your tab? I need more than one after what I been through."

Gus gave him a wave of his hand. "Tell Charlie to put two on it, but if you want more, you'll have to bum it off some other sucker."

Gus walked over to Doc Stevens's office, and Ruth looked up as he came in.

"Am I glad to see you, Gus. I know Doc wants to talk to you."

"Is the Cullen girl still here?"

She shook her head. "No. An ambulance picked her up about an hour ago and took her up to Mercy Hospital."

"How was she doing?"

"She's gonna live, but we're both worried about a pellet that's lodged in her spine. Right now she seems to be paralyzed from the waist down, but Doc hopes they can get it out, and that she'll mend in time. Have you got time to talk to Doc?"

"Yeah."

Ruth went and got Doc, and he came out to the waiting room and shook hands with Gus. "This thing is sure the pits," he said to Gus.

Gus nodded. "Did Derek tell you about Andrew?"

"Yeah. Sorry to hear about that. I wasn't real crazy about the guy, but that's a heck-of-a-way to die."

"It sure is," Gus said. "What about Lily? Ruth says she may be paralyzed from the waist down. Is there any hope for her to recover?"

Doc gave a dubious shake of his head. "I don't know. If they can get that piece of lead out of her spine without doing any further damage, she might be able to walk again. I sure hate to think of a pretty young girl like that being in a wheelchair the rest of her life. It just isn't fair."

"Nothing about this whole mess has been fair," Gus said. "I expected more out of a town with four churches in it. I understand Derek has lost his job out at White Swan over this too. Talk about '*cutting off your nose to spite your face*'. He's the best thing that ever happened to that school."

Doc gave a disparaging flip of his hand. "Don't waste your time fretting about it, Gus. Half the people in this town wouldn't even know what you're talking about. By the way, did Derek go over to your station to wait for you? I told him to."

"He probably went home when he saw I wasn't back yet."

Gus started for the door, then turned back. "I hope you and Ruth won't say anything about this to anyone until I can contact Mrs. Cullen. I wouldn't want it coming from anyone but me."

Doc looked surprised. "She doesn't know yet?"

Gus shook his head. "I came straight here from the fort to try to talk to Derek, but since he's not here, I'm going over to The Oaks right now. Where'd the ambulance take Lily?"

"To Mercy Hospital in Yakima."

"I'll tell Laura. Thanks again, Doc. I'll talk to you later."

Gus left and walked back over to the station. "Billy still over at Charlie's?" he asked Jerry.

"I guess so. He hasn't come back here."

Gus let out a little laugh. "I bet he's cutting quite a figure in those pajama bottoms. Look, Jerry, I've gotta go over to The Oaks for awhile. If anyone calls for me, tell them they can reach me there, and if Derek shows up, tell him not to go anywhere. I'll be back in an hour. Okay?"

"Sure thing, boss, but I wish I knew what was goin' on around here."

"What you don't know won't hurt you," Gus said. He parked Elmer's pickup next to the station and went around to the back of his house and got his new Oldsmobile out of the garage.

Jerry watched with a puzzled look as Gus drove off in his fancy car.

CHAPTER 50

Laura was standing with Max beside his car when Gus drove into the parking court at The Oaks. He climbed out of his car and started toward them, then saw Laura's blackened eye. "What happened to you?" he said, rushing over to her.

"It's nothing. I'll tell you about it later. Max is just leaving to go up to the fort to see if they know anything about Lily and Sam. Did you find them?"

He reached out for Laura's hand. "I don't know where Sam is, but it isn't good news about Lily."

Her eyes grew wide. "What's happened to her?"

"I haven't put all the pieces together yet, but it looks like she and Sam found Derek up at Spirit Mountain and talked him into coming back, but Andrew ran into them as they were coming down the mountain, and took a shot at them." Gus took both of Laura's hands in his. "I'm so sorry, sweetheart, but Andrew accidentally shot Lily in the back."

Laura started to slump to the ground, but Gus caught her in his arms and started up the steps with her. "You'd better come in too, Max. There's more."

"What?" he cried.

Gus carried Laura into the family room and laid her on the sofa. She had started to sob uncontrollably, and Gus knelt down beside her and took her hands in his. "Listen to me, sweetheart! Listen to me! Lily's not dead. Derek brought her down here to Doc Stevens, and he worked on her for over two hours before an ambulance took her up to Yakima. I'm here to take you up to see her right now."

"Where's my dad?" Max demanded.

Gus looked up at him. "I said there's more." He turned back to Laura. "I'm so sorry to have to tell you both this, but Andrew's dead."

"What?" Laura gasped.

"How?" cried Max.

"I told you he tried to gun Derek down while he was surrendering, but Derek returned his fire and hit him right in the heart. I got that first-hand from Billy Aimes who was with your dad and saw the whole thing." He paused a moment, obviously battling with what he was going to say next. "There's something else you both need to know too. Derek didn't kill Morgan. Sam did. He told the caretakers up at Fort Simcoe about it over a week ago."

Laura looked bewildered. "But why would he kill Morgan? He loved him."

"He didn't tell them why. He just told them he did it."

"Maybe they're trying to protect Derek," Max said.

Gus frowned. "I know them both, and they'd never lie about something like that."

"But Sam is such a good man," Laura said. "I can't believe he'd hurt me like this. He knows how much I loved Morgan."

"I know he does," Gus said, "but I think Lily knows why he did it. I've thought all along that she was covering for someone, but I didn't know who. Now I see she was covering for Sam."

"He's been like a father to her all her life," Laura said, "and he'd do anything to protect her from Morgan. Where is he now?"

"Nobody seems to know. I guess he'll come back when he's ready to face the music."

"Where's my Dad?" Max asked.

"Sheriff Lucas is bringing him down to the mortuary in Toppenish. I'm really sorry, Max. I know this must be very hard for you."

Max walked over to the window and stared out at the hop field. He stood motionless for a long time, his hands thrust into his pockets, his mouth quivering. "You don't know how hard it is, Gus. I was hoping to have a little more time to be a kid, but I guess I'm the head of the family now." He walked back over to the sofa and knelt down beside his mother, brushing the tears from her bruised cheeks. "You and Lily don't have to worry, Mom. I'll take care of you *and* the ranch. You can count on me."

She drew his hand to her lips. "I've always known I could count on you, honey, but I hope you won't mind a little help from Gus, because he's going to be part of our lives from now on. Is that okay with both of you?"

Gus let out a surprised laugh. "That's the best news I've had in years."

Max gave them a look of astonishment. "Will someone please tell me what's going on?"

Gus grinned at him. "We'll tell you all about it on the way up to see Lily. She's waiting for us at Mercy Hospital."

EPILOGUE

The Year of Our Lord, 2000

Mount Adams shone majestic in the distance, its snow-capped peak jutting out of the clouds like a diamond tiara. The meadows below it were covered with a dazzling display of wildflowers: lilies, poppies, daisies, bluebells, and numerous other exotic mountain flowers. The sight was breathtaking in the summer sun, but the tall, bronzed man, his long braids streaked now with gray, seemed only to be aware of the fragile woman he pushed along the dirt path in front of him. She reached a hand down beside the wheel of her chair and plucked a daisy and began pulling its petals off. "He loves me, he loves me not, he loves me . . ."

The man covered her hand with his before she could go any further. "He loves you more than life itself," he said. "He always has, and he always will." His dark eyes were softened now with time and love, but still inscrutable after all these years.

Laughing gaily, Lily pulled his hand to her lips and kissed it, then looked up into the face of the man who had shared her life for over forty years. "Do you swear that on the graves of all our ancestors?" she asked, with a mischievous grin.

Derek threw back his head and laughed, then bent down and kissed the top of her head. "No, my love. I swear it on the *empty* grave of the One who gave you to me."

ABOUT THE AUTHOR

I am not an Indian, but I was born and raised on the Yakima Indian Reservation in Washington State. In the early 1900s, my grandparents, Walter and Frieda Houghton, left Michigan for a promised job in Seattle, but on their way there, they stopped to see the Yakima Indian Reservation in central Washington. After a two-month visit, they fell in love with the friendly Yakimas and their fertile valley, nestled in the shadow of snow-capped Mount Adams, and it wasn't long before Grandpa bought ten acres of Reservation land from an Indian and built a little house and farm on it. My grandparents raised all five of their children on the Reservation, and all of them raised their children there, of which I am one.

I attended Harrah Elementary School and White Swan High School where I kept busy as a cheerleader, sang in the school choir, wrote for the school paper and the Yakima Morning Herald, played on all the girls' sports teams, and was awarded membership in the National Honor Society. In the summer between my junior and senior year in highschool, I was elected Governor of Washington's Girls' State and chosen to represent my state at Girls' Nation in Washington, D.C., where I got to meet President Harry Truman.

After attending Yakima Junior College, Whitworth College, and UCLA, I came back to the Reservation and taught school in Harrah, then spent many years teaching history and English in Southern California. I served on the staff of Campus Crusade for Christ, wrote numerous books with my husband Hal Lindsey, authored the WWII novel, *All the Dogs of Europe Barked*, and *The Last Renegade*. I have had many blessings in my life, but the greatest have been my three daughters and their familes: Robin and Stewart Young; Jenny and Ross Patrick; Heide and Russell Ziecker; and my grandchildren; Riley and Nicole Charters and my great granddaughter Noemi; Zachary Charters; Jameson Young; Hunter and Jackson Patrick; Madeline, Zoe, and Daisy Ziecker.